Laura Coburn worked for a number of years as a jour-
nalist before training at the Los Angeles Academy to
become a reserve police officer in West Los Angeles,
first on patrol then moving up to the detective division
where she handled her own caseload of battery and
felony assault cases for West LA Homicide. She
received a number of department commendations for
her work as well as two commendations from the City of
Los Angeles and was named Reserve Officer of the year
for West LA division in 1984.

Also by Laura Coburn

A Desperate Call

An Uncertain Death

Laura Coburn

First published in Great Britain in 1996
by HEADLINE BOOK PUBLISHING

First published in Great Britain in paperback in 1996
by HEADLINE BOOK PUBLISHING

A HEADLINE FEATURE paperback

10 9 8 7 6 5 4 3 2 1

ISBN 0 7472 5249 1

Typeset by
Letterpart Limited, Reigate, Surrey

Printed and bound in Great Britain by
Mackays of Chatham PLC, Chatham, Kent

HEADLINE BOOK PUBLISHING
A division of Hodder Headline PLC
338 Euston Road
London NW1 3BH

Dedicated to my father, Luther Dalton,
a good friend as well as a good parent,
who sacrificed so that I might achieve

CHAPTER ONE

They found her body shortly after dawn. It lay face down upon the grass, the dew of night still wet upon it. They didn't need to touch her to know that she was dead.

I jammed the sandwich in my mouth and headed out of the door, the sergeant's words still spiraling through my mind. 'We need you, Kate. We've got a female white, mid-teens, gunshot wound to the head. We're by the little stream that runs through North Meadow, just off the Canfield road.'

I wiped the honeyed crumbs away, then shifted into high. Five minutes later I was driving down a dusty trail that ended at a clearing in the woods.

A uniformed unit secured the scene, standing silently, legs apart, hands behind them. Nearby, two men in jogging clothes stood beside a tree, anxious looks upon their faces. I glanced at them and then stepped forward, past the waiting officers.

She lay ten feet from the stream, flat upon her stomach, her left arm flung straight out above her head, her right leg bent oddly at the knee. A thick dark substance soaked her

1

short-cropped hair and spread in a random pattern on the collar of her blouse. Her face, pushed deep into the grass, rested slightly to one side.

Carefully, I squatted down till I was only inches from her, and peered at her intently.

A bullet entrance wound, small and neat and round, marked the flesh above her open eye, and thin red lines of liquid, dull and crusting now, lay along her cheek and brow. Dried blood and other matter filled the nostril nearest me and trailed down to her parted lips.

I straightened up and turned to face the sergeant standing next to me. My sole sank slightly in the softness of the cool moist grass and I was glad I'd worn flats and jeans.

'Who found her, Harry?'

He nodded toward the joggers. 'Those two, Kate. Out for an early run and came on this. What a way to start your day, for Christ's sake.' He ran his beefy fingers through his iron-grey curly hair.

'Any idea who she is?'

'Nope. My men don't know her either.'

I glanced around, my eyes searching. 'What about the weapon? Did you find one?'

'We didn't search. We secured the area, then waited here for you. Didn't want to tramp around too much.'

'Okay, notify the coroner and keep an eye out for Mungers. He'll be along shortly.'

I looked at her again and took the scene into my mind. The morning light touched her hair and laid a silver sheen of dew across the grass around her. Her reaching hand seemed to grasp the fragile wildflowers growing close beside her. As I watched, a tiny butterfly settled on her arm, then flew away.

My eyes slowly moved beyond her. Tall and leafy trees rose beside the clearing and stood alongside the stream as far as I could see. The August sky, pale and high and hazy, showed through the leaves as they began to flutter in the warming breeze. The night had been a cool one, laden with the moisture of an early Baja storm, but that storm had moved eastward and the heat of late summer had started to return.

As I turned away and walked across the clearing, I could feel the muscles tightening near my temples. The joggers raised their heads as I approached, and their anxious looks seemed to deepen. One ran his tongue around his lips.

'I'm Detective Harrod. I understand you found her.'

They answered eagerly, in unison, and relaxed a bit.

'Right, we did.'

'Tell me what you saw.' My eyes narrowed as I concentrated fully on their answers.

The taller one took the lead. 'We'd never jogged all the way along the trail before. Wanted to see what was down here. We came through the meadow, past those trees, turned along the stream, and there she was.' He bit his lip nervously.

'What time was this?'

'I'd checked my watch a moment earlier. I'd say it was probably six-fifteen.'

'What did you do then?'

The shorter one stepped forward. 'I took her pulse, although I knew it wasn't any use. I could tell that just by looking at her. Like a broken doll lying there. Then we ran to

3

that house across the field and called the cops.'

'Did you touch anything besides the girl, or disturb the scene in any way?'

'No, ma'am, we did not. We got out of here pretty damn fast. We didn't even come back down until we saw the black-and-white arrive.'

'Did you see anything unusual or hear any movement in the area?'

They looked at one another solemnly. 'Nothing. No.'

I took their names, thanked them, and told them I'd be in touch. They nodded swiftly, then headed up the trail.

I saw a tan car coming toward them as they crossed the meadow. Mungers, my buddy, my second-in-command, had arrived. Like me, he parked well back from the woods and walked his way in, taking no chance of destroying possible suspect tire tracks.

I walked to meet him, circling around the body, barely looking at it as I passed. 'She's in there, Carl. Lying by the stream. Far as I can tell, it's a single shot to the head, but we'll know better when the coroner turns her over.'

'Suicide?' His large frame shifted slightly as he spoke and his face seemed ruddier than usual. I watched him light a cigarette, then stub it out and pick it up.

'I doubt it. No powder burns and no weapon nearby, unless it's underneath her.'

'What about the ID?'

'Negative so far. I don't know her, sergeant doesn't know her. Neither do his men.'

'Anything on her?'

'No sign of a purse or pocketbook. I haven't gone through

4

her clothes yet. Want to wait till the coroner arrives before I poke around too much.'

He nodded and we walked together to the clearing in the woods. I glanced at him. He seemed preoccupied, but maybe he was only gathering concentration for the work ahead. I recalled his unprofessional lighting of the cigarette and didn't think so. He approached the body slowly, viewing it from all angles, then crouched down carefully, as I had done, so he could see the staring eye beneath the small round hole. He studied the body for several minutes, drawing details into storage in his mind.

I waited, and a sixth sense suddenly told me he knew more than I did.

He swung his head around and squinted up at me. 'I know her, Kate, at least I think I do. I'm pretty sure it's Connie Hammond, that hot-shot pitcher on the girls' softball team.'

He rose and stuffed the back of his shirt back inside his belt, where it had risen when he bent down.

I'd heard of her but not paid much attention – I wasn't a big fan of girls' softball. As far as I knew, I'd never seen her or her picture, and I'd certainly never watched her play. 'Where does she live?'

'Dunno. I only know what I read in the papers and they don't give the home address. But if this is who I think it is, she was good, really good. The team won its league last year on her pitching and it's up there right now battling for another championship.'

'He's right, Detective Harrod, I'd bet my paycheck on it.' I swung around to face a uniformed patrolman standing next to me. 'She lives close to me and jogs past my house every morning. There was something about those legs – big calves, strong yet well-defined – that looked familiar, but I didn't put it all together till right now. And then the back of the head, that blonde square cut. I'm sure it's Connie Hammond.'

'Thanks, officer,' I told him. 'Stick around awhile. I may need you when we turn her over.'

I touched his shoulder and he walked back to his position. As I began to turn to Carl, I saw the San Madera coroner's van easing through the field, raising tiny puffs of dust that settled on its glossy black exterior. It stopped beside the two detective cars. An older man got out, followed by a younger one. Penross and MacDuff – I knew them well.

'We're over here,' I called, and waved to them to join us by the corpse. They hurried down the trail.

'Let's see if you make this one out the same way we do,' I said when they arrived.

Penross, the chief examiner, stood beside the body without moving. He was a little man, dapper in his dress, and he didn't miss a trick. He carefully studied the body, just as Carl and I had done, before he began to walk around it.

When he reached the head, he halted. He bent down, but where we had stopped at a visual examination, he cautiously touched the hair above the collar, parting it every quarter-inch or so to see down the scalp. When he lifted up his hand, the opaque fingers of his coroner's glove showed reddish-brown.

Satisfied, he turned the body over. Carl saw the lifeless face, looked at me, and nodded. No one spoke. The only sound in that small clearing was the low, sharp click of MacDuff's official camera.

Finished with the head, Penross undid the cotton blouse and tan twill shorts and concentrated on the torso of the victim. Then he glanced at me. 'Did you find a weapon with her?'

'There was none near the body. No bullet either. We haven't searched outside the clearing yet.'

He pursed his lips and raised his eyebrows slightly. 'No powder burns, no weapon. I'd say it's pure and simple, then – just like you've got it figured. Homicide, not suicide, with cause of death being a single shot to the head – possibly twenty-five, thirty-two caliber – entering just above the right eye and exiting through the back of the skull approximately three inches from the base.

'Post-mortem lividity suggests she was killed exactly where you found her, not done somewhere else and dumped. She's already in full rigor and the lividity's past the blanching stage, so I'd say you're probably safe to put the time of death well before midnight, probably as early as nine or ten o'clock. Let me do the liver probe and I can tell you more.'

He punctured the corpse's abdomen with a short knife ending in a tri-blade tip, then carefully inserted an eight-inch meat thermometer through the tiny opening, piercing the small intestine, and drove down into the liver itself. He waited a few minutes, until its moving gauge stabilized, then removed it and took the reading.

'Eighty-one degrees, consistent with what I'd already surmised. Death was probably ten to eleven hours ago, certainly not less than that.'

He straightened up, brushed his pants off, and gave his head a little shake. 'I say it's pure and simple, but you know officially it's never that. I've got to get her back to the lab and do it by the book. Right now, though, I see no other marks or wounds that would indicate to me that she died by any means other than the shot.'

'Right,' I said. 'Let me check her over for ID.'

I approached the body and stared down at its face. The square shape, set off by short fair hair, was not enhanced by makeup, and the features were much too ordinary to be considered pretty. The open eyes, blue and vacant, stared straight past me at the sky above the trees.

I couldn't let it bother me. The poor young soul was a teenage girl no longer. The instant of that fatal bullet had reduced her to mere evidence in a crime.

I bent down and looked along the corpse's length. I saw a stocky build and figured she'd stand five-eight or -nine. The legs, as the officer had mentioned, were strong and well-developed, and the tan and freckled arms showed muscle mass below the short sleeves of the blouse. A tiny silver chain, extremely feminine in its design, dangled from one wrist. She was probably sixteen, seventeen at most. Despite myself, I sighed.

She wore only the twill shorts, cotton blouse, and under-wear above her sandals. If there was any ID, it'd have to be in the large pockets of the shorts. I reached inside the right one. Nothing but a Kleenex and a set of keys. My hand touched the left one and I felt a thick square object. My fingers slipped inside and closed around a leather wallet. I flipped it open. The same square and plain face stared up at me from a California driver's license. I read the name beside it.

'It's the Hammond girl,' I said. 'No doubt.'

I motioned to the coroner. 'She's yours now,' I told him. 'We'll keep on searching for that bullet, but do me a favor and 'scope her for me as soon as you get back, in case it's still inside her.' I stepped away.

Penross moved quickly forward and laid a body bag beside the corpse. He pulled the zipper harshly downward and spread the plastic folds apart, then he and his assistant raised the body and moved it sideways into the bag. He closed the zipper, moving slowly this time as the tab locked the metal teeth together.

MacDuff took the top end while Penross grasped the bottom, and together they carried the bulky bag to the waiting van, their free arms swinging outward as they strove to balance themselves against the weight.

I turned my back on them. They weren't of any interest to me now. 'Let's get on with it,' I said to Mungers. 'You stay here and search while I inform the next of kin.'

As I turned to leave, a narrow path, hidden in the shadows until now, suddenly caught my eye. It left the clearing at an angle to the main trail and, as the morning sun fell full upon it, I saw that it cut between tall oaks, then turned sharply left and headed toward the meadow. Wondering where it led, I stepped around the imprint of the corpse and started up the path, walking gingerly and watching every step I took. From time to time I paused and looked around. Soft sunlight and the silence of the woods surrounded me.

The path was two feet wide at most, and apparently so little-used that in spots fresh grass grew in lush profusion, standing upright and untrampled.

As I moved past a towering pine I glimpsed the emerald meadow straight ahead, and quite suddenly I stepped from shadow into full and bright sunlight. Then a glint of light caused me to glance sideways. I saw a girl's bike, chrome-handled with a blue gym bag in its basket, parked beside a tree. Cautiously, I walked up to it.

'So this is how she got here,' I murmured to myself. 'I'd bet my bottom dollar. She rode up on this bike and never rode away. But why? To meet someone? To have a quiet think alone? And why walk down that thick shadowed path instead of down the wider, smoother trail?'

I hurried back to the clearing to tell Carl what I'd found. 'There's a bike up there, close to where that path meets the meadow.' I gestured toward the narrow opening. 'It's possibly the suspect's or the victim's, although I'd bet the latter. Hold it, print it, and take care of the gym bag in its basket. Better do it now, before the curious arrive and take it over for their own.'

'Done, boss.' Mungers called to the patrol to keep the scene secured till he returned. His earlier mood seemed to have dissipated and now his mind was solely on his work.

I drove slowly toward the address on the driver's license, loathing the task that lay ahead. There was no easy way to do it, I'd learned that long ago. It was best just to find the kindest words possible, and know that even they would not, could not, make it any better for the victim's family. No

10

matter how I phrased them, I'd be crushing the world they knew.

The drive took only fifteen minutes, down streets of older homes – not pretentious, but well-kept with pride. I pulled up beside a California ranch house, long and low and made of brick and shingle, and parked the car out front.

Walking swiftly, I rang the bell and heard it echo through the house. I waited, then I rang again. Still no one answered. I stooped and peered through a small side window into a cozy living room, and saw no movement anywhere.

I left the door and walked around the corner of the house, heading for the back yard. When I reached it, I glimpsed a person in the distance coming toward me. As she drew nearer, I saw it was a large round woman with freckled cheeks and dancing eyes, carrying a basket full of vegetables.

When she noticed me she stopped short and set the basket down, looking slightly bewildered. In the next instant, an expression of expectant delight flooded her full face.

'Why, Ms Graber, you've come early. But that's all right. I'll call my husband and tell him to come home.'

Now it was my turn to look confused. 'Excuse me?'

'You said ten-thirty, and here it is barely going on ten o'clock – or did I misunderstand you on the telephone?' She wiped her hands self-consciously on the folds of her cotton skirt.

'Are you Mrs Hammond?' I asked.

'Why yes, I am, but please just call me Janet.'

'We haven't spoken on the phone, Mrs Hammond. I'm Detective Harrod from the police department.'

'Oh, I'm sorry. A reporter from the San Francisco paper is coming to interview my husband and myself on what it's like to raise a teenage baseball star. I just assumed you were she. I'm sorry.'

'Don't be,' I said kindly, wishing I could make it all so nice for her. 'It's all right.'

Suddenly, she peered at me. 'Detective Harrod, you said? Katharine Harrod? Why, you're the detective who handled that case with the little boy.' Her eyes widened as she continued staring. 'I never thought I'd meet you. I mean, I thought the world of how you handled that case and tracked the killer down. And the way you were so gentle with the mother. I heard about that through a mutual friend. You must've been a great comfort to her.'

'Thank you,' I said, but to myself I thought, 'not great enough, though,' as I recalled her bitter end.

A moment passed as we looked at one another. I didn't want to rush it. Then I saw her smile disappear behind a cloud of doubt and her eyes no longer danced.

'But why are you here?'

'Ma'am, could we go inside and sit down?'

She motioned to me to follow her, opened the back screen door, and walked through the house to the living room. I heard a radio playing softly in the kitchen as we passed. She sat down on the gaily colored sofa and I took a chair beside her. She waited, staring at me, and I saw the fear gathering in her eyes. Her fingers plucked at threads along the arm rest.

'Do you have a daughter named Connie?' I began, speaking softly as I laid my hands along my thighs.

'Of course. That's the baseball star I was telling you

about. That's our Connie. Why?' She leaned forward, her eyes now wide and frightened and her fingers clasped together tightly.

'Where is she now?'

'She spent the night at Margie's house – that's a girlfriend – and I imagine she's still there. I expect her home around eleven-thirty.'

'Mrs Hammond, could I ask you please to call your daughter at her friend's house?'

'What will I say to her?'

'Just call her, please,' I said gently.

She walked to a phone sitting on a desk across the room and dialed a number. She spoke so softly I couldn't hear her words. After several minutes she hung up.

I looked at her. She still stood at the phone, her back to me. Then she turned. She moved toward me silently, her eyes fixed on mine, and I saw that her cheeks were wet with tears.

'She wasn't there, Detective. Margie says she never arrived last night. She hasn't seen her. What's happening? What's this all about?'

'Mrs Hammond, a body has been found in the woods off the Canfield road. We have reason to believe it may be your daughter.'

She looked at me and listened to me, but she didn't understand. My words numbed her mind. She heard me but she could not accept my meaning. I waited, for I had nothing more to say till she took in the budding horror I was handing her.

Finally, she could deny me no longer. Her mouth fell open and an awful wrenching sob filled the air as she threw her hands up to her face. I reached across the space between us and placed my hand upon her arm.

'It's a mistake, Detective, all a terrible mistake. It can't be true.'

'We need someone to come downtown, to see if he or she can identify this person. That's the only way we're going to know for sure if it is your daughter or not. Did you say you're expecting your husband home soon?'

'Yes, for the interview. Any minute now. We'll come, of course – we'll both come. Then we'll know it isn't Connie.' The words stumbled out with a rush of breath behind them.

As if on cue, the front door opened and a neatly-dressed man of slender build stepped inside and looked at me. His face was serious and full of questions. I stood up, but before I got a chance to speak, Janet Hammond ran to him and threw her arms around him, pressing herself tightly to his chest.

'What's happened?' he asked sharply as he held her. His eyes never left my face as his voice pierced the air.

'I'm Detective Harrod, sir. Are you Mr Hammond?'

'Russell Hammond, yes. I saw the car out front. I knew it wasn't the press. What's wrong?'

I told him what I'd already told his wife and they moved together to the sofa and sat down holding each other wordlessly. I let them have the moment as I watched their grief. An ache began deep within my innards and wound its way upwards till it filled my chest.

'This girl – whoever she might be – how did she die, Detective?' Hammond finally asked, lifting up his head.

'We're not entirely certain yet, but she appears to have been shot. Can you come with me now?'

They nodded without speaking and walked to the door, hand in hand. They'd forgotten all about the expected visitor from the paper and I didn't bother to remind them.

We drove downtown in near-silence. From time to time I heard hushed whispers from the back seat, and once a sob, but that was all. I could say nothing to them. Now was not the time for false hope and they didn't want to hear what I really believed had happened to their daughter.

When we reached the coroner's office, I led them inside and down a long plain corridor to a closed double door of stainless steel.

'Is this where she is, Detective?' Hammond asked.

'Yes,' I said. 'It should only take a moment.'

He turned to his wife, and I could see the tenseness in his body. 'Janet, you stay here. I'll do this alone.'

'No, I have to go inside. I have to see, to be there with you.'

'Please, please stay here,' he begged. 'Sit down and wait for me. Let me do this for the two of us.'

She obeyed and reached sideways to grasp a chair. She sat down clumsily, almost falling, her face twisted by her torment.

We went inside the still and chilly room and the door closed quietly behind us. A coroner's assistant led us to the waiting gurney and carefully removed the sheet.

Russell Hammond looked at me and then looked down. He saw the square and plain face, the short-cropped hair, the bullet wound that marked the flesh above the eye. He stared at them, eyes wide in shock, and then he stumbled forward, clutching at the edges of the table. I caught his arm and pulled him back toward me. I didn't have to ask.

'It's her, it's Connie. Oh my God, my God!'

He wrenched away from me and stood alone, doubling over toward the floor. Powerful racking sobs shook his body as his vomit spewed across the concrete. I handed him a towel and spoke to him gently. Gradually, the sobbing slowed. He wiped his mouth and we walked back toward the door.

I paused a single second before opening it. I'd played this scene before, far too many times, and I wasn't anxious to get on with it. Even after all these years on homicide, I never fail to feel the pain of the survivors.

The door swung outward, and as we left that cold and silent room Janet Hammond rose to meet us. Her eyes, fixed upon her husband's face, saw the answer that she'd dreaded.

'Connie, Connie, oh my baby Connie!' she screamed out, and she ran to him and threw her arms around him, clutching at him madly. I quickly turned away, leaving them alone with the horror.

CHAPTER TWO

Afterwards I took them home and told them I'd return within the hour. They needed time alone with those familiar comforts that would cushion them, and I needed answers to those questions that I had to ask. I drove quickly from the house and approached the woods for the second time that day.

Carl was waiting for me near the stream, his sandy hair disheveled, his white shirt wet with perspiration. 'Well?'

'It's her, all right – father gave a positive ID. But that's all I've got. I'll question both the parents in a little while – they're in no shape for it right now. What's happening here?'

'Several things. I ran the bike through Records and Identification and it came back to Connie Hammond. The gym bag held some makeup and a change of clothing. I sent them both downtown to check for prints.'

'What else?'

'We found a knife, a small-size pocket type with a single blade.' Carl held up a plastic bag and I saw an object approximately two inches long and half an inch wide with an oblong pearl inlay on its handle. 'It was lying three feet from the body, hidden in the grass, and the blade was folded, as you see it now. Can't know if there's a connection with the killing, but it gives us something else to check for prints, and who knows where it will lead?'

'Who knows indeed?' I mused. 'I've had worse starts before. What about the murder weapon?'

I knew the answer even as I spoke. He'd have marched that out up front if it had surfaced.

'Not a sign. Kent arrived an hour or so ago and the two of us scoured the weeds but came up empty. No bullets or spent casings nearby either. We're going to climb up those rocks behind the clearing and search there and down along the stream, in case the gun was tossed away deeper in the woods.'

'I doubt you'll find it anywhere around here,' I told him. 'If our killer didn't drop it by the body, he'd likely carry it as far as he could before disposing of it, not throw it just a little bit away. We'll search, of course. I just don't hold too much hope.'

'I'll give you hope.' Carl squinted hard against the midday sun. 'I hope he got so confident he kept it with him so he'll have it on him when we finally catch the bastard.'

'It's been known to happen,' I answered quickly. 'Remember little Henry Lawlor? He loved his piece so very much he slept beside it every night, even after pumping six fat holes in his old lady.'

Dan Kent stumbled down the hillside, stopping short when he caught sight of me. A pebble bounced ahead of him and rolled beside my foot. Tall and broad-shouldered, with thick dark hair and honest eyes, he would've been every mother's dream for her daughter to bring home.

His boyish face looked grim and pale, but I knew the harried look didn't come from homicide. He'd married just the year before and baby Kent had sallied in three weeks ago – a rowdy little infant who believed that nights were days and made for romping, who kept his daddy up from dusk till dawn, walking as hard a beat as any he'd ever pounded on patrol.

'So much for evidence,' I chided. 'Watch those feet and try to get some sleep.'

'I'd already checked this area, boss,' he answered earnestly. I watched him as he carefully laid his jacket on a stump and began to roll his sleeves up tanned and muscled arms – and I smiled at how easily I still could jerk his chain.

He'd briefly joined me last year, working on the death by strangulation of a brown-haired little boy, but he'd been just a trainee then and had soon moved on to other tables. When he made detective I requested him full-time, and he became my second man on homicide, replacing Steve Darrow, who'd been reassigned to burglary as a departmental hand-slap for conduct unbecoming.

'Relax, Dan,' I told him, an amused look still playing in my eyes, 'you're not a trainee any more and I'm not going to bite you. What've you got?'

'He tell you about the knife?' He jerked his head toward Carl. 'Well, that's all. We searched the area for the bullet, but *nada*.' He'd been taking basic Spanish at the local junior college and loved to throw in the odd word now and then.

'Let it go for now,' I answered. 'The coroner's 'scoping her to see if it's still inside the skull. I should have an answer shortly.'

I left them at the clearing and walked briskly through the silent woods. I felt good for my thirty-odd years – nearly forty, actually – good and strong and better than I'd felt at twenty. Physically, that is. Mentally, emotionally? Well, maybe there was another story.

My mouth set in a thin hard line and I felt the light leave my eyes as I remembered the tan envelope lying on the front seat of my car and my anger began to stir.

'Damn you,' I muttered hotly, 'damn you anyway. Get the hell out of my life!'

I flung open the door and looked down at the envelope's fatness before I climbed behind the wheel. I'd deal with all that later on, I thought. I was a cop and I had other things to tend to now. Defiantly, I drew myself up straight and shifted into drive. He'd never win, I told myself, *never*, because I simply would not allow such a thing to happen. I would not let him get the best of me.

I felt better, almost buoyant now, as I lay easy in my confidence. Once, he'd fiercely called me a strong-willed bitch. He'd meant it as a criticism. I'd taken it as a compliment and embraced it with loving, hugging arms.

I fixed my eyes on the road ahead and thought about the people I was going to see, thought how it must feel to learn your child had lain cold and dead and all alone, face down on the dank floor of the forest.

Did they hear the sharp crack of the bullet as it split the skull? Did they see the warm pure blood as it erupted through the hair and stained the creamy flesh? Did they picture how she'd staggered, perhaps clutching at the air, before finally falling forward? I was certain that they did. I was certain that, right now, they were torturing and tormenting their already battered beings with those very images. I know that's just what I'd have done if my Tommy had been the victim.

Tommy. My only son, my only child. A nine-year-old, torn between two warring parents. Tomorrow was the weekend and it was Jon's turn to have him. He'd pick him up at eight-thirty in the morning, barely nodding to me as I stood to say goodbye, and bring him back after dinner on Sunday evening.

When he'd gone, I'd walk from room to empty room, idly picking up Tommy's toys and straightening up his shelves, and I'd hear the silence and feel the awful aching loneliness, as if a part of me were missing. And I'd wait for his return. And wait for Wednesday. Again, I glanced at the thick envelope lying close beside me, then quickly looked away.

I braked beside the ranch house, pulled into the driveway, and parked beside a two-tone green sedan. A vintage black VW was pulled on to the grass in front of it. Friends, relatives, sympathizers, I thought. The clan was gathering to nurture and sustain its wounded members, to take their grief and forcibly weaken it by sharing it.

I knocked and the door opened slightly. Russell Hammond, his face gray and haggard, waved me inside. Across the room, I saw two women sitting with their arms around his wife, who raised a blotched and tear-stained face when she heard me enter. A picture of the Christ child hung above her head, and the infant Jesus seemed to stare down at her beatifically in her distress.

'I need to talk with you,' I said. 'I need to ask some questions,' and I heard my voice, cool and steady, break the silence of the room. The women slid their arms away from Janet Hammond's shoulders and glided backwards toward the kitchen. Soon, I heard the murmur of their voices from behind the swinging door.

'Tell me when you last saw Connie,' I began, as I took a seat beside the weeping mother. 'Tell me that and everything you can to help me out, even if you're not sure it really matters.'

The grieving woman inhaled deeply and leaned back against the couch. Her eyes stared straight ahead, and at first I thought she hadn't heard me. Then she swung around to face me and I realized she'd only been gathering determination.

'She left last night, just as it was getting dark, probably a little after eight or so. She was going to spend the night with her best friend, Margie Dawson – she's the catcher on the team – pop in here for a bite of lunch, and then go on to practice this afternoon.'

'How did she leave here? By car? On foot?'

'Oh no,' Janet Hammond answered quickly, for the moment in control of her emotions, 'she took her bike as usual. She threw a change of clothing in her little bag and put it in the basket, then pedaled off. Funny, I watched her going down the drive' – I saw her hands begin to tighten on the armrest – 'and I never thought, I never knew, that I'd not see her any more.' She began to gag on her saliva as choking sobs suddenly shook her body, and her husband rushed across the room to take her in his arms.

A young girl, no more than twelve, I guessed, walked through the hallway door. I saw the short blonde hair, the familiar squared-off face, and I knew I was looking at Connie's little sister. She came toward us and began to pat her mother's arm and hand.

Russell Hammond straightened up and introduced her as Darleen, the only daughter he had left – the only other child, in fact. She sat stiffly, awkward and extremely ill-at-ease, not knowing what was expected of her, how she was supposed to act under the alien circumstances that suddenly surrounded her.

'We found the bicycle,' I told them slowly. 'We found it near the clearing where your daughter died. It looks as if she pedaled there on purpose, left it at the trail's head, then walked down through the woods. Do you have any idea why she went there? Did she ever meet anyone by that stream?'

They looked at one another in bewilderment. Obviously the clearing meant absolutely nothing to them. I didn't need their quick denial to tell me that.

'I thought she'd been taken there, Detective. I thought till now whoever did this forced her to go down there, far away, where he'd be hidden . . .' Russell Hammond rubbed his thin gray moustache nervously, first one side and then the other, as his voice trailed off. His eyes showed confusion as he scanned my face.

'It doesn't look that way,' I told him firmly. 'I think she

went there voluntarily, probably very shortly after leaving here.'

I saw Darleen watching me, honest open eyes fixed on mine as I sat talking to her father. Her lips were slightly parted, but she didn't say a word, she only listened.

'Do you know about the clearing?' I asked her gently. 'Do you know if your sister went there often?'

She still didn't speak, but shook her head slowly from one side to the other, now pressing her lips together tightly. I thought I saw a shadow pass through those honest eyes, but I could not be sure. I watched a moment, but when she continued to remain silent I turned back to the parents.

'Tell me about her friends,' I said, leaning forward as I spoke. 'Did she have many, and what was your opinion of them? Did any jealousy exist because of her athletic ability?'

'Everyone was her friend, Detective – she was that kind of kid,' her father answered eagerly, and I sensed that, for him, praising Connie and telling how well loved she was somehow breathed life back into her again. 'As for jealousy, I guess there's bound to have been some grumbling somewhere, but nothing we ever heard about, nothing major.'

I jotted down Margie Dawson's address as well as the address of the third baseman.

'Of all the girls on the team, I guess you could say she was closest to those two,' Hammond continued. 'The three of them were together whenever possible – hanging out at school, giggling on the phone, sleeping overnight. It's been that way since junior high.'

The murdered girl would've been seventeen in December, yet nowhere had I seen any evidence of a boyfriend – no picture in her wallet and, now, no mention by her parents.

'Did your daughter date?' I asked. 'Did she have a steady, or see a lot of different boys?'

'No. Connie didn't date, Detective.' The mother spoke, uttering her words in a calm, controlled tone, the weeping past for now. 'Oh, not that she didn't want to, but she just didn't seem to attract the fellas. She was a dear girl, Detective Harrod, and inside she felt as feminine as the Rose Bowl queen, but I think the boys saw her otherwise. They saw the muscles and the throw, and they thought her a bit of a jock, just like themselves. They never tried to look beyond that.'

I recalled the tiny silver chain dangling from the corpse's wrist and remembered how its femininity had struck me, had seemed in sharp contrast to the thick muscular arm that bore it.

'Was she aware of how the opposite sex perceived her?' I asked.

'Very much so, I'm afraid. And it hurt her deeply. She felt dainty and vulnerable inside, but she knew the guys couldn't get past her exterior appearance. I often told her that some-day she'd meet a boy who'd look beyond all that and find out who she truly was.'

From the corner of my eye, I saw Darleen tugging at her mother's sleeve and whispering, and I thought I caught a name.

'Who's Larry?' I asked.

'A no-good nothing,' the father answered. 'Darleen's

25

thinking we forgot Larry when you asked if Connie dated and, in fact, I guess we did. Or wanted to, anyway.'

I waited. No one spoke. 'Go on,' I said.

'Well, she didn't go out with him very much, and I don't think she'd even seen him since school let out.' Again Hammond stroked his moustache, but this time in a thoughtful manner. 'He appeared in town last spring, did odd jobs here and there, and somehow met our Connie. He was a good-looking chap and she was smitten, as they say. But he had a sneaky way about him, and a glib tongue. I could never find out much about him and I could never get myself to trust him either, though on the face of it he did nothing wrong, nothing I could point a finger to.'

I felt my interest quickening as he verbally fleshed out the boyfriend and his opinion of him.

'Did Connie know how you felt?' I asked.

'I'm sure she did, Detective,' Mrs Hammond, still composed, answered readily as her open palms smoothed down her skirt, 'but we didn't make too much of it. She seemed so happy and delighted at the attention that we didn't want to come down hard on her. We just kept our fingers crossed it'd end before it went too far. And it did.' They told me they hadn't seen Larry Merchant in several months and didn't know where to find him.

'He used to have a room over near Oliva, but I think Connie said he was moving closer into town.'

'Just one more thing. Did your daughter own a knife?'

The three of them looked at one another, then slowly shook their heads.

'Like a big knife? A hunting knife?' the father asked.

'Any kind of knife.'

'No, we never saw one.'

I'd leave them now, give them over once again to the succor of the friends and neighbors murmuring in the kitchen near me. I doubted their composure of the moment would last for very long. I knew the road that lay ahead, and so I knew that their deepest grief was yet to come.

I laid my hand on Darleen's shoulder as I walked past. I'd seen the tears begin to fall. 'You're a brave young girl,' I told her quietly, 'and because of that you *will* get through this, but you can't do it alone. You need your parents now, just as they need you.'

She nodded slightly and brushed the tears away with the back of a tanned and childlike hand.

I started up the car and backed out on the street. I'd call Penross shortly to get the skinny on that 'scope, but first I wanted a moment to myself.

The Hammonds had lost their elder daughter to a cruel and hideous death. While that void would never fill, they still had another blonde-haired, blue-eyed child to stroke and hold and kiss. If I lost Tommy, I had no one.

I touched the envelope lying there beside me. The custody hearing was set for nine o'clock on Wednesday morning. I'd read the fitness reports, the psychological evaluations, the legal mumbo-jumbo that accompanied the thin white sheet that stated day and time for a court appearance that could change my life.

And I'd read the lawyer's covering letter: 'Be hopeful, Katharine, but don't be over-confident.'

I'd been born in this broad and sunny valley, near the rolling foothills of the Mariposa mountains. I'd spent my childhood and my schooldays in the patchwork of these fertile fields surrounding me. I'd become a cop here, when I was in my early twenties.

And I'd married here, nearly sixteen years ago, and thought that I'd live happily ever after. I had a job I loved, a husband and a little boy that I adored. Even Jon's breakdown of several years ago seemed only a fleeting marring of the perfect picture, which became intact again with his recovery.

But the fairy tale had ended suddenly some months ago, when Jonathan had demanded I give up my job, when his increasing anger toward me exploded with the revelation that he'd always hated what I did, always hoped that I would leave it. He could no longer live with me, he said, unless I quit my work and stayed at home.

I'm not good with ultimatums at the best of times, but even had I wished to acquiesce to this one, I knew I just could not. Without my job – no, not a job, a life, for that is what a cop's work is – I'd wither from the inside out and become a fragile husk of my former self.

He was asking far too much. Simply put, he was asking me to give myself away. But he would not believe, would not even try to understand, the sure and certain consequences that would tumble down upon us if I gave in to his demands.

My son had stayed with me in these lonely months of bitter separation, but now my husband had begun a fight for custody, claiming I could not provide a stable atmosphere

28

because of my erratic schedule as head of homicide for my division.

And so I found that I hadn't known Jonny after all, hadn't really understood the man I'd lain next to for so many loving nights. Underneath the skin, underneath the surface, a transformation had been taking place for months, perhaps for years.

Or had he always been this person, in hiding from me from the start? I didn't know. I doubted that I ever really would.

I turned a grim face toward the window. The summer sunlight streaked the growing fields with gold, and the jagged mountains, scarred by dark and dusky crevices, laid a periwinkle blue swath against the faded distant sky. Ordinarily I'd have reveled in this sight, gloried in the brightly banded vision of the glowing California landscape that I loved, but not today. A harder edge now defined my life and my feelings toward it. I'd lost the joy.

I got the good news from Penross on a corner phone – the bullet was still inside the skull. The fluoroscope, a constant, running X-ray rather than the usual printed picture, had revealed it lodged near the base at a slight downward angle.

'Doesn't look fragmented either, Kate,' he told me. 'Once I get it out, it should do a good match if you find the weapon.'

I'd have to wait for the autopsy before learning any more – caliber, special markings, whether it really *was* intact as the coroner suspected – but I had what I wanted for now.

I relayed the word to Dan and Carl and told them to concentrate their efforts on finding the gun, along with any other evidence, then I headed for the Dawson girl's house.

As I drove, I pictured the bullet lying inside the skull it had cracked but never exited. Actually, I wasn't surprised it was still there. Bone is the most resistant part of the human body, with skin a close second, and a bullet of a smaller caliber, as we guessed this one to be, often can't get out. It frequently happens that a projectile will go almost completely through the body, only to be stopped by the skin on the opposite side, where it can easily be felt.

I remembered the stark, emotionless words in my homicide manual, which achieved by their very simplicity the creation of a chilling picture of horror far more vivid than in any novel I'd read: '. . . as the projectile passes through the body, it packs the tissue in front of it. If it has enough momentum to go through completely, it will finally force its way out through the packed tissues, causing a ragged and torn exit wound. Often, shreds of fat or other internal tissues will be protruding from the wound.'

Although this bullet hadn't exited, the process inside the dead girl's head would've fitted this description as the bullet moved from front to back. And if the projectile had struck a bone at an angle, severe destruction of the surrounding soft tissues would have occurred. Again I recalled the cold and factual explanation from my manual: '. . . this is caused by the energy of the bullet being transmitted by broken fragments of bone, making each fragment an additional projectile. Not only do the bone fragments enormously increase tissue destruction, but the bullet itself is frequently sent spinning end-over-end, which greatly increases tissue damage and bleeding.'

Not a pretty business at all.

The Dawson girl was next on my list and I started driving toward her home. On the way I passed a little square, green and neat with a statue of a local raisin baron standing in the center. Reminiscent of squares in towns back east, it had once stood smack in the middle of San Madera. But our once bucolic little city, as cities tend to do, had started growing, and instead of reaching outward evenly from all sides of this park-like setting, it had spread only east, north, and south, leaving the square in its western end, not too far from my home.

I looked at its grass and trees and remembered all the Saturdays in my youth when I'd ridden into town with my parents for the weekly Farmers' Market. They, along with other farmers, would set up their booths early in the morning and sell their produce all day long. Occasionally, livestock would be offered too, and sheep and goats would prance around their pens.

I'd always loved those days – the happy, milling crowd, the slightly festive atmosphere – and was sorry when, some years ago, the square had been abandoned. Nowadays the Farmers' Market still took place, but in a large antiseptic gray warehouse on the other side of town.

Looking toward the far end of the square, my eyes fell on a broad dark California oak whose branches spread gracefully above the grass. The story was that this had once been the 'hanging tree,' and I had no reason to doubt it. Founded in the early 1870s, San Madera had meted out a brand of justice not uncommon to the West. Now the tree lent only beauty, not a limb to string a noose, and told no tales of what had happened in the past.

I crossed some deserted railroad tracks just past the square and remembered how the boxcars filled with produce used to rumble through the town. The vast-reaching San Joaquin Valley is one of the premier agricultural areas in the world, producing varied fruits and vegetables in abundance, and within its sprawling acreage every little region has its specialties. San Madera's has always been its raisins.

Nestled in a tiny valley of its own, with the foothills of the High Sierras not far out of town, the fields surrounding my city continue to produce fat fine grapes that eventually become plump morsels in a Sunkist box. But now the tracks that take them off to market lie well outside of town, and all that's left of yesteryear is the memory of those Saturdays in the square and these broken rusting tracks that run to nowhere.

Ah, progress, I thought as I eased into the curb. You gain a lot, you lose a lot.

I didn't know if Margie Dawson had heard the news or not, so I wasn't sure what I was walking into here. One look at the face that answered the door told me without a doubt.

She asked me in as she wiped a hand across her tear-stained cheeks, and I followed her across the tiled hall floor into a warm and cheerful living room.

Unlike the dead girl, Margie Dawson was pretty and

petite, with dark, gleaming curls ringing a pink-cheeked face. I imagined she had more success with the boys than Connie had enjoyed, and I wondered if her friend had been jealous of her.

'Mrs Hammond told me Connie was supposed to stay here last night,' I began. 'Did you see her any time at all?'

'No, and no message either.' She blew her nose softly on a limp and rumpled hanky. 'I was out myself, and when I got home around eleven I expected her to be here. She was going to sleep over and then we'd mess around and go on to early practice in the afternoon.'

'What did you do when you found she wasn't here?'

'Nothing, just went on to bed. It was too late to call over to her house. I figured something had come up or maybe she'd forgotten, and I'd hear about it today.'

I asked about friends, enemies, any odd occurrences lately in Connie's life, and drew a blank with every question. Margie Dawson seemed totally bewildered as to why the Hammond girl had been murdered.

'How did Connie get on with her parents? Any problems there?'

'Nope, they're very tolerant, loving people and they understand what it's like to be a teen. Not like my Mom . . .' Her voice died off as her lips began to pout.

'Do you know Larry Merchant?' I asked, and watched curiously for her reaction.

'That loser!' She snorted and shook her head as if in disbelief. 'I can't think what Connie ever saw in him.'

'Could he have anything to do with this?' I queried.

'I doubt it. Oh, not that he didn't seem creepy enough to

do something bad – but she dumped him early in the summer. I don't think she'd even seen him since shortly after school let out.'

'Tell me, did Connie own a knife?'

Margie drew her chin in and her eyes opened wide. 'Good gracious, no. Or if she did, I never saw it.'

We sat silently for a moment and she became agitated, twisting and tearing at the hanky's hem. I watched as her face contorted in uncontrolled anguish, then switched abruptly to a remote, far-off expression. I could only guess at the confusion of emotions that were assaulting her right now. Her next words set me back a little and made me take a second thought.

'What's going to happen to our team?' she whimpered. 'We're up for the state championship and we can't possibly win without Connie. Does Coach Branscombe know yet?' Immediately she realized the apparent impropriety and clapped her hand across her mouth. 'My God, that sounded awful. I didn't mean . . . My mind was wandering . . .'

Tears began to ease their way down the pink cheeks and I moved to sit beside her, to offer comfort. 'It's all right, Margie, that's how our minds work. We think of totally incongruous things in the moment of facing a death. I don't know why we do it, but I do know it doesn't signify any disrespect.'

Her next words did, though. 'Tell me, Ms Harrod, did she bleed a lot? Was it awful? I mean, she was my best friend. I need to know.'

I could understand that – the bit about wanting to know how your best friend died – but the tone put me off. It was peek time at the supermarket tabloids. I had to wonder what kind of buddy she'd really been to Connie.

'That's confidential information, Margie,' I said, and it wasn't hard to invoke my very best police-procedural tone. 'It has no relevance to our discussions here.'

Her greedy, ghoulish little mind wilted as I watched, or at least it withdrew to safer quarters for the moment, and I got up and left.

CHAPTER THREE

I dropped by a drab brown building sitting on a corner the other side of town. It housed the department's narcotics team as well as several other specialized units. In this day and age, especially when the victim is in the tender years of life, drugs inevitably come to the forefront of the mind as a possible motive for murder.

As I walked across the parking lot, a dressed-down gray Ford, unembellished in any way, spun across the pebbles and parked beside me. Even without the special license plate, I'd have recognized it as one of our detective cars – not from my division, but from somewhere in the city.

I knew him instantly when he jumped out and slammed the door. Gant, head of narcotics, a man driven by an unrelenting, all-consuming hatred of the filth who peddle drugs, hawked as high excitement, to the citizens of San Madera.

I'd seen him once, burly belly spilling over his straining belt, sticking his face in front of that of a suspect in the lobby of my station, and spewing four-letter words all over him as he told him what he thought of him and others like him. A big bull of a man with a hard glint in his eyes and a mouth that didn't smile, he didn't give a goddamn for the idea of treating arrestees with respect and letting the courts deal out the punishment.

And he didn't care if the startled citizens scattered throughout the lobby had caught his tirade either. He'd fought the fight too long, he'd seen too many wasted people, too many lives dirtied and destroyed, to be anything less than right up front about his hatred of narcotics and their pedlars, no matter where he was.

The hard glint lit on me and a slight look of recognition passed through the eyes.

I helped him out. 'I'm Katharine Harrod, Detective Gant. Head of homicide in the west end.'

'Yeah, I knew I'd seen ya.' He flashed a smile, spread his legs, swung his head around, and spat. 'Watcha' doin' over my way?'

'Got any idea who's dealing drugs to high school kids?'

Gant pulled in his chin and gave a rolling belch. I noticed brownish stains, like drying juice from hamburgers, on his T-shirt front, but I doubt he knew or cared about them. His mind was only ever on one thing and all else was non-essential, never worth acknowledging. 'Damn right I do, Harrod. No matter who's doing the actual selling – I'd lay odds it's coming from Dicky King. I've had him tagged as main distributor in town for some time now, but I just can't get enough to put the final screws in and take it to the DA.'

I didn't know the name and wondered if I should. 'Dicky King? Has he got a record?'

'Nickel and dime stuff, way back. He's been smart enough to avoid getting caught so far for the biggies. Puts up a really good front, too. Nice little family, regular church-goer, runs a thriving lumber yard, belongs to the Junior Chamber of Commerce. Hell, he even sponsors that hot-shot girls' softball team!'

'Screw it,' I thought as I drove away, 'another drug-related death.'

I found them so pathetic, so discouraging and disheartening . . . and so increasingly common.

Usually, both the suspect *and* the victim were caught up in the downward spiral of life, and had set the course for their own destruction long before the final act. I found little joy in the solving of such crimes. Instead I felt a sadness at the waste, the senseless and needless waste.

Not that Connie had died by drugs, but it now looked possible she may have died because of them.

Gant had laid it all out for me back there in the parking lot. King had been the suspected heavy in the local drug trade for some time now, and constant, dogged digging by the narcotics division was starting to pay off. Slowly but surely, evidence was building against him – solid, bona fide evidence they could take to court. It was now one step forward and no steps back, or, as Gant put it, 'The bricks are strong, the mortar's sound.'

I'd told him about my homicide and my victim being one of King's softball players.

'Fuck it!' he'd exploded. 'Maybe now the shit's gone too far. Oh, not him, Harrod. I doubt he's the one who squeezed the trigger. He stays standing in the shadows and does the string-pulling, that's his style. But he'd have found some

Laura Coburn

patsy that he had a hold on of some sort and gotten him to do it.'

'You think she was involved, then?'

'Not saying that—' vehemently he spat again – 'but we've good reason to believe King's using high-school kids as his pushers with their peers. What age was your gal? Fifteen? Sixteen? And she was already connected to him through softball. Yeah, I'd say there's a strong possibility.'

And so I'd left, the feeling of discouragement riding close beside me. Maybe she'd crossed him in a deal, keeping the money for herself. Maybe she'd botched a score big-time and he wanted rid of her. Maybe she'd wanted out and he wouldn't let her go alive, or she'd been getting ready to rat to the narcs and he'd got wind of it.

Or maybe none of the above. Maybe she was on the other side.

Perhaps Connie Hammond had never been involved with drugs at all, but had inadvertently stumbled across her sponsor's dirty little game, had seen or heard something so potentially dangerous to King it would destroy him. And he'd found out. And had her killed.

Either way, I doubted Dicky King was going to sit right down and tell me all about it. My best bet, I figured, was talking to the high-school kids Gant had named as his sources, as well as to Connie's friends and family. I'd give the kids to Kent and Mungers while I focused on the Hammonds and the dead girl's close acquaintances.

I headed toward my home, a beige green-shuttered two-story dwelling with a short front lawn and a deep one in the back, set on a quiet block of Marsh Road in the west end of

40

our town. I wanted to grab some clean shoes, the spotless flats of that morning having gained a crust of dirt from walking in the woods and ploughing by the stream.

I parked by one of the tall trees surrounding it, crossed the L-shaped porch, and walked quickly through the door. As I passed the phone it rang and I snatched it up. I heard his voice, cool and slightly hostile, and I winced.

'Katharine? Surprised to find you there. I was expecting Mrs Miller.'

I pictured him holding the receiver in his apartment on the other side of town, standing by his drawing board in the room he called his office, surrounded by architectural renderings.

'I'm passing through, Jon. In a hurry. A young girl's been killed. Can we talk later?'

'Always later, sweetie, that's the way it always is,' he answered in a deprecating tone. 'I only wanted to say I'd pick Tommy up at eight tomorrow instead of eight-thirty. We've got a big day planned.'

'I have no objection, Jon,' I told him. 'I'll make sure he's ready then.'

'If your time permits,' he answered airily.

Oh, give it a rest, I thought. Let it lie still for a moment and behave like an adult human being instead of always digging at me. Despite my weariness with this constant line of chatter, I could feel my blood start to quicken and my stomach tense, and I was angry he still could get a rise out of me.

'See you at eight, then,' I told him brusquely. 'I'm going now.' And hastily I hung up the phone.

★ ★ ★

I swung into the station lot, my emotions iced and put away. I'd learned early on in my embattled relationship with Jonny that I couldn't let my personal life impact on my professional one. If I did allow that to happen, I'd be doing only half-service for my victims, with little service to my other life either. I'd also start getting careless – and because of the perilous nature of my job, I'd set myself up for being dead.

The two-story brick building lay roughly a mile from my home. Our little city was divided into four divisions, easily named East End, North End, South End and West End. Each had its own captain and its own head of homicide, though I was the only woman of the eight. My entire career had been spent in the westside division, save for my probation days when I'd worked the east. I knew it inside-out and back-wards, knew each street by name and number.

I walked in through the back door with my special key, just as the p.m. watch was coming on patrol. They poured through a downstairs door from roll call and headed for the kit room to pick up their weapons.

I knew most of them by name, had worked patrol with many of them, and I hand-slapped and exchanged greetings as I moved my way through the group.

A young lieutenant, badge gleaming, woolens crisp, joshed with an old-time street cop about what the afternoon would offer. 'So, what're you bringin' back for us today? What good will you have done by the next time I see you in here?'

The cop pretended to consider for a moment, then

answered with a grin, 'Two drunk drivers, one stop sign runner, one petty theft.'

'That's all?' The lieutenant huffed in mock disgust. 'I bet you bring in at least one felony before the end of watch.' He clapped the street cop on the shoulder and walked into the watch commander's room.

I climbed the stairs to homicide, poured myself a cup of coffee, and threw myself into a chair. It'd been a hell of a day so far and I had to wonder what was coming next. I'd take a thirty-second break before I went to the computer and began to do my homework.

I sipped the coffee slowly, so hot it fired my mouth and tongue, and savored every swallow. The aching pains of tiredness began flowing through my muscles, and as I relaxed I felt them ease away. In minutes, I felt better.

I'd run Dicky King, get a print-out and a fix on him myself. And I'd run the Hammond family, to see if the parents had arrest records, outstanding warrants, or had ever filed a crime report. This was routine business in a homicide – the searching for a record or a warrant, anyway. And ever since a case the year before, when I'd failed to look for crime reports and wasted time I could've saved, that had become routine for me too.

Moving to the computer, I signed on and did my work.

Mr Dicky King came up the model citizen. Even the nickel-and-dime stuff mentioned by Gant no longer showed. Male white, forty-three years of age, address on the hill, vehicle registration and driver's license up-to-date. I printed out the info and kept it for my records.

I found nothing on the Hammonds either – no contact with

43

the police, their side or ours. I wasn't surprised, but I'd had to make the search because sometimes appearances can be deceptive. In this case, though, unless something suspicious surfaced in my inquiries farther down the line, I couldn't consider them suspects in their daughter's death.

Satisfied for now, I shut the system down and walked back to my desk. I'd check with Penross on the time of the autopsy, scheduled for tomorrow morning. I was anxious to learn about that bullet. The toxicological reports would be a while coming, I knew, but they weren't top priority with me right now.

Carl came across the room, his shoulders slumped, his face glum. I looked at him quizzically and waited for his words.

'Nothing more to give you, Kate. We did it by the book – searched grid by grid by grid – and the only thing we found was that little knife. The weapon's far away, in my opinion.'

'What about the creek?' I asked, tapping my pencil on my lips.

'Hell, that water's crystal-clear, running from a mountain stream. We waded through it all and it isn't there, not near the murder site anyway.'

'The knife's not hers, Carl,' I told him. 'I asked her parents and her best buddy and they've never seen it. It may be important . . . and it may be all we've got except the bullet. Did you hear from R & I?'

Records and Identification had found no prints other than those of the dead girl – on the bike, the gym bag and the makeup kit. We'd have to get our help from somewhere else.

'Carl, what's wrong? What's troubling you?' I knew him

like the back of my own hand, and I could tell he was in agony.

'Betsy.' He choked and looked away. 'Lila's taking her away.'

'For the weekend? For a trip?'

'No, goddamnit. For good.' His blue eyes swung around to mine, and I could see his anguish had dulled them, made them flat and pale.

I went to him and put my arms around him. 'Tell me.'

'She's moving down to Bakersfield and putting Betsy in some hospital down there.'

Long before I knew him, long before he had made detective, Carl had met and wed a long-limbed satin beauty with wandering eyes and the urge to follow them. Although all his friends had wondered at the union, he'd not seen through his sleek-skinned woman. Not until the day he went home early after an injurious struggle with a crook and caught her sharing all that satin with his child-hood best friend, a buddy who worked day watch and got off at four o'clock.

He'd forgiven her, even though she'd tossed her indiscretion in his face and told him about the others. But then one day Lila did the leaving – just shut the door and walked away from the best man she could ever hope to find.

In the midst of all this sorry mess there was Betsy, a child now twelve years old who was born retarded and had lived in hospitals ever since. A gracious, gorgeous child, who had no clue at all as to what was going on. Lila had primary custody, not that it'd ever really mattered, since the girl was being raised by doctors and nurses rather than by either of her parents. But now, suddenly and unexpectedly, it did matter very much to Carl.

He visited Betsy whenever he could and brought me vivid tales of hope, tales of how she'd responded to this or learned to do that. The stories were merely words shaped into dreams and wishes because he wouldn't accept the truth. His child would probably never progress beyond her present state.

'What can you do, Carl?' I asked, and my own troubles slipped away as I focused on the torment tearing at him.

'Nothing, not a goddamn thing. Legally, she has every right to take her.'

There was no answer, neither hard nor easy. Whether it was morally right or not didn't enter Lila's picture, but the truth was that she could move Carl's little girl anywhere she chose.

'You can be with her at least once a week,' I said, thinking of the hundred-mile drive down and then back again, 'and if you need more time the first few months, you know I'll do my damndest to cover for you.'

He nodded, didn't speak, walked listlessly to his desk and banged his fist down on the faded blotter.

He hadn't asked about my hearing coming up on Wednesday. He'd been my constant ally since my troubles had begun with Jonathan – listening, advising, being there as my personal tower of strength – and normally he'd have mentioned it. I knew he'd simply forgotten because of the emotional vortex in which he was caught.

Or maybe not. Maybe he knew that the news about Betsy had already woken the raw and constant fears that were dwelling inside me, and he didn't want to add to my anxiety. How could he reassure me now, when his own life showed how very wrong things could go?

I glanced up as the youthful face of Kent stood in front of me. I was glad someone on my team had a happy marriage, even if its product kept him up all night. I called Carl over and filled the two of them in on Dicky King and the possible drug connection.

'The two of you divide these names—' I handed them a list – 'and go talk to these kids. Nose around, see if you hear anything tying our victim to Mr King in a drug-related way. I'm going to see the third baseman.'

They hustled off to start the work and I picked up the phone to call Penross. I got MacDuff instead, but his word was just as good. The autopsy would be performed at ten o'clock tomorrow. One of us would be there – and then I'd start to get some solid answers.

I stuck a notebook in my pocket and clattered down the back stairs. Turning to go down the hall, I felt a hand touch my shoulder, and I spun around to face a tall, straight man.

Captain John Stratton would be a hard one to lie to. He was quick and he was bright, his mind digesting facts as fast as he received them. His eyes fixed on yours when you started talking and wouldn't let them go till you'd finished. You almost thought you could hear that mind crackle and sizzle as it worked, like a current racing down a live wire. He cut quickly through the chaff in any situation and went directly to the core, tossing non-essentials aside like so much garbage.

Unlike many captains, he'd worked the streets of San

Madera for years before ascending through the ranks. He knew the problems of the 'foot soldier' on patrol and of the working detective, and was always in step with their feelings. All his men respected him.

'What's happening with the homicide, Kate?' he asked, and I knew he wasn't just passing time. He wanted all the pertinent details without a bit of bullshitting. I gave him everything I had, succinct but complete.

'I didn't know the girl,' he told me, 'don't know the family either. Damn drugs . . . if it's true, then what a waste.' His mouth set in a bitter line and his eyes looked momentarily wounded. I knew he'd lost his oldest son to a narcotics overdose some years ago, and I still couldn't find the proper words, could only nod and wish the moment gone.

Then his eyes sharpened again, the pained expression shuttered from my sight, and he smiled at me. 'Sorry, Katharine, I know what you must be thinking. I didn't mean to make it awkward for you. I've pretty much put it behind me. Not forgotten it, but put it in the past.'

He could do that – effortlessly, gracefully, fluidly – put you at your ease and make you feel all right. I relaxed, and knew that if he wanted to talk about it again I could stand there comfortably and offer my compassion.

He didn't. 'Keep me informed, Kate. I want to stay on top of this.'

'I will, sir,' I told him, and he turned and walked away. I'd wanted to salute – that's the response he invariably evoked in me – but I quelled the urge. He wasn't the chief, after all.

Kerry Spaulding lived right around the corner from the

station. When I saw her coming down the walk, I felt we'd met before – not just passed each other on the street, but been introduced. This was confirmed when her eyes widened happily in recognition. The dark and puffy skin around them told me she'd been crying.

'I'm an Explorer, Detective Harrod,' she explained, referring to the police-sponsored civic club for teens that operated out of our community relations department. 'I met you last year when we handed out flyers for you on that missing child case.'

'Ah, yes,' I said, and I remembered the enthusiasm and the willingness of this big-framed, freckle-faced girl standing in front of me. She'd organized six kids under her and distributed more sheets and posters than any other group. 'I need to talk with you for just a few minutes,' I explained, 'about your friend's death. Is now a good time or were you going out?'

'It doesn't matter. I was going to a teammate's house – we were Connie's best buddies – but this is more important. Do you want to go inside?'

'Would you mind if we just sat out here on the grass?' I asked. 'It's such a warm and pretty day.' And we sank to the soft greenery beneath us, curling our legs under us, and relaxed like two old friends with nothing but idle gossip on our minds.

'I need your help,' I began softly. 'I need your help in finding out who murdered Connie Hammond. It was a wicked, violent death and I don't believe she was a random victim, killed by some irrational nut who didn't know what he was doing. I believe she was intentionally targeted to die.'

She winced and swallowed hard, but she looked me straight in the eye as she answered. 'I want to help you, really I do, Detective Harrod, but I've no idea who'd do this. Everybody loved her. She had no enemies.'

'Did she confide in you? Did she have any troubles?'

'We told each other everything – at least, I always thought so – and, no, there were no problems. We were going to the state championship and she was taking us there. I'd never seen her happier.'

She clasped her hands together and leaned forward earnestly. 'I want to be a cop, Detective Harrod, that's why I'm active in the Explorers. I've always wanted to be a cop, so if I could think of anything to tell you that would help you, you know I'd do it.'

'What about her parents? Did she get along well with them?'

'Oh, yes.' Kerry nodded. 'It's a very loving family. The four of them were very close to one another.'

I asked her if Connie had ever needed money – money that her allowance or babysitting jobs wouldn't cover.

She started and sat up straight. 'How odd that you should say that,' she said. 'Just last month, when we hit our winning streak and knew we were going to the state, she began to talk about wanting to earn nearly a thousand dollars, but she didn't know how she'd do it. I think she got obsessed with it and it started bugging her.'

Now we were getting somewhere. 'What was she going to do with all that cash, Kerry?'

'The national playoffs are held back east. She felt we had a good chance to go and she wanted to surprise her parents with air tickets to come see her play.'

I broached the next question in an easy, low-key manner. 'Kerry, have you ever heard anything – just a rumor, even – about a possible drug connection with anyone involved with your team?'

She reddened and became plainly uncomfortable.

'You know what you tell me is confidential. And you also know, because you want to be a cop, how important it is that you share everything you have with me.'

'I've heard a few things about Mr King, that man who sponsors us,' she said reluctantly. 'That maybe he's some-how mixed up with them.'

'What about the players?'

'Well, there was some talk early in the summer that several of them might be selling coke, but I never saw it. As far as I'm concerned, it was just talk, nothing more.'

'And the coke came from Mr King?'

'That's what they were saying, yes. But if it happened it was never around me.'

I can usually spot a liar, but I didn't see one here. Kerry Spaulding impressed me with her obvious sincerity. I didn't think she'd been included in the sponsor's inner circle.

'Did Connie know about the clearing?' I asked next. 'Did she ever meet anyone there?'

The girl relaxed, obviously glad to move away from the drug talk. 'She knew about it because she used to meet Larry Merchant there, when her parents thought she was seeing him too much. She didn't like to do it but she'd leave the house and say she was going somewhere else, then she'd go to the woods instead.'

Merchant again. 'Could she've been meeting him last night?'

'Oh, no, I'm sure not.' Kerry shook her head vigorously. 'For one thing, she'd have told me. For another, she broke up with him early in the summer.'

'Do you know where I can find this boy?' I asked.

'Nope, he just drifted in and drifted out. I'm glad, too. He wasn't right for Connie. I don't know . . .' She stumbled as she tried to put her feelings into words. 'He was pretty good-looking, but he seemed sort of, well, slippery. I think he lied a lot, about himself and everything else too and I never felt he really cared for Connie either, just used her and sort of toyed with her.'

Unexpectedly she began to cry and she burrowed her face into the purple sweater she was holding while her shoulders shook in sudden spasms.

I crouched beside her and put my arm around her, offering comfort but knowing it could do no good. Her friend was dead, and nothing could undo that.

CHAPTER FOUR

Who was Larry Merchant? I couldn't bring his name up on the computer, for either a California driver's license or in-state, out-of-state ID. I could find no rap sheet, no outstanding wants or warrants.

I phoned Margie Dawson, hoping Kerry would be there too.

'Did this Merchant boy work?' I asked. 'How'd he earn his money? Who was his employer?'

'We never really knew – maybe Connie didn't either. Perhaps he didn't work. He seemed to have a lot of spare time on his hands.' I heard a little clicking sound, as if she were rolling some sort of lozenge against her teeth.

'Is Kerry there? Does she have any idea?'

'I don't think so, but I'll ask.'

The click was starting to annoy me. 'No, put her on. I'll talk to her myself.'

She left the phone, and I heard the sad, soft voice of Kerry Spaulding.

She couldn't help me either. 'Sometimes Connie would pay for movies and eating out, but sometimes he would too. I

53

don't know where he got the money.'

'Well, how'd she meet him? How did she and Larry get together in the first place?'

'At softball practice last spring,' Kerry answered slowly. 'One day he just showed up at the field and started talking to her, and then every afternoon after that he'd be hangin' around when we started to warm up. Connie just fell all over him right away, even though the rest of us weren't too impressed.'

I hung up and sat there musing, my eyes staring straight ahead. The baseball field, no known ties to town, time to kill. Could this Merchant kid be one of all the King's men, dealing drugs to earn his keep?

I left it for the time being and walked away to wash my face, hoping the splash of freshness would lift my spirits and my tiredness. I raised my head to towel off the drops of water and took stock of my reflection in the washroom mirror.

I saw gray eyes, dark brown hair swept off an oval face, even teeth set in a firm and full-lipped mouth. The expression they presented was an honest and straightforward one, and though I'd never thought myself a beauty, I was pleased with my appearance and believed I looked like someone people might feel they could trust and would like to get to know. But I'd been screwed around a bit in the past year or so, and now a certain pain and wariness lay in the grayness of the eyes and at the corners of the mouth, filtering into a face that only rarely had known them before.

He leaned against the batting cage, his bulky frame immobile, his eyes staring out across the diamond. As I approached, I saw him raise his foot aimlessly and push a fallen bat back and forth in the powdered dust.

'Coach Branscombe? May I speak with you a moment?'

Kenneth Branscombe swung his head round and gazed at me, and I felt as if his eyes were looking through me and didn't really see me standing there.

'I'm Detective Harrod, San Madera homicide. I'd like to talk with you about Connie Hammond.'

He motioned toward a wooden bench and we sat down on it together, mitts and bats scattered at our feet. I looked at him and saw a stocky man somewhere close to fifty with ruddy cheeks and pale blue eyes peering out from a moon-shaped face. His slicked-back hair was blondish-brown and cleanly clipped around the edge, as if he'd just come from the barber shop.

His solemn eyes now focused on me keenly while his mouth stayed set in a pained and narrow line. 'What can I tell you? What can you tell me?' He spread his thick hands helplessly and moved them back and forth in front of him, finally resting them on his knees. 'Connie's dead, shot. That's all I know, but that's enough, isn't it? She's gone. A great kid, a great person, not to mention the talent, all that talent. She could've done anything, gone anywhere with it – scholarships, maybe even pro someday.'

I asked him how he'd learned about the murder.

'Some of the gang came to early practice. One or two had heard rumours. Then Margie Dawson showed up and told us what'd happened.' He'd sent the girls home after that, cancelling practice till the following day. 'But I told them to come back here tomorrow. They need this now.'

He waved his hand around the diamond. 'They need the structure to give a shape to their lives while they're getting through this.'

'What about the championship?' I asked. 'Is there any chance at all?'

'Not much, I'd say.' Branscombe looked at me bleakly, then picked up a straw and stuck it between his teeth. 'But if I can get them fired up for Connie, maybe we can win it yet – for her.'

'Who did this?' I asked softly. 'Do you have any idea?'

'Christ, no.' An anguished croak struggled from his throat. 'She was one terrific gal, no enemies, wouldn't hurt a fly herself.'

'You were her coach for several years,' I persisted. 'You must've known her better than many of her classmates. You must've been almost like a second parent.'

'I was, I was.' His blue eyes opened wide and stared straight out across the field, and he lay his palms flat upon the bench beside him. 'But that don't mean I know who killed her. Look—' he swung a beefy neck around and stared at me – 'I wish to God I could point a finger for you but I can't.'

I nodded silently and drew a little circle in the dust with the tip of my shoe. 'What about jealousy? If Connie were that great an athlete, attracting press stories and the like, it could've stirred some strong emotions in anyone who envied her.'

'Enough to kill her? Nah!' he said disdainfully.

I tried a different tack. 'Did she date?'

'No, she didn't. Her heart and mind were all wrapped up

in softball and she had no time for all that social stuff.' He got up and began to pace around in front of me, eyes looking at the ground.

'But what about Larry Merchant?'

Branscombe stiffened slightly and stopped the pacing. 'She didn't date him.' A flush began to flow above his collar, rising up into his cheeks, and his eyes now held a look I couldn't place.

'I was told she did,' I answered steadily, surprised at his reaction.

'He bothered her a lot, hangin' around practice till I shooed him off, but she saw nothing in him, never gave the creep the slightest tumble.' Branscombe snorted and shook his head vehemently back and forth.

'Not even a soda now and then?'

'Well, maybe that,' he conceded slowly, 'maybe just to humor him. But she was way above that jerk. He couldn't even start to touch her and she knew it. That's why she'd never've been attracted to him.'

'Where's Merchant now?' I asked, hoping that for once I'd get a solid lead so I could track down this kid and put some questions straight to bed.

'Gone, that's all I know,' Kenneth Branscombe answered. 'Haven't seen him now for several months.'

Listlessly, he started picking up the balls and bats, and I began to walk away, across the empty, silent field.

I glanced up and saw a crusty, grizzled figure walking toward me, then dumping a load of gear on the desk three down from mine. It's gotta be Meisner, I thought, looking at the mottled skin and the tiny round belly pushing out above his belt, and I got up to welcome the new head of robbery, who'd just transferred into division. 'Kenny Meisner? I'm Katharine Harrod, head of homicide. Welcome to the West End.'

He poked around the stack of files, then picked up his gun and vest. 'Thanks,' he muttered, not looking me in the eye, and that was that.

Great attitude, I thought. What the heck's his beef?

'If there's anything I can do to help you settle in, just ask,' I told him, still trying to be the perfect host. 'For starters, the coffee machine's right over there.'

He lifted up his eyebrows and nodded once or twice but refused to crack a smile.

Kent came through the door, his eyes lighting on the newcomer. Just as I had done, he approached him and stuck out his hand.

'You must be Kenny Meisner,' he exclaimed. 'We've been expecting you. Dan Kent, welcome to the West.'

'Thanks, buddy, glad to be here.' The grin came rolling out and Meisner grabbed Kent's hand, slapping him heartily on the back. I was starting to get the lay of the land and not much liking it. After Kent had strolled away, I walked over to Meisner again, determined to clear the air right now so nothing could start to lie and fester. 'Excuse me, Kenny, but is there any problem here? One perhaps I'm not aware of?'

He pursed his lips and slammed a desk drawer shut, then glanced over his shoulder as if to see who was listening. 'No problem, lady, except I don't like broads in the department.'

He couldn't get much clearer.

'Okay.' I smiled. 'Well said and fair enough. Now that's behind us, let's get more productive. The detective supervisors in this division meet once a week with the lieutenant. How'd they handle it in yours?'

I'd thrown him totally with my hale and hearty manner and my refusal to get stirred, and he didn't know quite what to do. He glanced at me sharply, inadvertently knocking a can of pencils to the floor with his hand. 'Once a week,' he answered grudgingly, 'unless, of course, a special case comes up.'

'Like the Davies case,' I said, referring to a crook who'd done a string of heists late last year in the East End. 'I admire the way you handled that, the way you got his buddy to co-operate so you could set the trap.'

'Thanks,' he told me, responding not quite as sourly as before. 'That was one tough nut to crack.'

I nodded and left him staring after me as I began to walk away.

I'd run into this sort of thing before, of course – men resenting women on the force. The younger guys weren't so bad, because most academy classes would now include a liberal sprinkling of women – and the men quickly saw what they could do. But old-timers like Meisner had come from a time when women cops were assigned only to juvenile units or the female jail and never worked the street. They didn't like the way things had changed, so they voiced their resentment. Sometimes they carried it even further, into mean-spirited practical jokes or – at the worst extreme – withholding back-up when a female officer needed it.

They had to be more careful these days though, with all the new laws about sexual harassment. Many women, not just in my profession, had slapped a lawsuit on the perpetrator without a second thought.

Good for them, but I personally preferred not to handle it that way. I preferred to deal with it quietly but firmly, one-on-one – and if it left a few lumps on their psyches, well, so be it. A sore burning was the price of the senseless game they played.

In this case, I doubted I'd bruised Meisner, only puzzled him a bit. Sometimes the cool smooth approach worked and saved coming down too heavy.

Sawing, cutting, grinding sounds echoed down the hallway. They were sounds I heard sometimes in my sleep.

I entered the antiseptic chamber and watched as Howard Penross sliced the head of Connie Hammond, separating skin from skull and laying it upon her chin like a doubled-over cap. Later it'd be sewn up again for viewing at the local mortuary – seamless, perfect, as if she'd never died from a gun blast to the upper cranial region.

'Katharine, come on over,' he called out. 'I'm just beginning.'

The smells of morgue chemicals and lifeless, opened bodies cloyed the air as I moved forward and looked down.

She lay there on the cold chrome gurney, limbs together, toe tag dangling from one foot. She meant nothing more to Penross than an experimental rabbit in a high-school bio lab.

He probed and sawed and pulled, talking as he worked into a microphone dangling from his neck. I could hear only snatches, and the terms sometimes escaped me: '. . . middle cranial fossa, no debridement present . . . adjacent medulla oblongata . . .' I didn't worry. He'd lay it all out for me in simple bloody words when he finished with the cutting up.

Finally, after carefully working through the violated cranium, tracing the wound path as he went, he looked up at me, grinned, and gave a tiny 'ahhhh'. Then, picking up some tweezers from a tray beside him, he reached deep inside the girl's skull and pulled out a single bullet from somewhere near its base. He held it up and turned it slowly in the light.

'It looks intact, just like I suspected, so it should do you a lot of good once ballistics gets hold of it. There're signs of hemorrhage and blood clot along the wound path, which also shows that your projectile ricocheted around a lot in there—' he gestured toward the head – 'forcing it to lose momentum. Came to rest against the back just above the base, causing all that blood and cracking that made me think at first it'd exited the skull.'

I bent across the body and took a good look at my bullet – a .32 if I was not mistaken. A pristine piece of evidence, one ballistics would analyze and catalogue and keep till I came up with the weapon it belonged to. The weapon that had shattered Connie Hammond's brains and drained her body's life blood.

'I'll send the full report when I've finished, Kate, but you've got what you need for now.'

61

I nodded my thanks and left Penross standing at the gurney. He began to make a Y incision to enter Connie Hammond's body cavities. Several pails, large and sturdy, stood beside him on the floor, ready to receive the organs. I gave one last look at the sad remains, then walked quickly from the sterile fluorescent room, and the sawing, cutting, grinding sounds receded slowly into the distance.

I flipped open the mailbox as I left the house and saw it lying there: a thin blue envelope, addressed to me. I pulled it out and saw its virgin right-hand corner. No postage, nor postmark either, so it'd been hand-delivered to my home. But when? Last night? Earlier this morning? I hadn't checked the mail since yesterday.

Curious, I turned it over, looking for a return address, but none was printed anywhere on the envelope. I ripped it open and pulled out a single sheet of paper in an off-white shade not matching its container. As I unfolded it, the letters leapt out at me, printed in a careful, bright blue block.

'Ask Coach Branscombe why he whacked the dead girl,' they read. 'We hear he slapped her in the face last Tuesday at the practice.'

I stared at the words, reading them again, then turned the paper over to the other side. Clean, just like the back of the envelope. I held it to my nose to see if it bore a scent, but no smell reached my nostrils.

I drove to the station, glancing often at the letter lying there beside me, wondering what it meant and where it came from. I had just settled at my desk when the phone began to ring.

The voice was low, even and deliberate. I could say it was a woman but I wasn't really sure.

'Did you get it yet?' it asked. 'Have you checked your mail?'

'I got something,' I parried, edging forward on my seat. 'What's it got to do with?'

'About the coach hauling off and hitting that Hammond girl. Did you get that?'

'I did,' I answered. 'Please tell me more about it.'

'No, no,' the voice told me firmly. 'Just follow up on it and see what you find out.' And then I heard the line go dead.

What the hell did all this mean? I asked, as I propped my chin on upturned palms and stared deep into space, mindless of the room around me. Was it a genuine tip, or just some phoney stirring up the air? I left my desk and quickly headed for Kerry Spaulding's house.

A jet soared high above me, roaring through the skies, and I wondered if the pilot could be Duane, a distant cousin of mine who flew for Delta out of San Francisco. Someday I'd have to take a trip, a real vacation. Someday . . . maybe Tommy and me . . .

Kerry's mouth dropped a little when she saw me, and I knew she wondered why I'd come, probably thinking, we'd already said it all. She pushed a shaggy grinning dog off the sofa and we sat together on the cushions it had warmed.

I dove right in. 'How did Connie get along with Kenneth Branscombe?'

'Real good. We all do. He's a really great coach – patient, positive, always encouraging the team even when we're off our game.'

'And how did he get along with her?' Casually I tucked one leg beneath me.

'The same – real great.' She answered easily, the words running right along.

'What happened Tuesday then?'

I watched her closely and saw the open candid face begin to close and shadow. Wary eyes looked up at me and her cheeks began to redden. 'I don't know,' she told me weakly.

'Why'd he hit her?' I drove on, ignoring her denial.

She sighed. Lying wasn't in her nature. 'How did you find out?' she asked, staring at me miserably as confusion filled her eyes. 'Oh well, it doesn't matter. I don't know – none of us does – and Connie was too shocked and too embarrassed to tell us why he did it. It isn't like the coach. I never, ever knew him to do a thing like that before.'

'Tell me how it happened, Kerry.' I spoke softly and moved a little closer to her.

'They were standing near the batting cage, right after practice ended. I saw the coach put his arms around Connie's shoulders, which surprised me because he never touches us. She jumped back, startled-like, and I saw her face flush as if she were uncomfortable. I knew she didn't like it. Then they began arguing.

'I could tell that they were fighting, though it wasn't loud enough to hear what they were saying, but the coach's face just looked so angry and Connie looked confused but also like she was standing up to him. And then he raised his hand, pulled it back, and slapped her really hard across the face.' Her words had raced out as she tried to understand the scene herself.

'What happened next?' I asked.

'He turned and walked away and left her standing there. We rushed up to her, but she said everything would be okay and not to make a fuss about it. We begged her to tell us why he'd hit her, but she just shook her head and made us promise not to tell her parents.'

I leaned back against the sofa, digesting what I'd learned. 'Did anybody see the slap besides your teammates?'

'Good gracious, yes. Probably ten or fifteen people who come out each afternoon to watch us practice. The stands hadn't all cleared out at the time it happened.'

Apparently, the practices that followed had been uneventful ones, with both Connie and the coach pretending nothing had gone wrong between them. Or perhaps it wasn't pretending – perhaps they'd worked it out and smoothed it over.

Quickly, I started back the way I'd come, the summer heat lying heavy on my body. An unexpected humid spell had settled in this morning, and I slowed and wiped the dampness from my neck, sweeping my hair up high and snapping it tight with the barrette I always carried with me. Better now, I thought, and looked forward to the shortened August evening and the coolness night would carry with it when it came.

Carl crossed the parking lot and disappeared inside the station, and I hurried through the door and up the stairs behind him. I found him sorting through some folders on his desk, a worried frown playing on his brow.

'Any luck with Gant's contacts?' I asked, leaning back against a cabinet and looking down at him.

'Nah, nothing worth a hill of beans. Kent's still working through them, but without a lot of luck. They can name names of kids they think deal for Dicky King but they can't point to Connie Hammond.' He raised his brows as if to say 'that's the way it goes,' and ran his fingers idly through his hair.

'She was clean then?'

'Far as they know. Didn't use, didn't sell. Not so much as a whisper about her along those lines. All she ever did, it seems, was smoke that ball like Tommy Glavine.'

Mungers was an unabashed Braves fan – no California clubs for him – and he'd slip the names of Atlanta players into his talk whenever even slightly relevant. And sometimes just to route the subject to his favorite team.

'Well, let me tell you what I've got,' I said, and eased myself into a chair beside him. 'The softball coach, Branscombe, whacked our victim hard across the face two days before the night that she was murdered.'

He raised his brows again, this time in pleasure and surprise at the tiny crack I'd opened in the case. 'What for?'

'Don't know, haven't talked to him about it yet. But I'm sure as hell going to. Who is he anyway? Do you know?'

'Only that he runs a farm machinery shop somewhere the other side of town. And he's been around town a long time too, maybe even born here. No dirt on him I've ever come across.' He shrugged and his expression changed slightly. 'Gotta start somewhere, Kate – but, hell, slapping's not grounds for the gas chamber.'

'It *is* a start, though,' I persisted, 'that's all I want for now. You've got to admit it's not your usual player–coach relationship.'

Carl's mouth tightened and his eyes narrowed slightly. 'No, ma'am, I'll give you that. It certainly isn't.'

Kenny Meisner still wasn't my best buddy, far from it. He'd sometimes challenge my remarks in front of others, and several times items on my desk had been misplaced in what I perceived as childish games.

His actions hadn't gone unnoticed. 'Kate, what's with you and Meisner?' Lieutenant Morris asked one afternoon. 'It seems he's always taking little digs at you. You two got some beef going I don't know about?'

'No beef,' I answered, 'it's the woman thing. He made it clear the morning he arrived he doesn't like females on the force.'

Morris raised his eyebrows. 'A hold-out from the caveman era, huh? Want me to talk to him about it?'

'Lieutenant!' I chided, opening my eyes wide. 'I can fight my own battles if I have to. I don't need a Daddy to do it for me.'

'Okay, okay,' he said, holding up his hands, 'I should've known better. I guess Kenny's still burned he didn't get your job.'

'Say what?' I asked.

'You didn't know? Yes, when the opening came up for head of homicide that time, Meisner was one of the Detective Threes who applied.'

Oh, that explains a lot, I thought. A double-barreler: not only am I a woman, I'm the one who got his job. Well, learn to live with it, Kenny, learn to live with it.

When I'd made head of homicide several years before – the first woman to hold that position in my department – I'd been acutely aware of a grumbling undercurrent among certain of my colleagues. Looks were cast, and coolness became the prevailing mood for several weeks. But soon it had all died away, or at least become well hidden, because they'd had to learn to live with it. You don't, after all, mess too long, too loud, with a detective supervisor before being brought up short.

I found him where I'd left him yesterday, on the baseball diamond picking up some bats. Nearby, several girls took infield practice while two pitchers and their catchers warmed up along the sidelines. He spun around when I called his name, and the large solemn face stared at me blankly.

'I need to talk to you again, just for a moment.'

Branscombe motioned to the splintered bench and I sat down carefully. I hesitated; I'd given this a lot of thought because I didn't want to scare him, but still there was no perfect way to do it. So I grabbed the reins and plunged ahead, hoping for the best.

'Was Connie an easy person to get along with?' I asked gently. 'Or could she be headstrong from time to time?'

'No more headstrong than the rest of us,' he answered willingly enough, 'not so it ever got in the way. Basically she was a good-natured girl who was extremely willing to take instruction.'

'If she'd been obstinate or stubborn – say, for instance,

when you tried to talk to her about a play or about her pitching – how would you have handled it, what would you have done?'

He looked straight at me, his face open, his eyes innocent and guileless. 'I'd have let her cool off, then sat down and talked it over with her calmly. That would've worked – it's never failed me yet.'

'Not even on Tuesday?' I asked quietly.

'How do you mean?' His startled eyes looked at me and a slow dark blush spread across his broad cheeks.

'I've been told by several people that you touched Connie in a rather forceful way that day after practice. I figured it must be some sort of disciplinary measure, easy to explain, but I need to know about it, to try to understand.'

The blush deepened. 'I slapped her. I won't lie to you, and I know they saw it happen anyway. I slapped her in the face and I'm so ashamed for doing it.' His own face contorted and he wiped his eyes hastily with the back of a beefy freckled hand.

'I'm sorry,' I sympathized, touching his shoulder lightly. 'But why?'

'Oh, because she was talking back to me, questioning some play I'd called. I'm all wrought up about this championship game comin' up and I just lost it for a minute and started actin' crazy.'

'But you've already told me you don't handle headstrong players in that way.' Indeed, Branscombe didn't strike me as the nervous, temperamental type. He seemed stolid and unflappable, the sort to lay an even edge on any problem.

'I did that time, though,' he insisted quickly, in a stubborn tone. 'That's what that was all about.' He set his mouth firmly and stared across the infield. Although I wasn't happy with his explanation, I knew he wasn't going to tell me any more. I'd leave it there for now, on the good footing I'd established, not keep pushing till I got his anger up.

'That's it then, Coach – and call me if you need to, any time at all.'

I waved at him and walked away, as he bellowed at his team to take the field.

I wanted to nose around a bit and not be caught doing it, so I picked up the phone and called Karen Windall.

We'd become friends when she'd covered a double murder for the local paper six or seven months before. Not close friends, but comfortable in each other's company. She'd ridden in late in life as far as finding a career was concerned. Like myself, she'd milled around a lot after her high-school days, and it was only after two marriages and two divorces that she finally took herself in hand, went to college – and came out in her early thirties with a way of putting words to paper that snapped you to attention.

Tall and slim, blonde and tanned, Karen was a no-nonsense, straightforward girl with a rowdy sense of humor and little patience with the foibles of the human race. She knew all about the troubles I'd been having with my marriage and kept a shoulder handy for any time I wished to cry on it – which she'd let me do, then dish out a scathing line of cynicism about the worthlessness of men that would usually turn my tears to raucous healing laughter.

Ironically, it was this very attitude of hers that also kept a wedge between us and held me back from fully embracing her as my friend. While I loved the quickness of her wit from time to time, I found I missed the presence of a sympathetic chord in her appraisal of her fellow man.

But all that didn't matter now. I didn't need a bosom buddy, I needed something else.

'Hi there, kiddo, going to be there long?'

'Just putting the polish on a feature for tomorrow,' she answered breezily, and I heard her inhale deeply on her cigarette. 'It'll take me maybe half an hour or so.'

'Stay there, then. I'll drop by and buy you coffee when you're finished.'

I headed for the brand-new *Sentinel* building near the city center, built recently to accommodate a doubling of circulation in the past five years.

My town had grown, sure, and it was very different from the way I remembered it when I was young. But I was pleased with its growth, pleased with the way it'd been directed. Instead of allowing it to sprawl aimlessly in an unorchestrated pattern, the city leaders had seen fit to enact strict codes, and today its layout was appealing, no building standing more than four stories high.

Although some examples of Spanish architecture sprang up here and there, San Madera didn't show the abundance of gleaming white and rich red tile you find along the coast – along the mission route stretching north from San Diego to Monterey. Most of San Madera's buildings were built of brick or wood, and the harshness of their lines was broken by tastefully-planted trees. All in all, a pleasant little city and one I loved. My home.

I found Karen hunching over the typewriter, eyes narrowed as she reviewed what she'd been writing. Seeing me, she jerked the paper from the roller and stood up, her arms stretched high above her head.

'That'll do it, let's grab that coffee. Marty's?'

'Sure,' I said, 'why not? It's got the strongest stuff in town.'

'Is that what you're needing now?'

'Not especially, but it tastes good too.'

We chatted amiably as we wove our way along a busy block filled with weekend shoppers, then passed through a green-framed door and took a table near a sunny window.

'What's up?' Karen asked, lighting up a long slim cigarette and blowing smoke away from me.

'What do you know about Kenneth Branscombe, the girls' softball coach?'

'Don't even know who he is. Is this about the Hammond girl? Wasn't she some sort of softball star?' She drew heavily on the cigarette and watched me closely.

'You know I can't tell you that, kiddo,' I answered her, 'but help me out here. Sniff around and find out what he's like, what his background is, and if there's any gossip, past or present – and don't say who you're asking for. If I can give you something later on, you know I will.'

'Fair enough,' she nodded. 'I'll build him up and flesh him out for you. Give me several days, or maybe only several hours – we'll see how fast it goes.'

We drained our cups, then filled them up again, talking all

the time about the murder. This time Karen hadn't covered it – she'd been out of town on another story.

When I'd finished the second cup, I set it down and laid some money on the table. 'I'd love to stay and chat,' I said, 'but there's too much work to do. Call me when you can, okay?'

'You know I will,' she assured me, and I left her there, lighting up another cigarette.

CHAPTER FIVE

It wasn't the hard, sharp crack across the face that Branscombe had given her. It wasn't because I couldn't tie her in as one of King's couriers. But for whatever reason, in one startling instant I came to feel beyond a doubt that this was not a drug-related murder. I saw a depth of darkness shadowing this death that went beyond a calculated, unemotional hit. I sensed the presence of a factor that I'd not yet found. My mind told me this hunch was not worth playing with, but my instinct told me I was dead on line.

I'd been walking back from coffee, heading for the station, when it had hit me – creeping up slowly, sneaking in the back door when I was unaware. The hunch was unsubstantiated, not based on any evidence – and yet it grew ever stronger and I could not push it back.

I thought about my victim, a guileless, clunky girl with feelings as feminine as a dainty ballerina's. I thought about intensifying jealousies – smouldering beneath the exterior, staying hidden deep down, out of sight. I thought about teammates, envious of superior ability, and I thought about a drifter named Merchant and a coach who'd lost his cool. Emotions, building and building till their pressure finally broke the bounds of civilized behavior, were behind the motives of most murders I'd investigated. And they were behind Connie Hammond's, too – I was sure of it.

Now I knew what I was looking for: a .32 caliber handgun with a six left-hand twist.

Ballistics had confirmed the murdering projectile's size and had given me something even more important – the description of the spiral markings etched into the bullet by the weapon's rifling pattern. It was these markings that would start to match this bullet to a gun, eliminating some makes and offering up others. When a possible was found, other unique tooling signs – as individual to every handgun as fingerprints are to a human being – would then let me know beyond a doubt whether it was the one that shot the life from Connie Hammond.

I found Carl holding a small framed photo of Betsy in his hands, staring steadily at it. He set it down hastily, almost guiltily, as he heard me coming.

'Could be a Colt, then,' he conjectured when he'd heard my news. 'Not a Smith and Wesson – that's got a five right-hand twist. You still betting on a revolver?'

'Sure am,' I answered. 'We turned every blade of grass and every nearby rock upside down and shook it, and no spent cartridge anywhere.' An automatic ejects its casing after firing while a revolver always keeps it in the chamber.

'Unless, of course, our boy picked it up and pocketed it to keep it out of sight.' Carl looked at me questioningly, waiting to hear my opinion on this possibility.

'That could be,' I conceded, 'but I don't think so. I think the odds are against his doing that even if he'd wanted to. Remember, it was dark or almost so, and the cartridge wasn't falling on to an open smooth space like a kitchen floor, it was dropping among leaves and stones and grass. I doubt the killer took the time and trouble to linger there and search. So if there'd been a casing, it'd still have been there for us to find.'

Carl drummed his fingers thoughtfully on the desktop. 'I wonder where the gun is, Kate,' he mused. 'Do you ever think like this? That right now, somewhere, it's lying waiting to be found. Underneath a car seat, at the bottom of a river, in the pocket of a coat, but it's there – it's somewhere right this moment but we just can't see it. I wonder what it's gonna be that leads us to it?'

As he spoke I visualized the murder weapon in its hiding place and had the teasing and tormenting thought that it was waiting patiently for us, ready to be picked up and entered into evidence, if only we knew where to look.

Carl swung round abruptly. 'Are you scared about this Wednesday, Kate?'

I grimaced. 'Of course I'm scared, who wouldn't be? You can never tell how a judge will act – we know that better than most.'

'I'm here for you, you know that,' Carl told me quietly.

'We're here for each other,' I assured him. 'We always have been and we always will be.' I squeezed his shoulder in silent gratitude and looked up to see Dan Kent walking toward us.

'I've got the knife report,' he said, waving a single sheet of paper, 'but I doubt it's going to do us any good. It was clean of fingerprints and not particularly distinctive. The manufacturer is a small Ohio firm who distributes only in the east. Used to sell to retail stores out west, including some in California, but hasn't since the company down-sized several years ago.'

'File it with the ballistics report,' I told him. 'The knife could be unrelated to the murder anyway – no telling how long it's been lying there. But if it *is* connected, we can maybe tie it to someone somewhere down the line, prints or no prints.' I shoved myself off the desktop I'd been leaning on and headed for the computer. Just an idle curiosity, just an unfounded need-to-know.

I pulled up the 'guns registered to' format and fed in the name of Kenneth Branscombe. The computer hesitated a moment, searching, then threw out its answer – no weapon of any kind, automatic or revolver, was registered to the softball coach.

'So what did you expect?' I asked myself sardonically. 'A big red flickering star beside a Colt, saying, "Come and get me, baby, here I am"?' I was wearing down. I'd wrap it up, go on home, fix a vodka-soda, run a long hot bath. And let the day's events just slip away, into another time.

Carl had left already, and only Kent, along with the solitary night detective, remained in the large and silent room.

'Go on home, Daddy, and do some floor-walking,' I kidded him. 'Junior needs you more than I do now.'

He quickly slapped some files into a drawer and we walked out together, into the dark and cooling August night.

★ ★ ★

She hadn't wasted any time. My phone rang shortly after eight, while I was making morning coffee, and Karen started talking without waiting for my voice.

'Knew you were an early riser, so I figured this wouldn't be disturbing you. How do you want it? On the line or face-to-face?'

'I've got an omelet ready for the pan,' I answered. 'Why don't you come on over and we'll share it while you tell me what you've got?'

'I'm on my way,' her voice said crisply, 'but skip the eggs. Just give me toast and lots of strong, black brew.'

Her small red sports car pulled up ten minutes later, and I saw her ease her body from its low-slung seat. Molly, the ragbag dog I bought for Tommy after Jon and I had separated, ran to meet her, jumping up on her slacks. Instead of pushing her away and moving on, Karen knelt and took the furry face in both her hands, shook it gently back and forth, then planted one long kiss atop the large moist nose.

I smiled. Karen's tendency toward brittleness, reflected in the harshness of her judgements, was often offset by spontaneous exhuberance that was a delight to watch.

I held the front door open and she marched straight in, followed by the panting dog.

Karen hiked herself up on a wooden kitchen stool, wrapped her long slim legs around its rungs, and began to sip her coffee. 'We've got to take time to catch a movie one night, Kate, or just hang out for a beer. We've both got to relax a little and not meet only when we're hashing over work.'

'Right on,' I answered, 'but tell me when. Ever since the separation, it seems all my time is taken up with Tommy and work. I'm not complaining, don't get me wrong, but I try to be a double parent so he won't feel the lack.'

'But you've got to take some moments for yourself or you'll wear out heart and soul, not to mention body.'

'I know. I don't even get much time to listen to my beloved rock 'n' roll or even clip my roses. Look at them.' I waved my hand toward the kitchen window. 'Those blooms should've been cut off long ago. But you know what?' I shook a finger at her. 'I'm optimistic things will level off and I'll have more time again. I've even been thinking, when that happens, I'll dig out my skates.'

'Oh, puhleeze.' Karen rolled her eyes skyward.

'No, really. I used to roller skate and I just loved it. Now, tell me what news you're bringing to the table.'

'Your Mr Branscombe is a perfectly ordinary middle-aged guy,' she told me, 'except in one respect. And even there, I'm not so sure that it's unusual, knowing men the way I do.

'He's a childless widower – been one for a decade – living with his sister on a spread outside of town. Was born and raised in San Madera, runs a little farm machinery business he's had for years, goes to church, coaches ball, belongs to the Lions Club, and all the rest.'

Karen had worked fast, talking to colleagues on the paper, friends of hers in town, contacts she'd used on several of her stories. She hadn't pushed, just casually dropped the Branscombe name and asked several questions here, several others there. So no one had even noticed she was digging. She began to light a cigarette, then frowned and stubbed it out. I hated smoking in my house, even if the smoker was a friend.

'Go on,' I told her lightly, 'just this once. I owe you.'

She picked it up but didn't strike a match, just rolled it back and forth between her fingers.

'So what's the one respect?' I asked. 'The only way he isn't ordinary?'

'It's your gal, your murder victim, Connie Hammond. Branscombe was smitten, besotted, head-over-heels in love with his ace girl – his star pitcher – and he mooned around like a little puppy dog.'

'Say what?' My mouth gaped. 'He's close to fifty years old and she was just sixteen.'

'That's what I mean, hon, about men. It doesn't surprise me one little bit.' Karen checked the paint on a long red index nail. 'And I bet it doesn't really surprise you when you stop to think about it.'

She was right. After nearly twenty years in this business, very little was news to me. 'Who'd you hear this from?' I asked.

'From just about everyone I talked to. It seems it's common knowledge, and he's the laughing stock of town.'

'How far did it go? Was there involvement on the girl's part, physically, emotionally – or both?'

'No one knows for sure, but the guess is no, none of the above. My sources think maybe the old fool wouldn't even admit his feelings to himself. But it was plain as day to anyone watching him panting all around her.'

I refilled Karen's cup while she carefully spread butter on

a slice of toast, then scooped up the excess with her fingertip and slowly licked it off.

'What else?' I asked.

'Do you know about the slap?' She looked at me and arched her eyebrows.

'Ah . . . yes, I do, but fill me in on the version you got.'

She repeated what I'd heard from Kerry Spaulding. With one important detail added. 'Seems the speculation as to why he lost it after practice last Tuesday afternoon is that he was totally off-his-head jealous of her involvement with another party.'

Larry Merchant, I'd bet my bottom dollar. And Branscombe had denied to me that Connie had ever dated him, had even been attracted to him. And all the time he'd known different, and hated what he knew.

He pulled up hard and fast and cut the engine at the curb. Since the start of the disintegration of our marriage, a certain arrogance had emerged in Jon, and I hardly recognized him as the fragile being who, curtailed by his imagined insufficiencies, had succumbed to that breakdown several years ago.

I hurried to the door and, when I saw the little face peering out of the right-side window, my heart warmed and pounded. My son was home at last.

I stepped outside and Molly raced past me, shaggy fur flying, pink tongue hanging out the side. Tommy squeezed her quickly, then ran up the path and threw himself into my arms. We whirled around in joyous spinning till both of us began to laugh and clap our hands to dizzy heads.

'I missed you, kid,' I told him. 'I missed you all the time that you were gone.'

Jon appeared behind us and stood aloof, several steps away. I asked if there was anything I needed to know about. No, he replied coolly, nothing unusual had occurred. I didn't ask him in – we were way past that point in our relationship – and he gave no indication of hoping that I might. Instead, he hugged Tommy stiffly, then straightened up and said to me, 'I'll see you Wednesday, Katharine. We'll get this all sorted out in court.'

I winced, hoping Tommy hadn't heard, and Jon headed for the car. I didn't watch him drive away, just took my son and went inside, where it was warm and comfortable and no threats lay in wait.

We played and ate and I listened to his stories about the movie that he'd seen, about the baseball glove his dad had bought him to keep at the apartment. Later on, as I watched him roll around with Molly and engage her in a tug-of-war, I suddenly realized he'd gotten taller – almost overnight, it seemed – and I marveled at how quickly he was growing up.

Lost in my thoughts, at first I didn't see him staring at me, but suddenly I noticed he was watching me intently.

'What's up, kiddo?' I asked, curious about the look.

'Mom, how come I don't live with Dad sometimes?' he asked, lightly twisting the dog's fur. He looked serious and slightly concerned.

'You *do* live with him,' I pointed out. 'Every other week-end.' Not knowing what was coming next, my heart began to quicken.

'But not like I live with you,' he said, shaking his blond

head firmly back and forth. 'Not like Andy Murray lives with his dad. He spends one week with him and one week with his mom.'

'Would you like that?' I asked, and now my heart was racing.

Tommy didn't answer, just continued twisting Molly's fur.

'Do you think you'd like that arrangement?' I asked again, very quietly.

'No,' he answered finally, swinging his blue eyes up to meet mine. 'No, Mom, not really. I like this house and all my things here. And I love you. It's just, sometimes with Dad it's extra fun. Like this weekend. Like we do different things together than you and me – so it made me wonder why I live here more than there, that's all.'

I felt a jolt of jealousy as I heard his words, upset that Jon could entertain him more than I. 'What do you do with him that's extra fun?' I asked, determined to delve into his feelings as deeply as I could.

'Play baseball, go to movies, always go out somewhere to eat,' my son answered happily. 'And Dad doesn't set a lot of rules.'

'But Tommy, if you lived with your dad for longer than two days you probably wouldn't be doing all of that, and he'd soon start *making* rules.' I didn't want to sound mean-spirited and put Jon down without cause, but I desperately wanted the boy to see the truth. 'It's precisely because your dad has only that short time to spend with you that he tries to cram so much into one weekend and lets you get away with murder. He couldn't keep up that pace on a daily basis and he couldn't ignore the discipline.'

'You mean it'd be just like regular life, like here?' Tommy asked, looking at me questioningly.

'Probably,' I replied cautiously. 'Yes, I'm sure it would.'

The dog got up and moved across the floor and Tommy scrambled after her. 'I guess you're right,' he said finally. 'I guess it *would* be like that if I lived with him longer.'

Suddenly he began to frown as a new thought crossed his mind. 'Do you think Dad's lonely, Mom?'

'I think he misses you when you aren't there, but he keeps himself busy with his work and that keeps him from being lonesome.'

Why these questions now? I thought. Tommy had always seemed to accept the situation, never before wondering why he didn't stay longer with Jon, never before worrying about his father's welfare. This sudden and unexpected concern with Jon's well-being, and my son's obvious delight with his recent visit, made me start to dread the coming court date even more intensely than before.

I watched him playing with the dog. He seemed happy enough now with the explanations that I'd given him, but suppose, as often happens in such cases, the judge called him to the stand? And suppose Tommy, in all innocence, uttered words that made it sound as if he wanted to start living with his dad? Even though he really didn't. Even though he was happy here. If that happened, Jon surely might win custody and I'd lose the center of my life.

My stomach tightened and I felt my worry rise. That can not happen, I thought quickly. I will not let that happen. But defiant though I was, determined though I was to make those words come true, the spectre of the court date loomed before me, and I had to wonder if forces I could not control would take those strong, brave words and turn them into whispers in the wind.

'I saw him turning down the path that leads into the woods. I know his walk, I know his clothes, and I partially saw his face. It was him, beyond a doubt.'

I'd entered the squad room the following morning and found a well-dressed man standing close to Dan Kent's desk, looking serious and gesturing while he spoke.

'Kate, come here a minute, I want you to hear this.' Dan waved me over, and I noticed his eyes were red and puffy, his expression pained. 'Mr Greenwell has something of interest for us. I'll let him tell you for himself.'

The man swung round to meet me and I saw anxious eyes above a firm set mouth. I didn't think he liked what he was doing. I motioned to a seat and he sat down uneasily. Fingering a short-clipped moustache, he began to speak. 'I saw Kenneth Branscombe heading toward the woods off the Canfield road the night before you found the girl's body there.'

I stiffened, and I felt my eyes widen slightly, almost imperceptively, as I took in what he was saying. 'Are you absolutely certain it was Branscombe?'

'Oh, yes. Like I said, I've known the man for many years and I got a pretty good look at him before he turned his back on me.'

'What time was this on Thursday night?'

'Around eight-thirty or so. Getting on toward dark, but

there was still some twilight left and I was pretty close to him.'

Stuart Greenwell had been driving down the Canfield road, on his way home from a late night at his law office, when he'd passed a pick-up truck he recognized as Branscombe's parked off the pavement a hundred feet or so from the dusty trail leading to the woods. As he'd neared the entrance to the trail itself, he'd seen a man walking quickly toward it, then turning on to it and heading toward the trees. He'd glanced at him and recognized the coach.

At the time, Greenwell had given scant attention to the matter, other than to think it slightly odd – but then he'd heard about Connie Hammond's death and the location where her body had been found, and suddenly the incident of Thursday night took on a fuller and possibly more ominous meaning.

'I didn't want to have to do this,' he said reluctantly, 'honestly I didn't. Kenny Branscombe is a good man, but I knew I had to tell you what I saw and let you sort it out and find out what it means – or even if it means anything at all.'

I assured him he'd done right, but I could see he was still not totally convinced or happy with himself when he walked away. I hurried after him, wanting to reassure him so I wouldn't lose his evidence. I caught up with him as he neared the stairs and we walked together to the lobby.

'Mr Greenwell, you're not accusing Kenneth Branscombe of anything, remember that. You're only telling us the literal fact of what you saw. The truth will rise from all the facts – you are not influencing or manipulating it. I'm a pretty good judge of character and I don't think you're the type of man who could rest easy with your conscience if you'd failed to come forward with that information.'

I saw him relax, as if a weight had suddenly lifted. 'You're right, Detective. I know that, but it was good to hear you say it. You're thinking I'll back down, weasel out, aren't you? Well, I won't. If it becomes necessary, I'll testify to what I saw.'

A woman stood as we entered the lobby, and I saw a little smile of pleasure touch her lips as her eyes met Stuart Greenwell's.

'My wife, Sara,' he told me proudly, as he put his arm around her shoulder.

She was a tiny woman with curly graying hair, who projected an aura of extreme delicacy and dependence on her husband. 'I'm so pleased to meet you,' she said in a gentle little voice. 'I hope it all went well.'

'It did,' I said. 'We're grateful to your husband for coming down.'

I watched them walk away and saw Greenwell spring forward to open the door for his wife. Once outside, he took her arm and whispered something in her ear.

His solicitude touched me. It didn't seem forced or over-bearing, and after having seen so much of men and women treating their spouses with cruelty or indifference, I found his actions heartwarming.

I went back upstairs, wanting to find out why Kent had looked so pained.

'Is something wrong, Danny? Are you okay?' I looked again at his unusually somber face as he shuffled papers on his desk.

'No, it's my dad,' he told me. 'I got a call from Chicago this morning and he's in the hospital with heart trouble.'

'Oh, Dan, I'm sorry,' I sympathized. 'Are you going to go to him?'

'Not just yet, not unless it gets more serious. They're monitoring him at this point and Mom advised I should stay here with Rena and the baby and wait for further word.'

'He's on the force, isn't he?' I asked, recalling Kent had been born and raised in Illinois and came from a long line of Chicago cops.

'Yep, for nearly twenty-seven years, along with my two uncles and a cousin. Kate, he's only fifty-three years old but I've been expecting this to happen for a long, long time.'

'Why?' I asked, surprised.

'Because it runs in our family, that's why. My granddad died when he was only forty-nine and one of Dad's cousins passed away at forty-two. Rena's scared to death something's going to happen to me.'

My God, I thought, I'd had no idea. What a cloud to live with, always hanging dark above your head. 'You take care of yourself, though, Danny, and you get checked out on a regular basis, don't you?'

'Sure I do, but in our family that doesn't seem to matter. The heart attacks come anyway.'

'Let me know if I can help you,' I told him, and gently pressed his arm. 'In the meantime, let's get Carl over here and go to work, help you keep busy and take your mind off it.'

I gestured to Mungers and he walked up to Kent's desk.

'Look at what we've got here,' I began. 'A man infatuated

with our victim and jealous of another guy, although he won't admit to either feeling. The smack across the face by him two days before she died. A visit to the woods where she was murdered around the very time the gun was pointed at her head.

'*But*, we've got no reason at this point to think that Branscombe owns a .32, so I can't get a warrant for a search. What do we do now?' I had my own ideas, but hoped that they'd come up with something better.

'Sniff around and find someone who saw the two of them together,' Carl suggested, 'maybe at a drive-in movie or parked somewhere off the road. We could use that fact as leverage later on.'

'I doubt there is such a person,' I replied. 'Word is the girl was not involved with Branscombe at any time, in any way.'

'Maybe he confided in a bartender,' Dan speculated. 'You know how people like to spill their deepest secrets to the man who pours their drinks. Maybe he confessed to his jealousy and anger.'

'Good idea, kiddo, but I don't think that would work either. Once again, the word is Branscombe probably never consciously admitted his obsession, even to himself.'

They sat quietly for a moment, their minds working hard. Kent screwed his mouth into numerous different grimaces as he concentrated, while Carl crossed his legs and stared straight ahead.

Finally, I broke the silence. 'Way I see it, there's nothing else to do but go straight back to Branscombe himself, even though we've only got a shaky hand to play. Maybe catch him off his guard, confront him with our knowledge of his feelings for the girl and his presence in the woods that night, and hope it jiggles him. Handled right, he might just spill the beans, or at least give out enough to lead us on to somewhere else.'

'Yeah, you're right,' they reluctantly agreed, 'that's the only way to go. There's nothing else open to us at this point.'

I clapped them both on the shoulder, satisfied that a decision had been made, even though I'd hoped for something better.

'Let's not go in like gangbusters,' I advised as we started to get up. 'This is definitely the sort of situation where one-on-one is called for. And, if I might suggest it, I'd like to be the "one" on our side and try the woman's touch.'

In splendid mocking style, Kent held out his arm and, bending low, made a grand, sweeping gesture side-to-side. 'Be our guest, Detective Harrod. Be the one who goes to bat against the coach!'

I took some time to be alone. We were in a dicey situation here. As I'd told my men, we had only flimsy stuff to work with – just some town gossip and a story of a man seen near some woods. Nothing that would even start to stand up in the DA's office, let alone in court.

If Branscombe tried to hardball it and refused to break down, my bluff would be effectively called and I'd have to back off and leave him alone till I got more solid evidence – against him, or against somebody else.

So I wanted to get my mental state in order. I wanted to step into my role well before I got to the theater. How should I approach him? I asked myself. What technique would gain his trust and cause him to confide in me? Or rattle him enough so that his mind went into swirl formation and he told me things he really didn't care for me to know.

I let my thoughts simmer just a little, until I felt them start to jell. I wanted to go warm and gentle, I decided, unless he made me show a fist of steel. I'd give him sympathy and thereby gain his confidence, I'd soothe a man in anguish because he'd lost the one he loved – even if that loss had come by his own hand.

Branscombe's farm machinery business wasn't hard to find. I parked my car, stepped around a yellow tractor and headed for the shop's front door. Balers, spreaders, and combines of all sorts – machines of every type a farmer needs to raise a healthy crop – stood ready for a sale. I found him locking up for lunch, just as I had hoped he'd do.

I asked if I could see him for a moment and we went back inside, although he left the 'Closed' sign on the door. Conditions couldn't have been more perfect for my purposes: we were all alone, with little chance of interruption, in a familiar setting where I hoped he'd be relaxed.

We walked into a tiny office, brightly decorated with John Deere tractor posters. The faintest smell of fertilizer, not entirely unpleasant, hung lightly in the air. Branscombe turned his large moon face toward me and waited patiently to hear what I would say. His expression was both serious and solemn, but I detected no uneasiness, no sign of wariness as he watched me. He sat down heavily in a worn wooden chair and I took a seat across from him before I spoke.

'I want to offer my condolences, Coach Branscombe,' I

began, in a soft and gentle tone. 'I've come to realize how very much Connie Hammond meant to you and how devastated you must be by her death.'

His eyes narrowed slightly and now he looked at me with some suspicion. Clearly, he didn't know quite what to make of this. 'What're you talking about?' he asked guardedly.

'You knew Connie for a very long time. You worked closely with her on the softball field for several years. By all accounts, she was a wonderful young girl, a very special person, and I've heard people say you looked on her almost as a daughter. That's why I've come back. I didn't realize your closeness and I must've seemed insensitive the times we met before and I failed to show more sympathy.' My voice sounded soothing, even to myself, and I knew my eyes projected an expression of sincerity. I waited quietly while he digested what I'd said.

Suddenly his body slumped and he ran a calloused hand across his face. 'I appreciate your words, Detective Harrod,' he told me in a choked and wavering voice. 'It's been so tough and no one else has known, no one else has said . . . I've just felt so alone, no one else to talk to. Your kindness helps a lot.'

Despite myself, I felt a shot of sympathy course through me for this large and blundering man and I felt the pain of emptiness and loss his life must hold. But then I saw the image of a young girl's lifeless body and my feelings quickly dissipated as my face began to harden.

He was still talking, in rapid rambling words and phrases spilling over one another. 'Like a daughter. Yes, that's what I always felt for her, how I thought of her – a dear, sweet girl.

No daughters of my own, you see. No children at all, in fact. My wife died ten years ago of cancer, but all that time before, we couldn't have a child. I miss her, I miss her oh so much . . .' And he convulsed and bent downward toward the concrete floor as powerful sobs wrenched his body. He'd retreated into a private world of misery.

I hesitated, debating what to do, and then I stood and went to him and laid my hand on his, to let him know he didn't cry alone. After all, he was a human being, hurting from an awful pain, and I could not withhold compassion from him, especially since I had no proof he'd been involved in Connie's death. And, on another level, I wanted Branscombe to regain control so he could hear the rest of what I had to say.

Gradually the sobbing and the shaking stopped and he looked at me, wiped his eyes, and nodded, as if to say 'It's over now'. I waited just a moment, letting the silence lie between us, then I spoke.

'Mr Branscombe, several people overheard your argument with Connie last Tuesday afternoon. They say it was about some fella, not about her pitching style.'

His head swung quickly up and his eyes locked tight on mine. I was reminded of a charging bull. 'What's that?'

'The argument between the two of you. I'm told it was about Larry Merchant.'

'They heard me, did they?' He slumped again and slung his arm along the chair back. 'Well, they were right. But what the heck does that have to do with anything?'

'Maybe nothing,' I replied, careful that my tone remained calm and sympathetic, 'but I need to know about it none the less.'

'He'd started hanging around Connie again. I saw the two of them together one day after practice and I was afraid he'd try to force himself on her just like before. He wasn't right for her – just a scummy little boy – but she was so kind and innocent she couldn't see him for what he really was. She might've felt sorry for him, taken him up like some stray puppy dog.' Branscombe's face was deeply flushed and a vein bulged, pulsing in his forehead.

'And you had to save her from all that?'

'I wanted to protect her, yes. I knew what was best for her with a guy like Larry Merchant. I was just trying to take good care of her, give her some advice and make her see some sense.'

'By smacking her across the cheek when she wouldn't understand?'

He covered his face with both his hands and, again, his voice began to crack. 'I feel so sorry about that, so very sorry. She wouldn't listen to me, she said I wasn't making any sense, and I just lost my head. Oh my God, Detective, I didn't mean to do it.'

I waited till he calmed a little, then began my move into chancy territory. 'Mr Branscombe, was your love for Connie Hammond that of a surrogate father, or did you care deeply for her in another, different way?'

He stared at me as if in total disbelief, and when he answered, his outrage was undeniable. 'I cared for her as if she were my daughter, damn it, and there was nothing more to it than that. What you're hinting at is ugly, unnatural. The very thought of such a thing tarnishes her memory. I won't let you talk trash and filth like that again.'

The pulsing vein had turned purple and Branscombe's eyes were bulging now. Quickly, he reached toward a drawer and I tensed, my hand moving toward my gun. He withdrew a large white handkerchief and wiped his face, and I relaxed.

'You tried to hold her that Tuesday afternoon when practice ended. She pulled away, rebuffing you, and then you slapped her – slapped her when you saw that you repulsed her, as well as out of hate for Larry Merchant.'

'I never touched the girl that way,' he shouted. 'Whoever told you that is lying.'

He could've said he'd tried to comfort her for some shortcoming on the field – a plausible enough explanation. His absolute denial of the holding made me know the lie was his, not Kerry Spaulding's – and that lie confirmed to me the truth about the nature of his love for Connie Hammond.

Retreating from the possibility of sexual yearning for the dead girl, I continued the attack from a different direction. Pretty soon, I knew, I was going to lose favor with him altogether, but that could not be helped.

'Mr Branscombe, would you mind telling me where you were last Thursday evening between eight-thirty and nine o'clock?'

'I was home, watching television, same as I do every weekday night.'

'Suppose I told you someone saw you on the Canfield road, near the path that leads into the woods.'

He rose from his chair abruptly, causing it to clatter across the concrete floor. 'They'd be lying,' he sputtered angrily. 'I was nowhere near those woods at any time that day or night. And now I want for you to go.'

I knew I'd gotten all that I was going to get, so I quietly rose and walked away. Ordinarily I'd have chatted around a bit to try to make him drop the fact that he owned a .32, but casual talk was definitely not in order now. And if I asked him outright about the murder weapon, he might get the wind up and hastily dispose of it before I got my warrant.

No, I'd have to leave with just the little I'd found out and try to learn about the gun some other way. If, indeed, the .32 was even linked to Kenneth Branscombe.

CHAPTER SIX

I knew he'd been deeply, emotionally involved with Connie Hammond, and I remembered what I'd suddenly felt while walking back from coffee with Karen Windall: that this was not a drug-related murder, that its roots lay deep in powerful feelings pushing past their pressure points.

But without probable cause to believe Branscombe owned a .32 or, at the very least, had access to one, what I'd learned wouldn't do me any good. Legally, I still didn't have enough to get my search warrant.

I began to pull lost or stolen reports, to see if maybe the man had reported a weapon missing that had later been recovered. I nosed around other detectives, asking if anyone had reason to believe he owned such a gun.

And then, almost as an afterthought – a straw-clutching, barrel-scraping, last-ditch effort – I fed Kenneth Branscombe's name into the computer to see if he'd ever been named as a participant of any sort in a crime. And the computer gave me my reward.

Two years earlier, Branscombe and his sister Mabel had frightened off a burglar at their farmhouse located several miles from town. They'd heard a noise late at night and crept downstairs to find a darkened figure raising a kitchen window. As the unknown intruder threw a leg across the sill, Branscombe had grabbed a gun and fired one shot, scaring off the perpetrator, who never bothered them again.

Drawing in my breath and holding it, hardly daring to hope, I moved my eyes slowly down the page, searching for the kind of gun he'd used. And, two lines from the bottom, I saw what I was looking for – the weapon fired by Kenneth Branscombe had been a .32 Colt revolver.

I hurried to my desk and wrote the affidavit for the search warrant, laying out probable cause in cool, factual words. Branscombe was seen entering the woods at the approximate time of Connie Hammond's murder, he admitted to deep feelings for the girl and deep concern regarding her continued involvement with another male, he used physical force on the victim following an argument regarding this concern only two days prior to her death, and he owned, or had owned, a .32 caliber revolver – according to a crime report signed by his own hand – a revolver that ballistics stated was the only type of gun that could've killed Connie Hammond.

I rushed to the judges' chambers and found Eli Wasson, a Superior Court judge with a fondness for the police, poring over depositions on his desk. I handed him the affidavit and he scrutinized it thoroughly, picking up a fountain pen when he was half-way through.

He finished reading and, without a word, began to write. Within moments, as the wall clock ticked toward three, he handed me my warrant.

AN UNCERTAIN DEATH

★ ★ ★

The farm lay low and lonely, several miles from town. Flat, fertile fields surrounded it, with only the trees and brush along the driveway to lend height to the tableau.

We approached cautiously, though we were fairly certain our man was still at work. 'Park right there,' I told Mungers, pointing toward a pull-off near a thick dark stand of foliage. 'We'll walk the rest of the way in.'

I knew Branscombe had a sister who lived with him, but I wasn't entirely sure they lived alone. I hoped we'd find her by herself, and also hoped no barking dogs would give away our presence before we wanted it known.

I'd gathered up Dan and Carl as soon as I'd returned from judges' chambers, talking at them as we wheeled the car around the station lot, then headed for the farm.

'We're looking for a .32, of course, and anything we turn up in the search for it that ties him in any way to Connie Hammond or her murder. Keep your eyes out especially for any note or doodling that might connect him to the crime.'

'Got it, boss,' Carl replied, 'but tell me this. Why would Branscombe kill the one he loved instead of knocking off his rival, Larry Merchant? And how'd he get her to the woods? She'd hardly agree to meet her coach in such a setting, since she didn't feel the romance. She'd have thought it mighty strange and not have gone.'

He was right, of course. I'd wondered about all of this myself but figured we'd work it out later. It was not unusual for a man to kill the girl he loved . . . if he took out her boyfriend and himself as well. That hadn't happened here. 'Maybe he didn't lure her to the woods. Maybe she'd

101

arranged to meet the Merchant kid, and somehow Branscombe got wind of it and decided to catch them there together. Maybe he just wanted to watch them with each other, to confirm that what he thought was true, and then he'd shoot them both. Maybe Merchant was there but got away and Branscombe killed Connie anyhow.'

'So why didn't he off himself, then?' Kent queried, leaning forward in his seat. 'That's the usual mode.'

'Perhaps he wants to wait around to finish off the boyfriend, because maybe he shot at him and killed Connie by mistake. I honestly just don't know. But I *do* know Branscombe had motive, means, and opportunity to do this murder.'

What *had* she been doing there in those lonely woods at night? I asked myself again. Taking time to do some thinking? Meeting Kenneth Branscombe? Rendezvousing with the Merchant boy? Or something else entirely different?

We quietly slipped open the car doors, then started up the winding drive. The golden light of afternoon filtered through the trees, and not a single sound except the muted crunch of gravel marred the silence all around us.

I saw the house, the wooden porch, the four steps leading up to it. 'Okay, let's go,' I said, and hands poised to reach our guns if needed, we climbed the stairs and pounded on the oak door. Almost instantly it swung swiftly inward and a woman stood there staring at us, her eyes open wide but never frightened, her feet planted firmly just a little bit apart. A fleeting thought ran quickly through my mind: had she been expecting us, had she known that we'd come?

The woman didn't speak but simply gazed at us, waiting

to hear whatever it was we had to say. Those eyes, dark and watchful, never dropped, never wavered, never left our faces. Of medium build and possibly sixty years of age, her coarsened skin, graying hair and plain farmhouse clothes told of years of work and little vanity.

'Are you Kenneth Branscombe's sister?' I began, watching her but looking past her for movement in the shadows.

'That's right, I am,' she answered, and the voice, just like the eyes, held neither terror nor anxiety. 'I'm Mabel Branscombe.'

'We've got a warrant to search these premises for a weapon,' I began. 'May we come in?'

She motioned us inside as she stepped back and pulled the door wider open. But suddenly her manner changed and she moved in front of us again and blocked our way. 'No, I can not let you do that,' she told us firmly. 'You've got no right, warrant or none, until you tell me what this is all about. And then we'll see.' Her mouth tightened in a little line, the blood draining from her lips, and her arms folded tightly in front of her, as if she felt an attitude of toughness would make us turn around and walk away.

'We have reason to believe your brother is connected to the death of Connie Hammond. And we're going to search these premises, with or without your permission. Do you own a .32 revolver and, if so, where is it?'

'Rubbish! There's nothing here like that and he had nothing to do with that girl's murder. He was her coach and that was it. My God, woman, what can you be thinking of?'

I stepped forward, took her by both shoulders, and set her to one side. 'We've got to look none the less.'

I motioned to Kent to search the living room while Carl tried the rest of the first floor. I climbed the stairs to the second-story landing.

Suddenly, a rush of air swept past me and the hurtling figure of the Branscombe woman barrelled into the room ahead. Pushing forward, I pounced on her and pinned her up against the wall, calling out for someone close to help me. Mabel Branscombe kicked at me and twisted back and forth in a syncopated rhythm of resistance.

'Stay still,' I yelled, bending toward her frantic face. 'Stay still or I'll be forced to cuff you.'

Footsteps hurried up behind me and I handed Branscombe's sister to Carl.

'Watch her and don't let her try to interfere with me again,' I said, and he led the frantic woman to an armchair near the door.

I was starting to go through the bureau drawers, meticulously turning hankies over and looking under scarves and gloves, when Kent came racing up the stairs.

'Katharine, look at this.' He held out a worn diary with a faded purple cover, opened to a page near the back. Eagerly, I took it from him and began to scrutinize the writing, set down in long and flowing script. I heard a quick intake of breath from somewhere near the door.

'I can't stand the thought of the two of them together,' I read, mouthing the words in whispers as I went along. 'I've got to do something about it quick, even if it's drastic action.'

The date, printed in cheap gold along the page's edge, was two weeks prior to Connie Hammond's murder.

'It's his?' I asked, raising up my eyebrows in a question.

'It's his. Look at the flyleaf, right here,' and Dan pointed to the name written in black ink – K. Branscombe.

'Take it in,' I told him. 'That's just the sort of thing I hoped for.'

My father had always kept a farm journal, noting dates of calf birthing, mare foaling, crop planting and the like, and it was possible this volume might hold little more than that. But just in case it contained more, we'd go ahead and seize it.

I heard a cry and then a muffled sob from Mabel Branscombe, and I saw her try to make a lunging motion toward the diary. I paid no mind, and continued turning over clothes in all the drawers.

Next, I opened the closet and examined every blouse, every coat, every skirt and suit. They all hung neatly, waiting to be worn, but none would give me any clue. Finally finished, I moved to the rear bedroom and began to search in there.

I pulled out the wide top drawer and saw a pile of gas and phone bills, miscellaneous jewelry, an old discarded wallet. But nothing else.

And then I bent down to the second drawer, jerked it toward me, thrust my hand beneath a man's thick sweater, and felt something hard and cold. My pulse began to quicken. Hastily I pushed aside the sweater. And there it was, waiting for me just as I had pictured it – a .32 Colt revolver, nickel-plated, with a dark brown plastic grip.

It went surprisingly easy, up until the end. We found him

tinkering with an overheating tractor engine, bending down and grunting as he worked.

I approached him first, with Carl coming close behind. When he heard our steps, he looked up, startled. Expressions played across his face like a kaleidoscope – surprise, fear, anger, doubt. He straightened up and waited, hands hanging at his side.

'Kenneth Branscombe, we're holding you for questioning in the murder of Connie Hammond.'

I reached around to grab my cuffs and ordered him to spread his arms and legs and stand up against the wall. Carl gave the pat-down for a weapon and I moved in to snap the cuffs around his wrists.

Suddenly Branscombe spun around, knocking both my arms away from him, and bellowed like an angry, cornered creature from the wild. The sound must've come from deep within his gut, judging from its depth and resonance. He charged past me, leaping and pushing to get free in a crazed and frantic motion, but Carl caught him by the shoulder and threw him to the concrete floor.

A plaintive gasp wheezed from Branscombe, and then he lay still and silent while we locked the cuffs around his wrists. We led him from his shop like some docile creature from a nearby farm.

'You lusted after her, you wanted her, you hated it when you knew you couldn't have her. So you shot her to make sure she didn't ball some other guy.' I'd tried calming him, cajoling him, nurturing his emotions in this raw and hostile atmosphere in which he'd suddenly found himself. But it hadn't worked, and so I'd had to try another tack.

Branscombe just whimpered like a baby and wouldn't play the game with me. 'I loved her like my daughter,' he cried out, 'and not the dirty way you're saying. I'd never have hurt her, no matter what she did. For God's sake, can't you see the way it really was?'

'So what does this mean, then?' I held a piece of paper out in front of me, pretending I was studying it. I let my voice simmer on a low and gentle purr. ' "I can't stand the thought of the two of them together. I've got to do something about it quick, even if it's drastic action." '

Branscombe didn't move a muscle – just a big dumb creature sitting there and gaping at me. But I knew better. I knew *he* knew what I was talking about. But still he wouldn't give it up. 'I never heard those words before. You're trying to trick me and I don't know why.' He threw both his hands to his face and covered it, so only the mussed and rumpled hair showed.

'It doesn't matter, not a bit. We'll just wait, then, for ballistics.'

And ballistics didn't disappoint me. The pristine bullet pulled from Connie Hammond's head precisely matched the .32 I'd found in Branscombe's bureau drawer. And it fitted the casing left inside its chamber.

That wasn't all, the clincher came later on that night. Only one print marked the weapon, according to the crime lab, but it was a perfect swirling from the thumb of Kenneth Branscombe.

I went back to him again.

'I know about your feelings, I know about the woods that

night, I know the gun you own is the one that murdered Connie Hammond. Your prints are on that gun – yours and no one else's. Make it easy on yourself, easy on your sister, and tell me now what really happened last Thursday evening off the Canfield road.'

He didn't give an inch. He sat staunchly in his seat, looking straight ahead, admitting nothing. I wondered whether he was dumb or just trying to be smart. I found my patience wearing very thin.

'Detective, I swear in front of God I just don't know what's happening here. None of this makes any sense, none of it at all. Just let me go on home, please. This isn't right.'

I tossed him a look of scorn and left the room. The motherfucker had drained the life from a girl who hadn't yet begun to live, and yet he sat here still, with his floundering face, and wouldn't start to tell me what he'd done.

I felt revulsion and disgust, I felt a pounding of my heart because he'd silenced her so casually and played the part of God in the taking of a human life.

Just as Jon had played the part in taking mine. Except that I was still alive, in my agony.

I'd wrapped it up and I felt good about it. I tucked my baby into bed, mixed a healthy vodka-soda, and slung my body into a chair with a sign of satisfaction. Even minus a confession, I had enough to take Branscombe where I wanted him to go.

I thought of Tommy sleeping upstairs. Once I'd started worrying about his possibly being called to court, I found I was treating him with kid gloves, trying too hard to please, trying not to set too many rules. Finally I'd told myself to stop the egg-walking. Just be yourself, I said, and act like you'd normally act with him. You can't behave in a fake manner. You'll just have to take your chances it works out all right with the judge.

As I hooked my legs across the arm in a pose of utter indolence, the doorbell rang. Karen Windall wanted to come in.

'So it was him after all,' she greeted me. 'I just heard you've booked Kenneth Branscombe.'

'We're holding him for questioning,' I told her, 'but that's all I can say right now. He's not been charged with anything.'

I fixed a scotch and soda and gave it to her, and she took it to the sofa and sat down; sipping slowly, eyes narrowed, long slim legs crossed casually in front of her. I looked at her and wondered what I'd wondered many times before – how much of Karen's pose was merely posturing, to perpetuate the hard-boiled newspaper woman image, and how much was actual attitude.

'The old goat!' she started. 'He had the hots for that young girl and couldn't stand to see her go to someone else. Can you just imagine it? Him slobbering all over her in his dreams and probably jerking off when he thought of her!' The slitted eyes suddenly zeroed in on mine. 'How'd you tie him to it anyway? Gun, confession, what?'

She was trying to trick me, catch me off my guard, and I didn't even attempt to hide my smile. 'Nothing doing, kiddo, you're not trapping me. Drink your drink and let's be sociable but you're not getting anything from me.'

She laughed herself and gave it up.

'It's pathetic really, when you stop to think about it – I mean just the part we knew before tonight. That he thought he even had a chance. Poor dumb jerk.'

I recalled what Carl had said on the way to the machinery shop: 'Women! They'll get you one way or the other.' His words were, for him, unnaturally bitter, and I knew he was thinking of Lila. 'But Jesus Christ, Kate,' he said, 'this old fart was hung up on a little girl, a kid a third his age. How'd he lose himself like that, what did he ever think would come of it?'

'Can't explain love, sweetie,' I'd told him, and reflected on my own predicament and how very true that saying was. Hot and cold, in and out, undying love, enduring hate.

Karen finished up her drink, set down the glass, and pushed herself up off the sofa. Her tailored jeans and denim shirt accentuated the slimness of her figure, and I felt a certain envy at the smooth and polished image she always managed to convey. 'Have it your way, Katharine,' she told me as she said goodbye. 'Tell me only when you're ready, but know you heard it here first – he'll be standing trial for the killing of that girl.' She'd come in but hadn't found out much, and, defeated, she gave a wave and closed the door behind her.

But she was right, of course. Kenneth Branscombe was charged the following day with the murder of Connie Hammond and held without bail in the San Madera county jail.

I'd been expecting a call from the DA, and I rummaged around my desk to see if anyone had laid down a message. I couldn't find one anywhere so I picked up the phone and dialed.

'So there you are,' the DA's office answered. 'Thought you'd gone out of town on some big case.'

'Why?' I asked, surprised. 'I've been waiting for your call.'

'Because we phoned yesterday and left a message on that Bonham prelim and you never called us back.'

'Who'd you talk to?' I asked, puzzled.

'Someone on the robbery table. Meisner, I think he said his name was.'

I finished my conversation, hung up, and strolled over to Kenny's desk.

'I think you've got a message for me,' I began. 'From the DA, on a case I filed a while ago.'

'Message?' His grainy skin showed sallow beneath the bright flourescent light. 'I don't think so.'

'I do,' I retorted. 'They gave your name.'

He pretended to think a minute, then his face appeared to brighten. 'Oh, yeah,' he answered nonchalantly, 'here it is,' and he held out a pink message slip. 'Musta slipped my mind.'

He'd known they'd call back if it was important, or that I'd call to see why I hadn't heard. This had been just a small jibe to annoy me, not a full-bore effort to waylay my career. None the less, this niggling, childish crap had gone on long enough.

'Kenny, I think we need to have a little talk.'

I pulled up a chair and placed it square in front of him, then started speaking in a low, firm tone. 'I don't want any

111

more trouble from you. You spelled out your feelings that first morning, and I accepted that and said fine, now let's move on past it. But you won't drop it, will you?

'Let me tell you this, then, kiddo: I prefer to handle things myself, in a civilized and professional way, but if I have to, I will not hesitate to go to the lieutenant or take this even higher, and ultimately to file a grievance. And knowing the tone of the times, if I do any of the above your career will go right down the tubes.

'Again I repeat, I do not want to do this, it's simply not my style, but if I must I will, without any hesitation. Now, do you think we can work this out some other way?'

He sat silent, his face darkening, and when I saw he wasn't going to answer, I continued talking in a steely tone.

'Here's what I want in order for you and me to co-exist. No more sniping in the meetings, no more little games like hiding messages, no more badmouthing me to anyone. You don't have to talk to me, you don't have to like me, but you *do* need to stay out of my way. Do you think you can comply with all that, Kenny, so we can keep all this between ourselves?'

The starch went out of him as I efficiently clipped his wings. He knew I was damn serious, and I'm sure he saw his thirty years flying out the window, envisaging spending his final days knocked down to Detective One handling stolen bikes and petty thefts.

He gave a grunt and I couldn't tell if it meant yes or no, but I really didn't need to hear it. I know a hit when I see one, and I was certain I had shut him down.

I hardly slept the night before. In the fleeting moments of disjointed dreams, I saw the shadowed image of a little boy being pulled away from me, heard the painful cry of a child disappearing into darkness.

I awakened well before the pale soft light of morning, drenched in sweat and wide-eyed with the fear that dawn brought with it. The day had finally come.

I dressed carefully, turning, twisting, primping to the mirror to make sure I put forth my very best appearance. My fingers trembled as I tried to do a button and I mentally slapped myself and told myself to pull it all together. I knew I could not afford to show hysteria or emotional instability. I needed to parade my strength and my serenity so the judge would see me as a deserving, stable parent.

Hurrying down the stairs, I stopped short as I neared the bottom and saw, through the archway of the dining room, Tommy eating breakfast at a sunny corner table. Mrs Miller, the woman I'd hired to stay with him following the separation, was busy at the sink, humming to herself while she did the dishes.

He didn't know about the fight for custody – there was no need to know till the decision had come down. Nothing, after all, might really change. And if it did? Well, there'd be time enough to tell him.

I went to him, put my arms around his shoulders, and drew him close to me. I felt the slightness of his body and the warmth that emanated from it, and my stomach tightened as my heart grew still. Suppose I lose it all, I thought.

'Tommy, I love you very much. You know that, don't you?' I bent down beside him and looked into his eyes. My own eyes must have shown something strange to him, for he stared at me, then began to pat me clumsily on the cheek.

'I know that, Mom. I love you too – all the time. Please don't look so sad. I get frightened when you look so sad.'

I hugged him to me once again and forced my lips to form a happy smile. 'How's that, Buster? Better?' I drew back and made a clown face at him, and he broke into pealing gleeful laughter.

Mrs Miller gave a silent thumbs-up sign as I left the kitchen and I nodded quickly, then walked outside into the brightening morning.

I met my lawyer on the courthouse sidewalk and began to talk to him, my throat dry, my voice tense. I didn't recognize the sound I made as mine.

'Will it take long before we know?' I asked anxiously, as I slowly wiped the wetness from my palms against my skirt, careful not to let him see my nervousness.

'We'll meet informally in chambers,' he informed me, and a rush of joy shot through me. No large and barren courtroom to add somberness to the session. 'We may find out today or he may need more time to deliberate. Whatever happens, Katharine, remember what I told you – don't speak unless you're spoken to and then do not engage in angry outbursts. Let me handle most of what goes on.'

I nodded silently and followed him inside and up the broad cold marble stairs. Jon waited at the top, his tall lean figure pacing back and forth. Suddenly his dark head turned toward me and he walked swiftly down the hall.

My God, he can't even stand the sight of me, I thought,

and recalled a distant, vibrant love, so long ago it might as well have never been.

'When will we know if he'll call Tommy?' I asked my lawyer. 'Will we know soon?'

'No way to predict that,' he answered succinctly.

We entered a small and paneled office, facing toward the far-off mountains. An azure sky, flooded with the warm soft light that seems to exist only in California, filled the window frame in front of me. But inside the room I saw no light, and I felt a darkness that I knew rose out of fear.

The judge – a small, quick man with smiling lips and piercing eyes – sat behind an oak desk. I took a chair just to the left, in front of him, and Jon and his attorney settled to the right.

My lawyer was the first to speak.

'Your honor, we believe it to be in the best interest of young Thomas Harrod that he remain in the custody of his mother, my client, Katharine. She has provided an excellent atmosphere for his nurturing ever since the separation and, in my opinion, any severance of his ties to her or to the home in which he has been raised would be to his extreme detriment.'

He then introduced several depositions from Tommy's principal and teachers, testifying to our son's normal undisturbed behavior in the months since Jon and I had parted.

My husband shifted slightly in his seat, a faint smile playing on his face. Whereas I felt undeniably afraid despite my earlier resolve of bravery, he seemed completely confident.

His attorney changed seats with him, placing himself

between the two of us, and focused on the judge. 'Your honor, Mrs Harrod works outside the home, in an extremely dangerous job. Her hours are erratic, unpredictable, and can not be guaranteed to present any sort of structure for the boy. She may be there one minute, suddenly gone the next. In my opinion, and the opinion of many experts, this sort of behavior will impact on the child later if not sooner. My client, on the other hand, not only works a steady structured job, but works it from his home, so he is able to parent the boy on a twenty-four-hour-a-day basis.'

Suddenly I heard my husband's voice. 'She neglected him last spring, and he fell off a cliff and put a spike right through his arm.'

I gasped and swung my head toward Jon. I could feel the blood draining from my face. Now I understood the smile I'd seen earlier. He thought he'd trot out that sad incident and lay the blame on me.

'Damn you,' I cried out, and my lawyer laid his hand along my arm in an effort to restrain me, 'that's not fair. We were both there when he hurt himself. We were both at home together.'

The smile fashioned itself into an awful curving smirk and he turned his shining eyes toward the ceiling as his lawyer cautioned him to be quiet.

The war raged on and on, with one side going up to bat, then giving over to the other. But my heart had suddenly fallen down and I felt hopeless in the bottom of my soul, for I was sure that I'd lost Tommy. All I needed now was for the judge to call my son and read the wrong interpretation into his innocent words.

Finally, as the clock hands climbed toward noon, the judge announced adjournment and advised us to be back by two.

I couldn't eat my lunch, couldn't talk to my own counsel – could only let my wheels spin helplessly in suspension and pray that it would soon be over so that motion, any kind of motion, could begin again.

We returned to judge's chambers, only now the outside light had shifted and patterns of afternoon shade were playing through the window frame. I was scared, like an anxious rabbit, and I shifted often in my seat. I didn't look at Jon; I didn't pander to the smirk.

The judge gave his opening smile, then got down to business. 'This is a rather complicated case,' he said, piercing all of us in turn with the sharpness of his eyes, 'because of several unusual factors it embraces. The mother, for instance, works a high-risk job outside the home, while the father, in a role reversal, works a more conventional job within it. In my deliberation, I have come to the conclusion that a decision of permanent custody is not advisable at this time.

'I am going, therefore, to grant a temporary custody today, and urge the two of you to try and reach a permanent agreement on your own, always keeping in mind, above and beyond all else, the welfare of your little boy. In some cases I would call the child himself, to hear his side, but I feel confident in my mind I do not this time need to do that.'

The judge paused a moment and drew in his breath as he prepared to hand down his verdict. My mouth opened slightly and I felt my heart stand still.

'I conclude that the boy's mother, despite the unusual nature of her work and despite the allegations you've presented here today, has done an excellent job in providing a stable, loving atmosphere for her son to grow up in, and I can find no negative impact whatsoever from her care of him. I therefore award temporary custody to Katharine Harrod, with weekend visitation rights of every other weekend granted to the father.'

My mind whirled and a faintness filled my body. I felt as if I existed in a vacuum and all of this was happening somewhere else, to some other person. I was dreaming – of course, it must be that, because surely this shining, magic present could not be mine to have and hold.

And then I looked at Jonathan and knew I wasn't dreaming after all. It was real. His face showed an anger I'd never seen before, even in those tumultuous days of verbal violence before he'd left me. It was a deep, explosive anger stirred with hate and mixed with disbelief.

He rose up from his seat and pushed his lawyer to one side.

'You're crazy,' he shouted at the judge. 'She'll destroy him, she's all wrong for him.'

The lawyer pulled him back and shoved him toward the door, but he wasn't leaving without getting at me. 'You heard the man,' he told me sneeringly. 'Work it out ourselves, he said. Well, we'll do just that – damn right we will.'

The menace didn't worry me. These were idle words born from disappointment, exploding into shattered fragments to be heard no more.

I didn't care, I didn't even listen. I was wrapped in warm euphoria and nothing else could touch me. I hugged the certain truth I suddenly knew – that there is always a light that shines, always a flame eternal. And today that light had blazed and burned for me.

CHAPTER SEVEN

She raged into the room, scattering papers from the desks as she stormed a path straight toward me. Her eyes, dark and wild, fixed on mine like magnets on to metal.

'Let my brother go,' she demanded as she stood above me. 'He didn't kill the girl, he had no reason to. Can't you see the truth? It was her no-good violent boyfriend!'

Mabel Branscombe's lips tightened as her face grew tense and rigid, and those forceful eyes took on a begging, pleading look. I was reminded of some creature fending off attack against its young, and reminded of something else too, a fleeting feeling that I couldn't put a finger on. I frowned, wondering, and then I let it go.

She sat down heavily beside me, as tiny drops of sweat glistened on her forehead and coursed along her cheeks. She bent her body toward me and the eyes beseeched, implored. 'I saw him with the gun, I saw him with it in his hand after she was dead. Find that boy and make him tell you what he did!'

She straightened up and moved her feet, clad in plain chunk-heeled shoes, so that they rested quietly side-by-side, toes exactly aligned as if waiting for an order to set them into motion.

'What boy, Miss Branscombe?' My mind whirled, then settled, as I grasped the import of her words. 'What boy, and where did you see him with the gun?' My eyes were now riveted on hers and I felt my pulse quicken. I already knew the name I was just about to hear.

'Larry Marchand, that ex-convict who was dating her. She threw him over and it really, really bothered him. He couldn't let it go.' Mabel Branscombe drew her sweater tight around her, despite the warmth of the day. She wet her lips while she waited anxiously for me to speak.

'Larry Merchant? How do you know him, and can you tell me where to find him? I've not been able to turn him up anywhere.' I felt as if I'd just been handed an early birthday gift on a sterling silver platter.

'That would be because his name is not Merchant, it's Marchand. M-A-R-C-H-A-N-D. And he's got a room over near Jacinto. Here—' she fumbled in a worn leather purse and pulled out a tiny slip of paper – 'this is his address.'

I took the paper from her and saw that she was trembling. Her hands with their squared-off nails, were shaking slightly and her shoulders shuddered as she spoke. The potent rage that had pumped her up to come here, then powered her across the floor to stand in front of me, had now deserted her, and new emotions, more tentative in their intensity, had moved in to take its place.

I laid my palm across her forearm, comforting her, and felt the roughness of the dark brown handknit sweater.

'It's going to be all right, Miss Branscombe, don't distress yourself. Just start at the beginning, as slowly as you like, and tell me all you know.'

I found it easy to be sympathetic toward her. She was an unsophisticated farmland woman whose mundane world had suddenly pitched and spun and assumed dimensions of tremendous horror when her only brother was routed from the simple life they led and charged with the awful crime of murder.

A bulk loomed behind the seated woman and I saw Carl staring curiously, his strawstick hair standing out behind one ear. The pale green tie he wore was ill-suited to his light blue shirt. Always clean but rarely neat, he'd become even more careless of his appearance since Lila and the child had moved south. On several mornings I'd seen a show of golden stubble on his chin – absolutely *verboten* for a detective in our department unless he was working vice. I'd give him one or two more days to pull himself together and then, reluctantly, I'd have to talk to him about it.

He must've heard a glimmer of our conversation and wanted to hear more. I waved him to a chair and silently he sat down, then crossed his beefy calves and listened while his eyes began to narrow.

My touch must've calmed her, for when Mabel Branscombe began to speak her voice was strong and steady. I left my hand where it was, resting on her forearm.

'Larry asked me that Thursday morning if he could leave a note with me to give to Connie. He knew I sometimes saw her on my way to church meeting. As it happened, I passed her that very afternoon and gave it to her. She read it quickly, then asked if I'd be seeing Larry later on. I told her yes, I expected he'd drop by again, and she scribbled a reply for me to give to him. Which I did when he came by the farm at four o'clock.'

She paused and touched a tiny mole at the corner of her mouth. 'The following day – Friday – I went upstairs and saw Larry standing by the bureau with Kenneth's .32 in his hand. I thought he was just looking at it – he knew we kept it there – but now I think different. I think he'd used it to murder Connie, then wiped it clean and was putting it back from where he took it. Don't you see? I didn't read their notes – was none of my business – but I'm sure he was asking her to meet him by the stream that night and she was saying that she would.'

I saw a lot of gaps to fill in here, but I'd work on them later. 'Why didn't you come to me with this before, Miss Branscombe? You didn't have to wait until your brother was arrested.'

'Because I didn't put two and two together till you took Kenneth into custody and found the killing had been done with that gun. Then it all flashed in my mind – the note, the day he wrote it, seeing him with the .32.'

Carl hitched his chair forward and began working on the gaps. Apparently they baffled him, too.

'I don't get it. How do you know this Larry in the first place?'

'My brother met him last spring when he came into town. We didn't know it then – maybe Kenneth still doesn't – but he was fresh out of state prison. We *did* know he needed a job, and though Ken didn't have anything steady, he let him do odd tasks around the farm.'

Something wasn't lying right here. 'Your brother told me he hadn't seen Larry Marchand in several months, and he never mentioned to me that he'd ever hired him.'

Mabel Branscombe sat silently for a moment. A light flush tinged her face. 'That's because Kenneth turned against him – for no good reason I could see – and fired him in early June. But I felt sorry for him and maybe it was wrong, but I'd still have him drop by from time to time while Kenny was at work so he could do a few chores and earn a little money. It seemed the Christian thing to do.'

'How did you find out he was an ex-convict?' I asked curiously. Usually they don't advertise themselves.

'Because he told me so himself. We'd have a glass of iced tea occasionally and sit on the porch together between chores, and I think he began to trust me. He had no one else, really, and I myself lost my parents at an early age, so I could easily relate to him.'

I thought of my own parents – lost to me, too, while I was growing up – and felt a fresh pang. I knew the pain and emptiness this woman talked about. I thought I'd hidden it, buried it down deep a long time ago.

'Weren't you afraid to have an ex-con around, Miss Branscombe?' Carl queried. 'Especially living so far from town and with a weapon on the premises?'

'Oh no, because he told me he'd never done a violent crime, only burglary to get cash for food and rent, so I wasn't worried. Anyway—' she paused and pursed her lips, looking straight ahead – 'I believed he'd changed. Until this happened.'

I called the contradiction. 'When you came here today,

you labeled Larry Marchand as a "no-good violent boy-friend". I don't understand that if his only crime was burglary.'

'Because he had a temper, though he was learning to control it. And because he told me he'd beat up a person once – someone who attacked him first – although he didn't use a weapon. A bum . . . bum . . . bum something, he called it.'

'A bum rap,' I told her. 'A sentence he thinks he didn't deserve.'

She bobbed her head in quick agreement.

'Let me clear up a few more things, Miss Branscombe. First, why didn't Larry simply phone Connie, instead of going the circuitous route of passing notes through you?'

'Because her parents didn't think a whole lot of him, even before she broke off with him earlier this summer. He knew he wasn't welcome there and he didn't want to stir up trouble.'

Or could it be, I wondered, that he didn't want anyone else to know about the assignation in the woods?

'Did Larry tell you why they stopped seeing one another?'

'No, he never would say much about it, but I know she was the one who ended it and he didn't take it very well.'

I mulled that over a moment, then returned to something she'd said earlier. 'You didn't read the notes? Either his or her reply? Weren't you awfully curious? I'm not sure I could've resisted just a peek myself.'

She drew herself up stiffly and gave a little cough. 'I am of the old-fashioned school, Detective. I am a principled woman, or try to be, and those notes were none of my business.'

She could've come off stuffy and self-righteous, but the impression she made on me was quite the opposite. I began to feel that here indeed was a woman I could trust.

'Where was your brother on the night of Connie's murder?'

'He was at home, watching television with me.'

'And Larry Marchand? Have you seen him lately? Has he talked about the murder?'

'Well, that's another thing,' she answered. 'I've not laid eyes on him since that Friday morning. He's not called, not come by. He's dropped completely out of sight.'

I dug them out from where they'd lain for years in a box behind some rolled-up carpet in the attic. My skates, bought when I was nearly twenty, unused since I was twenty-five.

I'd always loved skating as a child and as a young adult but, as so often happens, work and marriage intervened and suddenly a joy I'd cherished for so long made way for new demands that needed meeting.

But now I felt an urge to strap them on again and fly like the wind right down the sidewalk. I wanted to feel the tension leave my body as a glorious sense of flight and freedom filled my soul.

'You fool, you'll probably break your leg,' I warned myself, but none the less I happily carried them down the stairs. My son was off playing at a pal's house and Mrs Miller had gone out shopping, so no one was here to see the spectacle except the dog.

I sat on the front steps and slipped a foot into each white boot, then tightly tied the laces. Carefully I stood up, holding the rail, then let go and started gliding down the walk. I didn't try to lift my feet, not yet, just let the pink wheels roll along and take me.

Gradually I gained confidence and began to skate, my arms flailing madly and my body trying to fall backwards.

Lean, I cautioned, lean into the wind and you'll keep your balance. And it all came back, the knack of how to do it – and the minutes passed and the cares lifted as I reveled in the wonderful fun of flying back and forth with a spirit of abandon.

'Every day,' I chortled, 'I'm going to do this every day! I love it just as much as ever!'

And with a joyous, childlike whoop, I rolled through my gate and out on to the sidewalk.

'Jesus H.C., Kate, look at this. Our boy's been busy.'

Carl held a thin computer sheet high between two fingers, and I watched as it unfolded to become a four-page rap sheet.

'Larry Marchand's been a player from the time he learned to hustle, which was probably early in his twenty years on earth.' Most of the earlier crimes were petty ones – misdemeanor theft, vandalism, battery – but around the age of seventeen he'd moved into heavier territory – burglary, grand theft auto, one count of robbery. I had to wonder what he'd been up to the past few months in San Madera. I didn't believe one bit in sudden reformation.

'Get your coat,' I said to Carl, 'we're going calling.'

Kent was in court today, testifying on a year-old assault-with-deadly-weapon case – ADW – but I didn't think we'd need him. All I wanted was a little chat, a finger in the water to catch the mood of Larry Marchand. I wanted to sit back and let him talk and see where he would take me.

I'd asked Dan how his dad was doing when I'd come in that morning. Immediately, his face had begun to brighten. 'He's going home tomorrow. They did their tests and found there'd been no apparent damage to the heart.'

'Dan, I'm so delighted. And you must be relieved beyond words.'

'God, yes. But now Rena's getting on at me about quitting the force. She knows the family history and this thing with Dad has given her a scare. She's afraid the stress of the job will take its toll on me sooner rather than later.'

'What are you telling her?' I'd asked, understanding how she felt but scared I was going to lose a good investigator.

'That I couldn't even begin to think about it, at least not now. I love the job too much.'

'I understand,' I'd told him, thinking of my own situation with Jonathan. 'Brother, do I ever understand.'

Meisner glanced up as I walked by, then put his head back down. Since our little chat, he'd given me no trouble – no nasty digs, no messages mislaid. And also no words of recognition. Fine with me. Like I'd told him, he didn't have to love me, just stand clear when I came past.

The pale gray road ribboned out before us as we left the town behind and headed for the flatland. The mountains to the east stood hazy in the summer sun, patched with bits of green among the harsh and jagged pinnacles, while the langorous heat of August filled the car and shimmered in the distance as it hung above the road and fields. A somnolence enveloped us, making us content to ride lazily along, saying little.

Abruptly I rolled the window up and turned the air conditioner on. Immediately I felt better – crisp, alert, focused on the task at hand.

Carl straightened up and cleared his throat. 'I'm glad you got Tommy, Kate. For once, you found a judge who knew what he was doing.'

I smiled, and felt the grin stretch my lips until they hurt. I still could hardly believe the way it'd all turned out. 'It makes all the difference to me, Carl. I didn't realize till it was over how much the fear of losing him had colored everything I did.' I smiled again. 'Oh, the relief, the wonderful relief I felt that afternoon.'

'I've been toying with the idea of trying to get custody of Betsy,' he volunteered, staring straight ahead through the stone-chipped windshield, 'but I don't know, I think my situation's a little different . . .' His voice trailed off.

'If that's what you really want, Carl, then go for it. You can never tell.'

'Ah, well, I'll give it some more thought anyway.'

We drove for several miles, comfortable in the silence as only two old friends can be. Then quietly, almost apologetically, Carl surprised me. 'I'm seeing someone, Kate. Sandy, that little girl in records.' He squirmed on the upholstery, much like a teen caught by his parents in some lie. I smiled at his obvious discomfiture, but my voice, when I answered, was serious.

'I'm glad, Carl. How did this happen?' I'd never known him to have a date since he and Lila had split. Sandy, the 'little girl', was actually a tiny woman in her early thirties with a wispy voice and a penchant for four-inch sling-back heels. I knew her only in passing but had always liked her friendly, open manner, unmarred by any hint of pretentiousness.

'We got to talking one day about Betsy,' Carl explained, 'and it turns out she's had it tough too – divorce, some physical abuse along the way, no kids to keep her company. One thing led to another and so I asked her out. I needed someone, Kate, and she's easy to talk to, like you. I just wanted you to know.'

'Heavens, Carl, you're not a kid and I'm not your mother. You don't need my approval to date a woman.' Then, fearing I sounded overly strident and might offend him, I continued soft and easy: 'But I'm glad you told me and I'm glad for you it's happening. You're right – we all need someone.'

He relaxed and tried to make light of his confession. 'We're just dating, Kate. Don't try to get me married off.'

'Okay, okay, you won't even hear me mention it again. But seriously, I *am* happy for you. It's about time.'

Jacinto lay low against the sky as we came around a bend. A little town from early Western days, it was made up of flat wooden buildings with a narrow main street running through it and several others crossing it along its ten-block length.

We cruised slowly, necks craned, till we found the block we wanted, then eased against the curb and cut the engine. The street was canopied by California oaks that shaded worn rooming houses with broken screens at their windows and wooden steps that sagged and creaked as they led up to littered stoops.

I stepped on to a dusty strip of ground that paralleled the sidewalk and toed aside an empty beercan. The air was still and fetid, and I tried to keep it out of me, inhaling only slightly and breathing out deeply, in a rapid series of sucks and huffs.

'It's the blue one, second from the end,' I said, counting down the numbers. 'I wonder if his room's up top or down below.'

The railing shook beneath our hands as we climbed the splintered stairway. I watched a tailless pale-furred cat slither past the corner of the house, scurrying in wide-eyed worry as we neared it.

The flimsy door was standing back, its opening covered by a grimy woodframe screen. I knocked loudly near the handle and heard a shuffling sound coming toward me down the darkened hall, followed by a sudden silence as the shuffling halted. Then it started up again and a leathery little man without his teeth pushed his head around the door and gaped at me. He sized us up and down and I knew he knew we were cops, probably from San Madera – but he didn't give a hint, just played it cool and straight.

'Watcha want, Missy? Can I help you out with something?' He edged his way on to the porch and let the door slide slowly shut behind him. He wore a cotton T-shirt, grimy as the screen, and a pair of torn chino pants. His feet were bare and I tried not to look at the filthy broken toenails.

'Does a fella named Larry Marchand room here?' I asked, Carl standing a step behind me.

'Does he want to talk with you?' the little man asked saucily, watery eyes fixing on me meanly. His skin, wrinkled on his cheeks and folded on his forehead, reminding me of a turtle's hardened head and neck.

'San Madera detectives.' Carl stepped around me, whipping out his ID. 'We'd like to see him if he's here.'

Sourness replaced sauciness and the landlord – for I was sure that's who he was – swung his head inside the door and bellowed with a depth I would've thought impossible from such a small frame, 'Yo, Marchand, you got company!'

Too quickly and without a sound, another figure moved toward us down the hallway, then hesitated and started to hang back as it neared the screen. A face, indistinct behind the matted wire, looked toward us, but no move was made to come outside.

The silence built and thickened as we waited for the door to open. It didn't, so I thrust my hand down and grabbed the rusted metal handle, and jerked the screen forward to reveal a dark-haired boy of medium build watching me with wary, shifting eyes.

Dense, stale heat swept past him from interior reaches and pummelled me with its intensity. I ignored it and concentrated on the male in front of me, as he leaned against the doorframe and waited for us to make our move.

He, too, was barefooted, and bare-chested as well, with faded jeans covering narrow hips and thin straight legs. I saw thickly muscled arms beside a pale and hairless chest, narrow lips with a tiny scar near the right-hand corner, and a nose just a little bit too long. Stubble covered sunken cheeks below the deep blue eyes, and the hair, cut short above the ears but worn longer in the back, was tossed and tousled as if its owner had just recently awakened.

The overall effect was of a certain physical attractiveness, seasoned by the sensation that some features were just slightly off, that the whole look somehow didn't hang together.

I could smell distrust, dishonesty, and knew I probably wouldn't get a straightforward answer to any of my questions, if there were any chance at all that answer would place this boy in jeopardy.

'Larry Marchand?'

'Yeah, right. Whaddya wanta see me for?' He looked me up and down, as the eyes narrowed and became more sly, less wary. A gleam of insolence began to glow. He was puffing up, prepping to brazen his way out of any verbal trap we set.

'Relax, son, we're not going to bite you,' Carl toned in. 'We need your help on something and we just want to talk with you a little bit.'

I caught the deep blue eyes and held them tight. 'Do you know a girl named Connie Hammond?' Cool and level, my voice flowed out easily. There was no need to anger him, to get his back up. Not yet, anyhow.

'Maybe, maybe not. I meet a lot of chicks, don't always know their names.' Evasiveness oozed out with every shift from foot to foot.

'I think you *do* know Connie – we've talked to several of her friends and to her parents. There's no need to stall with us, Larry. We just need a little information.' I smiled, trying to keep my eyes kindly, and motioned toward several broken kitchen chairs sitting near the far end of the porch. 'Let's sit down and talk awhile.'

I waved him off in front of us, noting no telltale weapons bulges in the pockets of his jeans, and we settled in like old friends as the weary chairs creaked and groaned.

'When did you last see the Hammond girl, Larry?' Carl began.

'Yeah, well, I *did* know her a little, you're right there.' Marchand raised his eyebrows high and ran his fingers through the tousled hair, staring all the while across the street. 'But I haven't seen her in a long time now, maybe several months.'

'We heard you had a thing with her, Larry,' I followed up, 'that she was your girlfriend.'

He fixed his gaze on me and an easy flirting look rested in his eyes. I was used to this by now. Male suspects often mistakenly believed I'd fall for their sexual appeal and put my questions – and maybe my body too – to bed and they'd get to walk away scot-free. 'Not my girlfriend,' he answered glibly. 'We maybe dated several times but then I just moved on.'

'We heard she dumped you, son,' Carl interjected.

'Hell, no, she didn't dump me.' Marchand spat out the words in short staccato cracks. 'I don't get dumped. If there's any walkin' away to do, I'm the one who does it.'

I leaned toward him, purposely locking eyes with him, purposely inviting that flirting look again. I wanted a velvet passage here, a smooth and pleasant interchange that would con him into opening up to us. 'Why did you tell us you didn't know the girl?' I asked quietly.

'Because I didn't know what you wanted to know for. I wanted to find out first. I still don't know. What's Connie done? What's this all about?'

The eyes that looked at me were guileless, innocent, and

135

yet I sensed the lie that lay beneath their surface.

'Do you know Connie Hammond's dead, Larry?'

He jerked back, and a flush began to build beneath his eyes. The evasive look was back full-force. 'No way! When? How?'

I ignored him. 'Do you care to tell us where you were last Thursday night?' My tone was still soft and easy, still the puzzled cop just looking for a little information. We had no hard evidence to charge him with the crime, so we had to watch our step here.

'Yeah, I was right here, watching TV with the guys. They'll vouch for me.'

'Right, I bet they will,' Carl said drily. I knew what he was thinking – a bunch of cons taking rooms together and covering each other's asses when the need arose.

'Tell me about the Branscombes, Larry. Are you still friends with them?'

The eyes weren't flirting with me now. He'd given up on that approach and gone back on the defensive. 'You sure know a hell of a lot about me, lady.' He began to pick a crusty scab on the inside of his wrist and I saw the spidered lines of muted blue beneath the soft skin of his forearm – the signature color of the crude tatoo artwork done by one prisoner upon another.

'You're right, we do. Even more than that.'

He sighed and gazed again across the street. The bobtailed cat, afraid no longer, strolled desultorily across the patchy yard. 'Old man Branscombe gave me a job around the farm when I first came into town. That sorta slacked off, but I still do a little work from time to time for the lady.'

'Were you at the farm last Friday?'

'Maybe, maybe not. I don't remember.' He was dancing with his words, looking for the trap again.

'Think a little.'

'I just don't know.'

'What about Mr Branscombe's .32 revolver? Do you know anything about that?'

'Yeah, well, I saw him with it once or twice, but I didn't pay no nevermind. None of my business, was it?'

'Where did he keep it, Larry? Do you know?'

'Beats me. Maybe underneath his pillow.'

He'd gotten the game down good now, and I knew the verbal sparring could go on indefinitely without us learning anything this boy didn't want us to know. I had enough anyway to back the deep suspicion that he'd handed us a phoney crock of answers to confuse the issue. Out of habit, or because Marchand had a lot to hide? A little bit of both, I'd bet.

We stood up to go and Carl laid his hand on Larry's shoulder. 'Thank you, son. You've helped us see things a little clearer now. And we're real sorry about your girl-friend.'

We'd play the kindness act until the end because we wanted him to stay in place, didn't want him getting the wind up and fleeing before we figured out what to do with him.

We left the porch, walking quickly toward the car. I heard a screen door bang behind me and turned around to see three empty chairs, with the pale-furred cat jumping up on one of them.

'What a bunch of crap,' Carl blurted out, kicking at a

pebble with his toe. 'Are they born lying or do they all wait and pick it up along the way?'

I didn't answer but started laying out my own thoughts. 'He denies knowing Connie, then admits it, though he puts a different spin on their relationship than what we've heard. He knows about the gun and he has a nothing alibi for Thursday night. He dances around a simple question like was he at the farm on Friday, and he says he knew nothing about the killing when this whole county's been abuzz with it. What we got here, Carl?'

'I think you can take this one and run with it, Kate. Get a warrant, search his room, jack him up about that flimsy alibi, his anger toward the girl for jilting him, the wit who saw him with the gun.'

I stopped beside the car and banged my fist lightly on the roof. 'And Kenneth Branscombe? His motive, his prints upon the murder weapon, the guy who saw him in the woods that night?'

'On one hand we've got strong evidence, Kate, and possibly stronger evidence waiting to be found on the other. All we're doing here is exploring – opening up another option we didn't know we had without closing down the first one. I think you've got enough to get your warrant.'

'And find the note asking her to meet him in the woods last Thursday night.' I set my lips and nodded once or twice before getting in the car. 'That would just about make this a whole new ballgame, wouldn't it, Detective Mungers?'

CHAPTER EIGHT

I felt slightly guilty even as I did it, but that feeling didn't stop me. I picked up the phone and dialed Mabel Branscombe's number, to thank her for the help she'd given me. Unwarranted, unnecessary, certainly unprofessional – for at this point nothing had been started, let alone finished, about pinning the murder of Connie Branscombe on the ex-con drifter Larry Marchand. Nothing had occurred that would free Kenneth Branscombe from that cold mean cell in the county jail.

And yet I couldn't see the harm. How would I feel if I were sitting in her place, alone in that desolate farmhouse, a lonely frightened woman whose only brother, only living relative for all I knew, was being held for a murder that maybe, now just maybe, he had not committed? I'd feel scared, confused, despondent, probably helpless and devoid of hope. I'd want to know if the slightest murmur in the stirring wind of whispered possibilities said it might not, after all, be true. Surely I owed her that much – and so I dialed the number, cupping the receiver, keeping my voice low and my back turned toward Dan and Carl.

'Miss Branscombe, Katharine Harrod here.'

I heard a quick intake of breath. I visualized the graying hair, combed neatly back behind both ears, the stolid legs and feet, the coarsened working hands. 'Did you find him?' she asked breathlessly.

'We found him. I know nothing yet, but I wanted you to know that we're on top of it.'

I couldn't tell her what we'd learned from Larry and his lies; I couldn't – wouldn't – tell her about the warrant. I just wanted to bring a little comfort, to ease this woman's suffering just a bit.

'You'll let me know, won't you, what you find, let me know when Kenneth can come home?' Her voice implored me and I guessed she was clutching the receiver tightly with both hands, holding it so close that the breath that eased between her lips created moisture on the mouthpiece.

'I'll let you know if anything develops,' I reassured her. 'Right now I just wished to thank you for your help and make sure you were all right. I know this situation isn't easy for you.'

'You're very kind, Detective Harrod, very kind and thoughtful.' She paused, then said, 'Kenneth didn't kill that girl, you know. Soon you'll see for yourself.'

I mumbled something and hung up, glad now that I'd made the call. I imagined an easing of her worry, a lightening of her tension and her fears. Perhaps now she didn't feel so alone. No harm done, I thought, just a little bit of simple human kindness.

I glanced across the room. The man's face was bruised and broken, his left arm encased in a cast and sling. He sat talking to the victims' assistance coordinator, filling out forms for compensation from the state.

Attached to the DA's office, Gena Barnes had set up a desk in our squad room, to help the maimed and savaged people who'd fallen prey to violent crime get some redress for their ills. Like this wretched man, they could gain some monetary relief and could also be counseled, to help them deal better with their trauma.

Victims, I reflected – so often the forgotten ones when the case moves on to court. This little bit of help, though welcome, was far from what they needed, for long after their visible wounds had healed, their psyches, despite the counseling, often remained scarred and tremulous for months. Their dreams would become crashing nightmares and their daytime thoughts would sustain a sudden jab as they recalled that terrifying moment when they'd been violently assaulted or stared down the barrel of a loaded gun.

And far too often they missed the satisfaction of seeing the perpetrator dealt with harshly by the courts. Probation instead of hard time, years knocked off a sentence – these were the affronts they witnessed over and over, effectively telling them their hurt wasn't really all that great.

The victims, standing in the shadows, fading fast from the minds of judge and jury, were made to feel the fault was theirs. I glanced again at that poor broken man. We can't do enough for you, I thought. Whatever you end up with, it'll be far too little.

I was gathering up my things when the phone rang, and when I answered, a woman introduced herself as Mrs Aston, principal of Tryon High. Located about six blocks from my house, on Morro Street, it was one of San Madera's two high schools and the one closest to me. Tommy would probably go to it one day.

'Detective Harrod,' she began, 'we're having Career Night two weeks from Thursday, and we wondered if you'd agree to speak to the students about your job. It would be our pleasure because you're so highly thought of here in the town, respected for your work and the way you handle people, and we think you'd be a real inspiration for our boys and girls. Not to mention the fact that you're a woman succeeding in a man's field.'

I blushed despite myself. I still sometimes find it difficult to take a compliment, especially one as full-blown as this. I was just doing my job, after all, and was always surprised to find how others – complete strangers – perceived me.

I wished I could help her out but I couldn't promise. 'Mrs Aston, I'm going to try to do it, but I may have to let you down at the end. I really would love to promote law enforcement to those kids, but in my business I just never know what's going to come up. Right now I'm in the middle of a case I can not leave, but if it clears up and nothing else occurs I'd be delighted to come. Could we leave it like that, or does that make it too difficult for you?'

'Oh, no,' she assured me in understanding, reverend tones, 'your job's a most important one. You must go when you're needed. We'll keep our fingers crossed that you can come, but we'll understand if you can't.' She hesitated a moment, and then a question that apparently had been pushing to be heard suddenly came popping out. 'I've always wondered, Detective Harrod, do you get scared?'

I smiled. 'Of course I get scared,' I answered honestly, 'and any cop who tells you he's never been afraid is either new on the job or not telling you the truth.'

I hung up and thought about the strange, unwanted fame that had come with my position. Because I was a woman in a job at the top end of my profession, and because in that job I'd handled a number of high-profile cases, I'd become known to a lot of folk around town I'd never even met. And I still found it odd and slightly unsettling when they caught up with me and bathed me in a verbiage of praise.

I left Dan working on the affadavit for the search warrant. Crisp and cleanly dressed as always, his face had regained its relaxed and healthy look since the latest news about his dad. As I passed his office, the lieutenant waved me in and I stood before his desk.

'Meisner seems to have calmed down a little,' he commented. 'Did he back off himself or did you use persuasion?'

'Persuasion, if you call it that. I made sure he got the message.'

'Who else knows about your chat?'

'Absolutely no one,' I replied, 'unless he ran his mouth, and I don't think that likely. It was one-on-one, swift and strong, with very little fallout.'

'Good kid!' Morris clapped me on the back. 'I like the way you handle business. By the way, what's happening with the Hammond case?'

'We're getting a search warrant for another possible suspect,' I told him, and filled him in on Marchand. We'd serve that warrant first thing in the morning, with the full, bright light of day to flood the room. I'd take the chance that lover boy wouldn't run away. Not much chance really, I decided. I didn't think we'd stirred him up too much or made him overly anxious.

I wasn't holding back because I needed sun to work with. Rather, I wanted to check out something potentially important that had occurred to me. I headed home, stopping on the way at the Hammond house. I'd seen the family at the funeral four days after Connie's death and spoken to them by phone when we'd arrested Kenneth Branscombe, but this was the first time I'd been by the house since the day the body was discovered.

Janet Hammond was at home alone, scrubbing down the kitchen floor. The dancing eyes were dull now and the freckles on her face had faded. 'I just need to clean, clean, clean, Detective Harrod,' she explained. 'It helps me to keep my mind off Connie and her suffering – it helps to pound and scrape and rough up dirt real hard.'

I nodded, understanding how she felt, and then I told her that the toxicological reports had just come in. 'They were negative, Mrs Hammond. They found no drugs, no foreign substances of any sort in your daughter's body.'

'I didn't expect there would be,' she replied. 'Connie took great care of herself because she loved her sport. She wouldn't take anything that might impact on her ability to play.' The mother wiped a hand across her forehead and set the mop against the sink.

'Mrs Hammond, I need your help on something,' I continued. 'We know your daughter was wearing that little silver bracelet at the time she was discovered, but could she have been wearing anything else? Any other jewelry that was not recovered at the scene?'

The sun fell full and strong against the kitchen window and laid a shaft of shining gold across the newly polished floor. Mrs Hammond moved across the swath of brilliance, pacing back and forth as she considered what I'd asked.

'Take your time,' I counseled, 'take your time and try to visualize what accessories she was wearing when she biked away that night.'

Janet Hammond pursed her lips in thought, then made a little sound. 'I remember now – the silver necklace. I don't know if she was actually wearing it when she left here, but I *do* know she had it on at dinner just a little earlier. They were a matched set, you see, but sometimes she wore just the bracelet because the dangling chain around her neck interfered with her delivery when she pitched.'

'But you *are* sure she wore the necklace earlier Thursday evening?' I persisted.

'Absolutely. I sat across from her and noticed it while we were eating. And since she wasn't off to any game that night, I'd say she didn't take it off before she left the house.' She paused and shook her head as if to clear her mind. 'Funny. With all that happened afterwards I just never thought to wonder what became of it. Where is it, do you know?'

'No – no, I don't, Mrs Hammond, but now I *do* know what I should keep my eye out for. Was that all? Were there any rings or watches?'

'Nothing else. Connie never wore a ring and the watch's strap had snapped several days before. She hadn't yet replaced it.'

I laid my hand lightly on her shoulder. 'How're you doing, Mrs Hammond? Are you holding up okay?'

She looked at me and her mouth began to tremble as her eyes filled up with sudden tears. Perhaps I should've let the matter lie, I thought, instead of bringing raw and tender feelings to the surface, where their pain could lie there, naked and exposed.

Then I saw her thrust her chin up fast and square her shoulders defiantly. Her voice, when she began to speak, was firm and clear. 'I'll be all right, Detective, all three of us will be all right. Russell and I have got to be here for Darleen after all, if not just for ourselves.'

She paused, and then a new sound – a low, guttural, roaring sound – emerged from deep down in her throat, spouting words I'd never have guessed she would ever use. 'But we'll be a whole lot better when that fuckin' bastard prick gets fried. That's when this family will finally start to heal, and not before!'

She suddenly pushed my hand away and threw her arms around me, catching me completely off my guard. 'God bless you, Detective Harrod,' she cried, hugging me tight and rocking me back and forth. 'Thank you and God bless you for catching that slimy pervert before he could destroy someone else's little girl!'

But did we have the right man? Naturally I wasn't going to tell Janet Hammond about the new developments, but I had to wonder. A lot of questions would be answered with the serving of the warrant and probably not before.

It was not quite four o'clock. Tommy was at Cub Scouts

and wouldn't appear till sometime after five. I decided to take the long way home and soothe my psyche with the vision of the far-off mountains, the purple sage among the foothills, the broad bleached fields and flatland, and the pale blue endless sky that covered all the rest like some huge inverted bowl.

Those sprawling open spaces of the valley floor stretched to a horizon so distant it sometimes seemed invisible. But today the bordering mountain ranges stood in sharp relief, a particular clarity of the air seeming to move them closer. I could rarely look at them and not feel reassuring comfort in their silent, stolid vigil, their enduring permanence. They nurtured me with their stability, imparting a sense of calm to my inner self. I drew strength from them and from their constant presence, as they cupped the bright and burnished fields of the San Joaquin Valley within their rugged creviced peaks.

This landscape that I loved made me feel clean and pure and free, with no confines upon me. When I was low in spirit, I could leave the streets of San Madera and go to it and raise my eyes to it and draw it all in. And I would feel a healing of that spirit and a resurgence of energy and hope.

Only once had these fields and mountains failed to comfort me, and that was during this past year, when I'd been too immersed in my own misery even to think to look to them for my rejuvenation. I'd turned inward on myself, as I descended to the depths of my despair.

I'd come off a case that had wrenched my heart – the murder of a little blue-eyed boy by a sociopathic monster – and I'd nearly lost my life myself as I fought to bring that case to its conclusion. Inextricably woven into that investigation was the disintegration of my marriage, for it was in that period that Jonathan delivered his ultimatum and, when it wasn't met, moved out.

I'd taken some time off after those tumultuous events and, at first, I thought I'd be all right. But the horror of that particular murder, the memory of my own near-brush with death, and the failure of a solid loving union combined as constant spectres in my mind, coming to me in sleep, appearing out of nowhere as I bent across my desk, pruned my flowers, played with Tommy. As the days went by, instead of growing weaker they grew stronger. I'd become disillusioned, bitter, a tattered, fractured woman distrustful and suspicious of every person, every situation. I'd temporarily lost my way and I felt brittle, cold, and hollow in my soul.

Some days would be bright ones, and I'd think I was on top again, but then the sick despair would hurtle in and drag me even further backwards. I felt I didn't know who I was any more. I was alternately whipped and chained, caressed and coddled, by the warring emotions that raged deep within me.

My music – the roaring, raucous beat of rock 'n' roll – held no joy for me during those days of darkness. I, who used to twist the knob and set the dial the moment I slammed the car door shut, now seldom played the radio at all. The uplifting sounds of celebration that always used to make my spirits soar suddenly seemed a mockery to me. For the first time in my life, I had felt my music failed me.

And just as it had failed me, men had failed me too. Jonathan had raped me emotionally with his cold manipulation, and my body had been violated physically in a way I'd never known by someone close to the murder of that little boy.

I'd felt I could never trust a man again, especially a man outside my field. I'd never take the chance again of being misunderstood, of getting mixed up with someone who'd never seen the dirt and the horror, who'd never felt the blood upon his hands, who didn't know the hell a cop like me must live in.

After several weeks I'd returned to work, and the discipline and concentration of that duty enabled me to perform professionally much as I had done before. But inside, caught in the downward spiral of a life emotionally mangled, I wasn't healing, and it was weeks before I started coming out of myself and connecting with the world.

And now I realized I'd not begun really to heal until the other day in court when I found I wasn't losing Tommy. Till then, that fear had blighted every aspect of my life and kept a shadow resting far too long on a soul already suffering.

I straightened up and brought my mind back to the present as the road began to make a sweeping curve. I was deep in the country now, driving on a narrow lane between the patchwork planted fields. High clouds moved ahead of me and the sun dipped slowly toward the west.

I began to head for home while my mind filled with pictures of my loving little boy. A smile broke out across my face and I felt a massive joy expand within my chest. I rolled down the window and, while the cooling wind whipped through my hair, clicked on the FM station, spun the tuner knob, and filled the car with music.

CHAPTER NINE

We parked far down the street and approached cautiously on foot. I didn't expect any trouble from the Marchand kid, but you never took the chance. Besides, the rooming house, from what I'd seen of it, probably held more than one or two who had a grudge against the police or didn't want us poking in their business.

I sent Dan around to cover the rear while Carl and I walked up the steps in front. It was barely eight o'clock and the heat of day hadn't started rising yet.

The flimsy wooden door was shut behind the screen, and I banged three times on it, then stepped off to one side. The same pale-furred cat appeared around a corner, but this time it strolled nonchalantly past us, as if it'd gotten used to our presence on the porch.

The door swung slowly open and the little leathery face looked out. He grinned a sly, salacious smile and I saw the teeth were in this time. 'Not had enough of that young boy? My, my.'

I held the warrant in his face. 'Show us Marchand's room, please.'

'Oh, right away. Yes indeed. Please follow me, madam,' and he began his crab-like shuffle down the hall. I could've knocked that grin right off his face and stuffed his smart-alecky talk and tone straight down his throat, but he wasn't worth the trouble.

I stepped in front of him, breathing in the thick and fetid odor of the house. 'Just tell us where the room is. We'll go on from here ourselves.'

He gave a little shrug. 'If you say so, Missy. It's up the stairway – number seven, in the back. Hope he's dressed this time of day. Likes to sleep in, that one does. But maybe that would suit you fine.'

We ignored him, climbed the stairs in silence, and walked down another narrow hallway toward the rear. A grimy window at the end gave out the only light and I had to peer closely to read the cheap brass numerals.

I saw the rusted number hanging by a tack from the middle panel of the door beside me, and I pointed to it and motioned Carl to one side while I went to the other. I knocked three times. The doorknob didn't move and I heard no sound coming from the other side.

'Marchand, open up. Police – we've got a warrant.'

I waited five more seconds, then reached my hand around and twisted at the handle. The paint-chipped door swung back before us.

I saw a small and narrow room, an unmade single bed with graying sheets pushed near the foot, a bureau standing in the corner. But I did not see Larry Marchand.

We entered carefully, our hands held toward our guns. I whipped the closet door wide open while Carl bent beneath the bed. The room was empty and the cigarette butts on the dimestore plate were cold and stale.

'Whaddya think?' I asked. 'Did he get the wind up or is he just taking a power breakfast somewhere?'

Carl shrugged his massive shoulders. 'Can't tell at this point, Kate. Maybe he's not come home yet from a wild night on the town, or maybe he's sleeping it off somewhere else. Or, yeah, maybe he's scampered.'

I left the room and went downstairs, wishing now I'd moved quicker with that warrant. The gnome stood waiting at the bottom of the steps. I doubted he'd moved away for long.

'Have you seen Marchand this morning,' I demanded.

'Me, Miss?' His wizened face showed mock astonishment. 'I don't poke my nose in my roomers' business.'

I got right up close to him and asked again. 'Have you seen Larry Marchand today?'

'No, Miss, no I haven't. Not since you came calling yesterday afternoon.'

I turned away and went outside. Why bother asking? I couldn't count on anything that one said to be the truth.

I found Dan waiting in the rear. 'Any action back here?' I asked.

'*De ningún modo* – not a movement. Wasn't he upstairs?'

'The room's empty. There's no sign of him. Come on up and help us search.'

We went upstairs and joined Carl, who was slowly, painstakingly, going through the closet. The landlord had quietly disappeared. Dan began to check the rest of the room, inspecting the narrow bed, the area beneath the shabby rug, the single drawer in the battered nightstand. I concentrated on the bureau.

'Hey, look at this,' I called out as I held up a cheap ten-shot photo album for them to see. 'A remembrance of happy times – his days in prison. Look at those muscles and tattoos.'

They gathered round to see snaps of dead-eyed guys with their arms draped around each other's shoulders, the guard towers of some prison, most likely Folsom, plainly visible in the rear.

'Ain't that sweet?' Carl commented. 'That's his high school yearbook, full of cherished memories.'

I laid it down and began to turn over the other contents of the drawer – some cheap underwear, another pair of jeans, several IDs with descriptions roughly fitting our subject but with names on them other than Larry Marchand. And then I saw two wallets lying in a corner of the last drawer from the bottom, and I pulled them out, wondering if an answer lay inside.

At first glance they appeared discarded, flat and light with no papers peering out. I flipped the black one open and confirmed that it was empty. Then I unsnapped the tan one and examined it. No pictures, no money, no ID. Nothing except a little piece of folded paper resting where the dollar bills should be. I felt my heart do a flutter and I pulled it out and carefully unfolded it.

'Come here,' I called to Dan and Carl. They peered across my shoulder and began to read the words, written in a small neat script in the middle of the page. 'I don't know what good it will do, but if you want I'll meet you in the clearing like you asked. I can't get there at eight. Eight-thirty would probably be the earliest. See you tonight, then. Connie.'

'Just like Mabel Branscombe said,' I murmured. 'And the fool kept the note.'

'There's no date on it,' Kent pointed out. 'It could be from any day in summer, not necessarily from last Thursday.'

'I know that,' I said impatiently, 'but I'm willing to bet this *is* the note that Connie sent through Branscombe's sister, and I'll find a way to prove it.'

The remainder of the room yielded nothing, and Carl and I drove back to town, leaving Kent on stake-out down the street.

'We've got to talk with him, Carl,' I said as we drew into the station. 'Not just because we think he might be involved in Connie's murder, but to get this whole mess straightened out.' I thought of Kenneth Branscombe sitting in his cell, a great caged bull wondering at his fate, and I felt deeply disturbed.

As soon as I got inside, I poured myself a cup of coffee and picked up the phone. I'd had an ugly ulcer earlier in the year and had been warned to lay off caffeine. I'd obeyed at first, but slowly I'd let the habit form again. The fiery jolt it gave me also gave me strength.

'Miss Branscombe? Katharine Harrod again. Can you describe for me the type of paper Connie Hammond wrote her note on? The note he gave to you to give to Larry?'

I wet my lips and drew them tight together as I listened to her answer. When she'd finished talking, I hung up and turned to Carl. 'The paper was pale pink, approximately four inches by four inches, just like this piece we found in

Larry's wallet.' I held up the plastic evidence bag. 'Mabel Branscombe knows this fact without a doubt because Connie had nothing to write on and Miss Branscombe gave her a page from a little notepad she always carries in her car. Which makes it highly unlikely our victim ever used a piece of paper like this one at any other time in her young life.'

I felt smug, triumphant, and elated, and it showed. 'I'm going looking for the necklace. Want to come?'

'You think it's pawned, Kate? It'd only bring a coupla bucks, outside, if it's a match-up to the bracelet.'

'They'll pawn for less than that, Carl, you know that yourself. It's worth a try. It certainly wasn't in his room, and if I find it hocked and he's the one who hocked it, that'll tie Marchand even tighter to this crime.'

'You go on, I've got some junk to finish up for court on Monday. Keep in touch.'

I booked the packaged note into evidence and turned to leave the station.

'Katharine? Got a minute?'

The deep voice made me spin around and I found myself staring into the penetrating eyes of Captain Stratton.

'So, it wasn't drugs after all?' he said.

'No, sir, it doesn't look that way. We're holding Branscombe, as you know. The gun was his, his print was on it, he had motive, and we've got a witness who places him at the location. But now another factor's entered in and it's awfully interesting.' I quickly briefed him on the Marchand angle, and he listened with keen interest, focused totally on what I said, not just politely feigning interest.

'Could be one or the other was acting alone,' I concluded, 'or could be, for some reason as yet unknown, they were in concert.'

He nodded thoughtfully. 'You love your work, don't you, Kate? You've set a great example for every other woman who wants to be a cop and to advance in that field. You took on a tough challenge and you've succeeded with dignity and intelligence.'

I blushed, used by now to occasional accolades but still humble enough to feel a bit embarrassed and on-the-spot when they came my way. I always found myself wondering if my shoes were tied properly, even when I wasn't wearing lace-ups.

'Thank you sir,' I said. 'I deeply appreciate your saying that to me.'

He smiled his broad, warm smile and strode away. I headed for the parking lot, walking just a little bit taller.

I was looking for the needle in the haystack, one I wasn't even sure existed. The silver necklace with the fine links could be lying anywhere: in the deep green grass in the meadow near the clearing, in the pocket of the thief who took it, around the neck of another girl. But I'd give the shops a shot, just to put my mind at ease.

I started with the pawnbrokers in eastern San Madera, a seedy little row of gray and faded buildings brightened only by their shining tri-ball symbols and the crimson lettering of their names set in big block letters on their windows.

I was betting on the fact that if he'd hocked the jewelry, he'd have done it here in our town where it'd find anonymity among the larger inventory of our dealers and thereby make it harder for anyone to spot. If I had no luck here, then I'd go to the one or two dreary little pawns I knew existed in Jacinto.

I worked my way down the row, peering in the glassed-in cases, visually sorting through the piles of memories and mementos now abandoned by their owners. I saw rings with brilliant stones, knives with inlaid lustered handles, scarab bracelets from another time, but I didn't see a fine-linked silver necklace with a tiny rose-shaped pendant hanging down.

I questioned several owners without much success, and after searching for an hour I gave it up. I felt a sense of disappointment, a little bit of letdown. Of course I'd known all along I might not find the jewelry, but deep down a hope had flickered and now I had to start to stamp it out.

I stepped outside the last depressing pawn shop, then stopped to check the time. My hands and face were dusty from the grimy atmosphere I'd spent the last hour in and I thought I'd pack it in and go on home. Then I pushed myself a little further, got into the car and headed out of San Madera. I might as well wind up the job I'd started, wind it up right now and put it all to rest.

For the second time that day, I drove along the curving roadway to Jacinto. I parked near the end of Main Street, in front of two more shops with three round balls. Again, I looked carefully through cases filled with odds and ends from people's changing lives, again the little chain eluded me.

And then suddenly there it was, a tiny rose-shaped pendant partially hidden by a rounded wide-band bracelet lying in the last case from the end. I bent down and peered at it and saw the pendant was suspended from a fine-link silver chain. I'd seen its match one time before, dangling from a dead girl's wrist in a grassy clearing near an emerald meadow.

'San Madera PD,' I told the owner. 'Pull the paperwork on this one, please.'

The woman nodded quietly and turned her back to me, reaching out across a desk. When she turned around again, she held a large, thick ledger in her hands. She laid it down in front of me and began leafing through it.

'Here we are,' she announced as she ran her finger down the page. 'Class C California driver's license number N2687541, in the name of Lawrence W. Marchand. Pretty little thing but not worth an awful lot. Couldn't give him more than a coupla bucks for it.'

'When was it brought in?' I asked. 'And did you handle it yourself?'

'Came in last Friday afternoon and, yes, these are my initials.'

'Can you recall what the person looked like?'

'Only vaguely. For a town this size we get a lot of coming in and going out, but he would have fit the description on that license and looked like its photo. You know we're required by law to ask for picture ID, and I'm always careful to make sure the person standing there in front of me matches up to it. It's my ass on the line if I'm careless here.'

'I've got to take the necklace in,' I said. 'It's possible evidence in a crime.'

The woman snorted. 'Probably half of what's in here is evidence in some crime. Not that I know anything about that when they bring it in. As long as I give a close check to their ID, I've done my job and I'm covered. Unless it stands out in my face, of course. What was it? Some residential burglary?'

'Something like that,' I answered vaguely as I took the necklace from her hand and dropped it in my bag.

I had to talk to Kerry Spaulding, to find out more about her friend's relationship with Larry Marchand. There was more depth there than I knew about, and if I could plumb that depth I might begin to find a motive. I could've gone to Margie Dawson, and maybe I'd have to later on, but something about the girl's personality turned me off so I'd leave her resting on the shelf for now.

I drove directly to the house, pulling up beside the curb as the sun diffused behind the clouds, flooding them with rich warm rays of gold. I saw her coming down the walk, a softball glove swinging from her hand.

'Kerry, may I talk with you a moment? I won't take long.'

'That's okay,' she said dejectedly. 'I was just going to evening practice but it doesn't really matter, does it? Connie's gone and so's the coach so the team's just falling apart.'

She dropped down on the grass and I settled close beside her, sitting as we'd sat one time before.

I sensed a certain reserve I hadn't sensed on that occasion. Just as I was wondering about it, she raised her eyes and looked directly at me.

'I think you're wrong, you know. I don't think you

should've arrested him. I just don't believe the coach could do a thing like that.' She began picking at the grass blades as she cast down her eyes, and I knew she felt embarrassed at questioning my judgement.

'I can't discuss evidence with you, Kerry, you know that. Just trust me when I say that we don't act in haste and without sufficient reason.'

'Without probable cause – I learned that term in the Explorers. Yet sometimes mistakes are made. You must know that yourself, Detective Harrod.'

'Well, we'll see,' I answered noncommittally, and let the conversation drift away. I waited just a moment, then brought it back again on a different subject.

'I need to know more about Connie's relationship with Larry Marchand. About the reason for the break-up. Can you help me there?'

She shifted slightly and squinted at me. 'How d'you mean?'

'Well, were they lovers or hadn't they reached that stage before they split? And did she ever talk to you about what broke them up?'

'Is this important, Detective Harrod? I mean, if it is I'll certainly tell you what I know but, if it's not, I'd just as soon not gossip about my friends' personal lives.'

Her discomfiture was plain. I hated to make her squirm but I had to know.

'I don't ask idle questions, Kerry, they're always for a reason.'

She sighed deeply and hunched her shoulders as her arms hugged her knees. 'I know you see it on the TV and in the papers,' she began, 'about teens sleeping around and think-ing nothing of it. But it wasn't like that with us. Connie, Margie and I had never, you know, been with anyone.' She blushed deeply. 'And then Connie met Larry and they went all the way. She fell for him hard and she thought she really loved him. And then she thought he got her pregnant.'

'Was she pregnant, Kerry?'

'No, thank goodness. Her period was just three weeks late – she never *did* find out why – but she was so scared during those three weeks she could hardly eat or sleep.'

'How did Larry take all this?'

'She never even told him. That's when she decided to break off with him. She'd gotten in way too deep and she was frightened. When she thought she was going to have a baby, she realized how that would kill her parents and mess up her own life. That sort of thing doesn't happen to us because we think it's wrong – but here it was, happening to her, and it really brought it all home to her and she knew she didn't want it, she didn't want to stay involved with him.'

'Did she break it off right then?'

'Yes she did, but right before that happened he got really mad at her for no good reason, and I think that made it far less difficult for her to say goodbye.'

'Tell me about it, Kerry.' I started picking grass blades too. Not in nervousness, but because we'd settled into the goodness of a casual, trusting conversation and I wanted to maintain the easy feelings.

'We were all sitting in the small café right across from school. Not Larry – he wasn't one of our crowd – but some of the girls from the team and a few fellas. Just sitting and eating and telling jokes. Connie was in a really good mood that day. Her period had come the night before so she was really in high spirits.

'He walked in and kinda signaled to her to come and talk with him. She called out, just jokingly, "Buzz off, mister, can't you see I'm busy with my friends?" She didn't mean it, not at all. Even as she said it, she was getting up to go to him. But we'd begun to laugh, and Larry got furious. His face turned almost purple and his eyes were flashing full of anger.

' "Smart-ass high school kids," he yelled, "thinkin' you're so fuckin' good!" And then he turned around and stormed away, throwing the door real hard behind him so it banged and shook.'

I was fascinated by the story and the insight it gave into Larry Marchand's manner. Of course his rap sheet had already told me he had a violent temper, but here was not only an eyewitness account but also one that showed my victim to be the object of his wrath.

'After she broke off with him, did Connie ever talk about getting back with him again?'

'No way. She'd been bowled over by his attention right at first, and the fact that he was goodlooking and a little older, but once she realized what could happen if she stayed involved with him, she never gave a second thought to going back.' She picked up her glove and swung it back and forth.

'Kerry, we now have reason to believe Larry might've met with Connie on the night she died. If this is true, why would she agree to get together with him?'

The girl frowned and shook her head. 'I don't know. Maybe if he's the one who asked to meet, she just went out of curiosity to see what it was he wanted.'

'Maybe,' I replied. 'Tell me, did Connie have any other boyfriends this past summer, after she broke off with Larry?'

'No, none. Just pals, not guys to date.'

'Could it have been that she was missing having a relationship, and with no one else to fill the gap Larry Marchand began to look awfully good again? That maybe after a few months passed, she began to forget about the bad part or gloss it all over just a bit?'

Silence followed while Kerry did some close considering. Then she answered, slowly and reluctantly. 'I guess it could be, yes. And she was ashamed and embarrassed about it so she couldn't tell me anything because she knew I'd disapprove and would discourage her from seeing him. Yes, I can see now that maybe that could be so. But I sure do hope that's not the way it was.'

'It doesn't really matter, does it?' I said quietly. 'He can't cause her trouble any more.'

I didn't need to talk with Margie Dawson; I didn't need to talk with Connie's parents. I knew enough right now to know that Larry Marchand had a reason that could make him kill the Hammond girl.

He'd told me himself – proudly, even arrogantly – that *he* was the one who walked away, his ladies didn't do the leaving. And yet Connie had been the one to dump *him* and, on top of that, humiliate him, though unintentionally, before her friends. She'd never really meant it but that didn't matter. All he needed to know was that she'd showed him up.

Premeditated murder? Maybe, maybe not. Suppose he'd

gone to the clearing to ask her to get back with him and she'd refused? Maybe even been insulting? And he'd stolen the Branscombes' gun for some other reason, then used it on her in the furious heat of anger when she rebuffed him again? Something to think about, for sure.

A weekend at last alone with Tommy, a weekend to make up for the one I'd missed before. But that didn't really matter any more – I bore no grudge for what I'd lost. After Wednesday's court date, I had no time for rancor, no time for self-destroying feelings of resentment, only time for loving and appreciating the way my luck had turned.

And turned it had. Jon's lawyer had called mine to tell him his client had decided to abide by the judge's decision and would not try to appeal. He'd accept my gaining temporary custody but would, perhaps, ask for an extra weekend now and then. I'd grant that, of course, for Tommy's sake.

So like my husband, I thought, to be so very flip-sided, and I remembered the chameleon qualities he'd displayed while our marriage was deteriorating – how one moment he'd lure my trust with his loving behavior, and the next he'd turn mean and cold.

Wednesday's final show in court followed by his subsequent reversal showed the same kind of see-sawing – vocal threats springing from a powerful rage, a rage soon to be replaced by a calmer sensibility. I gave a happy little sigh. I felt so very glad.

I'd been late getting home. After leaving Kerry Spaulding's, I'd booked the necklace into property, then checked up on Kent's surveillance. Still no sign of Marchand. I sent a member of patrol, working undercover, to relieve Kent for the night. By the time I turned the key in my front door, Mrs Miller had already helped Tommy with his bath.

He met me at the door with a fresh-scrubbed face and small white terry robe tied tight around his waist. He looked for all the world like a little man playing big, and I put my hands above each hip and lifted him above my head, then spun him around.

'We'll have such fun tomorrow, kiddo. Any idea what you want to do?'

'Let's go see Aunt Joan, Mom. I want to ride the horses.'

'You got it, sweetie. We'll eat breakfast, then head right out there. She'll be so glad to see us.'

Joan wasn't really Tommy's aunt, she was mine – my mother's sister – but he called her auntie all the same. She lived a few miles out of town, down a winding country road that ran behind the Branscombe farm. I was glad he'd suggested visiting her. She was part of all my good intentions; I didn't pay as much attention to her as I should.

I tucked him into bed and changed my clothes. I was fixing my nightcap vodka-soda when the doorbell rang and I opened it to find Karen Windall standing there.

'I'm not fishing, Katie,' she said, swiftly. 'Your case is all your own. I just want a little human company for a while.'

As if in quick defiance to her wishes, Molly sprang up from her wicker bed and pressed herself against her, a black moist nose sniffing at her shoes.

'Fine,' she said wryly, 'I shouldn't be so choosy. I'll take any company I can get.'

166

She settled back across from me and looked at me with an eye that mirrored a question.

'So what's up?' I asked, wondering what this was all about. Surely she wasn't going to hit me up about the crime so quickly after stating her good intentions to steer clear.

'What do you think of Steve Darrow, Katharine?' The cool, composed, sleek-faced woman that I knew was looking slightly flustered.

'He used to work for me. He's a good detective with a couple of flaws but not so much they matter. Have you had a run-in with him on a story?'

'No, I'm seeing him . . . on a strictly non-professional basis.' She seemed a little bit embarrassed and I knew she badly needed an answer to her question.

I gave it to her, true and full. 'Stand clear of him, Karen, he's trouble all the way. God's gift to women and all the rest of it. If you want an easy lay, no strings attached, go take his body – but I can tell by your expression you're looking for a whole lot more. You won't get it from that one, even on the smallest scale.'

'So maybe you didn't know him on a personal level. Maybe you just thought you did.' The one who'd been asking my opinion was now fighting my answers all the way.

I shrugged my shoulders. 'I knew him well enough to tell you what I did. He's trouble. Take him for a one-night stand or leave him all alone. I care about you, honey, I wouldn't steer you wrong.' I shook my head in wonderment. Here was the tough-talking woman who'd railed against all men. And now she was finally falling, and falling for the one who'd only re-confirm her worst beliefs. Her next words told me I hadn't made a big impression.

'I'll handle it, Kate, don't concern yourself about me. I've always been able to take care of myself.'

I listened to the feminine bravado while we sat together quietly, sipping at our drinks and feeling easy in each other's company. Then she swung her feet up on the chair arm and got a new expression in her eyes.

'Okay, I didn't come here for this – I swear I didn't – but is there anything new about the case?'

'Nothing worth mentioning, Karen. We're still going through with the prelim on Kenneth Branscombe.'

'Well, yeah, that's a given, isn't it? I meant had you dug up any tighter evidence against him? Like are you getting close to a confession? That sort of thing?'

She watched me closely and I realized I'd almost given myself away. I'd almost acted as if there were another possibility besides the guilt of the man sitting on the thin hard cot in San Madera County Jail.

'Look,' she said, homing in on the homeward track to get me talking, 'I write a serious story, I only use what you can give me, I treat it with respect. I don't just write some fluff and snort, I only deal with facts and I can be discreet.'

I almost had to laugh. 'Karen, we've worked together for some time now. I know the caliber of your work – you've got nothing left to prove to me. It's just there's nothing new, nothing that's worth mentioning.'

'But there's something, right? It's not all crisp and clean right now, like it was before?'

I'd had way too much of a conversation that could only get me into trouble. 'Shut up right now, drink your drink, then go screw Detective Darrow. We'll have lunch one day this week and get our friendship back on line.'

She relaxed and swung her feet back down, then got up to mix herself another scotch. We chatted like old pals for half an hour, then I saw her out and locked the door behind her. Steve Darrow – I couldn't yet believe it. She was just like Connie Hammond, except she should've known better. Both had let a man of shallow depth and endless wiles take their willing foolish hearts and twist them tight.

I washed up the empty glasses, went upstairs and brushed my teeth. Then I looked in one last time on Tommy before I went to bed, bent to kiss his forehead, tucked his sheets in tight. So we were going to see Aunt Joan, I thought, and found I was really looking forward to tomorrow. Maybe on the way there, I'd drop in on Mabel Branscombe, to find how she was coping with her trouble and her pain.

CHAPTER TEN

Larry Marchand had not returned to the rooming house by eight the following morning. We put out an all-points bulletin for him – wanted for questioning only in the homicide of Connie Hammond.

I'd have the eyes of law enforcement in all surrounding counties watching out for the ex-con, so, without feeling I was shirking any duty, I set out to enjoy my day with Tommy.

'Get up, you lazybones,' I called to him as I tossed a pair of faded jeans across his bed. 'You can wear these while you hold your horses.'

'Maaaaam!' he wailed, and looked at me and grimaced. He pretended to hate the puns I often made.

He breakfasted on waffles while I nibbled at some toast, then we left Mrs Miller with the dishes, gave the dog a kiss goodbye, and headed for the country. The warm soft breeze of an early summer morning moved through the open windows of the car and Tommy edged forward on his seat.

'Gonna be fun, Mom. Are you going to ride too?'

'Maybe, hon. Or maybe I'll just chat with Auntie Joan. By

the way, I've got a stop I'd like to make along the way at another farm. It won't take long. Anyway, I think that you'll enjoy it. There's a nice lady, some lambs to pet. Okay?'

'Okaaay. I guess.' He seemed in the mood to agree with anything I said, and I knew he loved our outings just as much as I did.

I still felt a little funny about it, keeping in personal touch with Mabel Branscombe, though for the life of me I couldn't see why. I was doing nothing wrong. In fact, I might gain some more damning information on her brother by befriending her. And yet I knew that wasn't the reason I was riding down this road, on my way to the lonely farmhouse.

I swung into the driveway with Tommy hanging out the window. I slowed as I reached the clump of bushes where we'd parked the day we'd served the warrant, then drove right on up to the house. This time I didn't have to knock. I saw her in a pen near the rear of the yard, scattering grain to several chickens.

'Where're the lambs, Mom?' Tommy asked impatiently.

'Around the back. I saw them the last time I was here.'

'How do you know this lady anyhow?' he queried. 'Does she work with you?'

'No, no she doesn't. It's a long story, kiddo. I met her on a case of mine, but she wasn't really involved with it, just standing on the edges.'

'The edges of what?'

I was starting to realize I'd raised a very literal child. 'It's just an expression,' I explained, 'meaning not actively taking a part in something.'

'Like when I'm sitting on the bench in Little League?'

'Yeah, sorta like that.'

She must've heard the car because I saw Mabel raise her head, then turn the bucket upside-down, emptying out the last kernels of grain before coming through the gate. I cut the engine and started toward her, holding Tommy by the hand.

'Miss Branscombe? I hope I'm not intruding. We were on our way past and I just thought I'd stop in and say hello, see how you were doing.'

The eyes that looked into mine were no longer dark and wild. Instead they held a somber stare. 'Detective Harrod.' She paused and laid her hand along her cheek. 'You're holding my brother for a murder he didn't do and yet I find I'm glad to see you. How very odd.'

I didn't know whether to stay or go, but her next words decided for me. 'Please come on up to the porch and sit awhile. I'd be happy for your company. Is this your little boy?' She bent over and placed a hand on Tommy's shoulder, smiling straight into his eyes. 'How are you today, sweetheart? Would you like a glass of lemonade or maybe go around to see the lambs?'

Her attention now seemed totally focused on my son, and I sensed that she possessed a depth of warmth and caring for young children. As far as I knew, Mabel Branscombe had never married, never had youngsters of her own, and I imagined she sorely felt the lack.

She confirmed my thoughts as she straightened up and looked at me. 'Although I raised Kenneth from a little boy, just about the age of this one, I was never fortunate enough to have a child of my own. It must be a wondrous thing, Detective Harrod. You're a very, very lucky woman.'

The three of us walked around the back, coming to a roomy pen holding seven fluffy lambs. They *baaaaed* and pushed against each other, their bodies clothed in tight white fleece, their legs and faces carbon black.

'I'll open up the gate, dear, and you go right on in,' Mabel offered. 'Play very gently with them, they're only little babies. And don't be afraid of them. They won't hurt you, but they expect you to be kind.'

Tommy darted forward eagerly and we shut the gate behind him, then returned to the cool and breezy porch where we sat on the white wooden swing, sipping ice-cold lemonade.

'Have you found Larry yet, Detective? Because when you do, you'll let Kenneth go, I know you will.' She bit her lip earnestly, and looked at me as if she was hoping she could convince me with her words alone and her wishes would come true.

'Not yet, Miss Branscombe, but I'm certain we will within the next few days. Wherever he's gone, we'll catch up with him.'

'So he's scampered, then? He's not over at Jacinto? Doesn't that show you something right there?'

'Miss Branscombe, your brother's prints were on the gun, not Larry Marchand's.'

'Fiddlesticks!' she cried. 'And why shouldn't they be? It's his gun, isn't it? Who else's prints would be on it? I told you that murderer Larry Marchand wiped his off, so Kenneth probably picked it up after that to clean it or something.'

'It wasn't cleaned.'

'Well, to shift it in the drawer then, to find some clothes.'

She was becoming agitated and seemed close to tears, so I gently changed the subject. 'You mentioned raising Kenneth. I don't mean to pry, but was he very young when you lost your parents?'

Her eyes took on a strange look as she swung her gaze full upon my face – a wary, unsure, questioning look. 'Yes,' she answered slowly, 'yes, he was. I'm a good bit older than Kenny. I'm sixty-two and he's twelve years younger. When it happened, I'd just turned eighteen and he was only six, and the courts decided I could raise him. He was my baby brother and I adored him so. No foster home was going to take him from me.'

'He was married once,' I ventured.

'Yes, to a lovely girl, a member of my church group. But she died of cancer ten years ago, without having any children, and he's been without ever since. Oh, those were happy times.' Her voice began to lilt and her eyes brightened. 'They lived out here with me the six years they were married, the three of us together.'

I didn't want to start on Connie Hammond and the love the coach had felt for her, and yet the true detective in me couldn't let it lie. 'The dead girl, some people say—'

I got no further. Mabel Branscombe laid her hand on mine and told me slowly and decisively, 'He felt nothing for her. Those are dirty lies, told by vicious filthy people. There was nothing to it and that is all I'm going to say. And I will not speak of it again.'

I left it alone and did what I'd come here to do in the first place – enjoy a casual visit.

'Were you raised on this farm, Miss Branscombe, you and Kenneth?'

'Oh no. Several miles from here, deeper in the foothills. Do you know where the San Luis turnoff is?'

'Why, yes,' I answered. 'I have an aunt who lives down that way. That's where we're going when we leave here.'

'Who would that be?' the woman asked curiously.

'Joan Tabor. Like you, she's lived around these parts all her life. She's a widow now but Dalton was her maiden name. My mother was her sister.'

A silence fell and deepened. Then, 'Was your mother Chrissie Dalton?'

I felt my eyes involuntarily widen and my mouth drop open. 'Why, yes, she was. She passed away many years ago.'

Mabel Branscombe leaned slowly toward me and laid her hand upon my knee. 'I knew your mother, Katharine.' I hadn't realized she was aware of my first name. 'I knew your mother and her sister. We grew up together. Our families' farms were not that far apart. I remember when your parents died. I remember hearing there was a child, a little girl. I didn't know till now that child was you.'

'Yes,' I answered, stunned. 'Yes, it was me, but I wasn't very little. I was in my teens when the accident occurred.'

'Ah, well, I'd forgotten or else I'd never really heard. The three of us had drifted apart long before that time and I knew only that your mother had married someone from Oliva and had a youngster, then had gotten killed in that unfortunate wreck. I'm so sorry for you, child – she was a lovely woman.'

All the pain, all the sorrow, all the anguish I'd kept buried for so long rose quickly to the surface of my soul, just as an object long-submerged then suddenly released rockets to the surface of the sea. I choked as I fought back the tears, and for a moment I was rendered speechless.

And then a bolt of realization struck me, and built and swept all through me – and I knew beyond a doubt why I'd been drawn to this woman, why I'd felt an empathy for her beyond all reason. She reminded me so much of my mother – her caring ways, certain small gestures she made, even, at some angles, her looks – as if she were Chrissie grown older.

I recalled the day she'd stormed into the squad room, proclaiming Larry Marchand's guilt. I remembered the feeling I'd had then, something far away and fleeting that I couldn't put a finger on. And this was what it was. I could put a finger on it now.

I felt an emptying inside me, as if the stuffing had been pulled out and I was left a limp and useless rag doll. 'Do you see Aunt Joan now?' I asked, weak-voiced, passing time while trying to regain my equilibrium.

'Only at a distance, several times a year. At least I think it's her. I'm not really sure I'd recognize her or her me. As I said, we've gone our separate ways.'

I wanted to go then, not to stay there any longer. I craved to get away, to be in private and begin to sort my feelings.

'Let's see how Tommy's doing with the lambs,' I said, and began to rise. Just at that moment, a young man passed through the yard, leading an old and haltered cow by a thick hemp rope. His blond hair gleamed reddish in the sun and his freckles stood out like small tan full stops across his face. As we watched, he gave the cow a quick hard tug, causing her to stumble on the rough uneven ground.

'Kevin, stop jerking her like that,' Mabel called out sharply. 'Lead her gently and let her set her own pace.'

The boy slowed immediately and he and the ancient animal ambled slowly toward a nearby field.

'He didn't mean it,' Mabel Branscombe said as she turned toward me. 'Ignorant, that's all. He's taken Larry's place. We always need an extra hand around here. And especially now.' She cast a quick, uncertain look at me. 'All in all, he's a hard worker, but, oh, some of them . . . She winced and set her lips and I saw tears begin to flood her eyes. 'Some of them can be so cruel to the poor animals, cruel on purpose. You could not believe the way they'd treat them, the things they'd do, till I caught them at it. I had to let them go, to fire them right away.'

She began to tremble and dabbed her eyes. 'Forgive me, Katharine, please forgive me. It's just that I cannot bear anyone being cruel to the animals.'

I longed to comfort her, to take her in my arms and soothe her, to drive away the anguish and the ache. But I knew that I'd be out-of-bounds, because of who she was and my own emotional reaction to her. I settled for a non-committal murmuring, assuring her I shared her point of view, then we began to walk around the back.

Tommy was sitting on the grass inside the pen, a little lamb held tightly on his lap. When it began to struggle, he released it and sat contentedly where he was, reaching out to pat the ones that came in reach.

'Tommy, it's time to go see Aunt Joan,' I called. 'Come on out.'

Reluctantly he rose and left the pen.

Mabel Branscombe started toward him, holding out her hands. 'Did you have fun, dear? Maybe your mother will bring you here again. Would you like that?'

He nodded enthusiastically. Once again she bent down till she was on eye level with him. 'I found out today that I knew your grandmother when she was a little girl, just about the age you are now. We played together. Isn't that surprising? She was a very, very nice person. You would've loved her very much.'

Tommy looked quickly up at me, his eyes questioning.

'She knew Grandma? The lady in the photographs?'

'Yes, Tommy,' I said softly, 'she knew your grandmother. Auntie Joan too.'

'Wow,' he said, and looked back at Mabel Branscombe. 'I sure wish I could've been you.'

She walked us to the car and waited while we got inside. 'Please come back, the two of you,' she said earnestly. 'I've so enjoyed your visit and getting to meet your little boy. He's such a little gentleman. I'd love to see you both again, if you're passing by this way.'

'We might just do that,' I found myself saying to her, as I looked up and saw her smile – a smile that took me back a long, long way to a long, long time ago.

We left the farm behind and began the drive to Joan's, and as we drove my thoughts turned inward.

I'd lost both my parents when I was only fourteen years of age – a fragile time for any child who's just starting to try to find her way in life, let alone deal suddenly with a devastating tragedy. I loved my parents, but of course I'd taken them for granted, and it was only after they were gone – wrenched from me with undeniable finality – that I truly realized the magnitude of the empty place they left within my life.

Especially I missed my mother. My father, at least several years her senior, seemed kind but more remote. I believe he wasn't certain how to deal with me at times, fearful he might bumble whatever approach he chose to take. Instead of reacting naturally to me, he seemed to feel there was a set of rules and regulations for bringing up a child that somehow he couldn't learn, so instead of plunging in and building our relationship, he chose to stand off in the background. He loved me, I knew that without a doubt, but I think I baffled him.

My mother, on the other hand, wrapped her love around me and wholeheartedly embraced the act of raising a child. She was always there for me, with laughter and with kindness and with comfort. Gently, she'd point the way in which I should try to grow – but she never pushed, never attempted to shape me into her own image.

And then one day she was no longer there. Gone, when I was just beginning to walk the long, confusing path from adolescence into womanhood. Aunt Joan, her younger sister, took me in and cared for me as if I were her own, but it was never quite the same. She was a different type from Chrissie and, while she fed and clothed and counseled me to her very best ability, there was an unpleasant sharpness about her that lay just beneath the surface. And, quite simply, she was not my mother. No matter what else she was, she was not my mother.

Slowly, I buried the sadness and the pain, until whole days would go by when I didn't feel them. They were still there, but they were hidden in the farthest corners of my soul with fences all around them so that they couldn't reach me. I couldn't feel their strength unless I wished to take them out and feel it.

And so the months passed by, and then the years, and I released the pain and sadness with decreasing frequency, so that I seldom felt their force and fury. I finally believed I'd muted them for good and they were only memories, like other recollections of my childhood. Until now. Until I met a woman who mirrored the persona of my mother.

Why, I wondered, at this point in my life? Surely there'd been other women earlier with whom I could have identified. Was it because I was especially vulnerable right now, made that way by the disintegration of my marriage and my own near-brush with death in my previous case? I didn't have the answer. I knew that all the hurt and sorrow, buried for so long, had now suddenly poured forth and I felt badly shaken. The feelings had stayed fresh and strong through all these years. They had not diminished with my careful 'fencing', I'd only hidden them extremely well – and now I missed my dear beloved mother as if her death had happened yesterday.

'Mom!' Tommy was pulling at my arm. 'Mom, slow down. We're almost there!'

I jerked back swiftly from my reverie and began braking for the turning into Joan's.

'I hope she'll let me ride Romper,' Tommy bubbled happily, referring to a chestnut gelding standing nearly sixteen hands.

'I think Sox is more your style, Sonny,' I advised him, picturing the little bay with the blaze upon her face.

'Okay, but someday I'll be up to taking Romps,' he announced with confidence.

I'd called ahead, and she came out of the farmhouse door as we parked the car. A tall, thin woman dressed in jeans and a checkered shirt with rolled-up sleeves, we bore a family resemblance, especially around the eyes, but I was more fleshed out than she.

'Ready to ride?' she called, as she tucked a strand of iron-grey hair back into its ponytail.

'He is, but I think I'm just sitting,' I replied. 'Sitting down and yakking.'

'Too bad,' she answered ruefully. 'I was looking forward to some exercise, and so were Sox and Dusty.'

'Sox will get hers,' I told Joan. 'Tommy's set to ride 'em cowboy.'

We saddled up the little mare and Tommy mounted her. He began to ride around the paddock while Joan and I settled on a nearby bench to watch.

'His arm's doing well,' she noted as she watched him take the reins. 'Much better than I'd ever have expected.'

'It's a miracle,' I said. 'Even the doctor can't believe it.'

I marveled at it every day myself. His forearm, injured when a spike had pinned it in a nasty fall the previous spring, had hung partially useless by his side for many weeks, and therapists had told us never to expect full healing. But suddenly the strength had started coming back and was increasing in leaps and bounds on a daily basis.

'Joan,' I said, turning to my aunt, 'I understand you once

knew the Branscombes. That you and mother both grew up with them.'

'We did,' she said. 'We were slightly older than Mabel was and, of course, a whole lot older than Kenny but, yes, for all practical purposes we *did* grow up with them. And now look what that one's gone and done. Like father, like son. I guess what they always say is true.'

'I don't understand,' I said, frowning. 'What do you mean? What're you talking about?'

'Don't you know about it?' she asked, narrowing her eyes. 'No, I guess you wouldn't – it happened more than forty years ago. Jason Branscombe slit his poor wife's throat, then turned a shotgun on himself and blasted out his brains.'

I sipped my coffee slowly as I looked at her across the room. We'd moved indoors to be more comfortable, while Tommy groomed the horse and put away the tack.

When I'd heard what Aunt Joan had to say, my mind had reeled and spun. It was almost too much to take in.

'I never heard of it,' I'd said. 'I never heard a single thing.'

'Ah, well, like I said, it's past history now. No one talks about the old murders. Though I certainly can see why *you'd* want to know more about it. Interesting coincidence, isn't it?'

'Where were the children when this happened?' I asked her now, as she cut some sandwiches and poured some milk.

'In the house with their parents, as far as I can remember. I don't recall hearing any different. In fact, I think Mabel was the one who found the bodies and called the police.'

'Why did he do it? Did he have a history of violent behavior?'

'Jason Branscombe was the meanest man I ever met,' Joan said slowly and emphatically. 'Hard, cold, cruel – a right bastard, as they say. He was certainly mentally abusive and probably physically as well. Treated his wife like dog dirt. Just about wore her into the ground with his constant criticizing and haranguing.

'I think he was crazy too. Had to be, hadn't he, to do what he ended up doing? He didn't leave a note, as I remember, so no one ever really knew why. Most people figured he'd just had it up to here one day—' she laid a finger flat against her throat – 'and decided both of them should leave this world for good.

'It was a pretty ghastly business, as you can well imagine. The wife was in the kitchen, lying near the table soaked in blood, with her head hanging by a thread from her body and laying to one side with the eyes open wide. Her blood had splattered up against the stove and spurted on the wall above the sink. I knew a cop who was early on the scene and he said it was like swimming in a sea of red.'

'And the husband? Was he found beside her?'

'No. He'd gone out on the porch and sat down on the steps, then placed the gun between his knees with the barrel shoved in his mouth. They found him sprawling backwards on the wooden floor with half his head and brains spread across the window panes behind him.'

'My God,' I murmured slowly, taking in the picture. 'My God, I had no idea.' I paused a moment, then, 'Why weren't the children killed along with Jason and his wife?'

'I don't know,' Aunt Joan replied. 'Maybe they were hiding with all the ruckus going on, or maybe in his insanity he wasn't even thinking of them. Remember, this was all a long, long time ago and I'm no longer clear on all the details.'

The door slammed back and Tommy raced inside and threw himself into a chair. 'She's all cooled off and put away, Aunt Joan,' he said, looking longingly at the sandwiches. She picked up the plate and let him choose the one he wanted, then placed a glass of milk beside his hand. He munched happily away while flipping through a Batman comic.

'There's really not much more that I can tell you, Kate. If you're truly interested, the library should still have it all on file.'

She stared into the distance and a far-off look came into her eyes. 'That poor, poor woman. She was the kindest, sweetest person you could ever hope to meet, but oh so fragile and so indecisive. Against Jason Branscombe, she didn't stand a chance – he tore down any confidence she might've tried to build. And then he slaughtered her and brought her living misery to an end.'

CHAPTER ELEVEN

Mabel Branscombe had lost her mother and her father, just like me, and now she was about to lose her brother – unless someone had made a bad mistake, unless there really was another killer, as I was starting to believe might be the case.

I strode along the long hard hallway in the county jail and paused beside the cell of Kenneth Branscombe. He sat dejectedly on the side of his small cot, his head hanging down between his hands.

'Mr Branscombe, you don't have to speak to me without your attorney being present.'

'I don't care. I've got nothing at all to hide from you.'

'How did the print get on your revolver? I mean, how precisely?'

'Because it was layin' on the bureau top on Friday evening and I picked it up and put it in the drawer where it belongs. I've been thinkin' about it and that's the last time I touched it. And the first time too, in many weeks.'

'Why wasn't the revolver registered?' I asked, curious as to why I'd not been able to bring it up in the computer.

'Oh, I just got careless, never did it. After that prowler, the detective warned me I should do it, but I put it off again, then just forgot it.'

That explained that, but other matters needed sorting out. 'You lied to us about knowing Connie was seeing Larry Marchand again. Why would you do that if you didn't care, had nothing to hide?'

'Because I didn't want to look like the interfering fool I was. I didn't want to get you on the subject, so I didn't tell the truth. I know now I messed myself up by doing that, but at the time it seemed the smart thing to do.'

I studied him. He'd lost some weight and a lot of ruddy color. A jail cell didn't suit him any better than it suited most men.

'Your pick-up truck was seen beside the field. You were positively identified turning to the path.'

He rose ponderously to his feet and shook his fist. 'I . . . wasn't . . . there!' he shouted out, pausing for emphasis between each word. 'Whoever says so is a goddamn liar!'

I left him roiling at a high simmer and went back home to call Stuart Greenwell. The gentle voice of his wife Sara answered but he quickly took the phone from her when he found out who it was.

I minced no words.

'Mr Greenwell, are you absolutely certain you saw Kenneth Branscombe in the meadow off the Canfield road?'

'One hundred per cent, no doubt about it. Him and that pick-up truck of his with that busted left-side fender. It's been like that a long time. Look, Detective Harrod, I told you right up front – this really pains me. Kenny Branscombe's always been a fine man up till now, but I've got to do what's right and tell the truth.'

So there it was. My prime suspect gave a perfectly logical explanation for his print being on the murder weapon, but an unprejudiced – indeed, an unwilling – witness stuck like superglue to his contention that Branscombe was heading toward the murder scene that night.

And so? I asked myself. What does that exactly mean? Had I rushed on too fast, eager in my desire to find the murderer? After all, a man turning down a path leading to a clearing in the woods does not necessarily have to be the man who fires the gun. Suppose Kenneth Branscombe had gotten wind that his beloved Connie was going to meet Larry Marchand that Thursday evening. Perhaps Mabel had sneaked a peek at the note after all, and mentioned it to Kenneth, or perhaps Kenneth had come across the piece of pale pink paper himself.

And then he'd gone to watch, to eavesdrop, maybe even to have it out with Marchand – but when he got there Connie was already dead, lying face down on the cool, soft, fresh grass, and he became too scared to admit he'd been any-where near the murder scene, for fear we'd really hang him then. So he was stonewalling it. And waiting for a miracle.

'Damn it,' I said sharply to myself, 'we've got to pick up Larry Marchand.'

I got to the station bright and early Monday morning, but Carl was there ahead of me, working through the diary we'd taken from the Branscombe house. He'd started fine-tooth-combing it, to cull all additional damning evidence from its pages and help us build our case. As I reached my desk and slung my bag across it, I saw him frowning as he ran his finger across its pages. He heard my step and called me over.

'Kate, come here a minute. Something's funny. See what you . . . Hold on a second.' His phone had begun to ring before he'd finished, and maybe it was my imagination but I thought I sensed an urgency in the strident trill.

I was right. Carl dropped the faded diary, grabbed a pencil, and began to write frantically. His face had suddenly grown serious and his eyes were riveted on the scribblings he'd made. He swung his head up, looked at me, and nodded up and down in triumph.

'We've got Marchand, Kate,' he told me as he banged the phone back in its cradle. 'That was sheriffs over at Oliva. They've found him in another rooming house, apparently bunking down with some ex-con friend of his. They got a line on him earlier this morning, then staked out the joint and saw him going in just now. I told them to keep it covered front and back, but not to take him in. Let's roll!'

We ran into Kent as we were going down the stairs two at a time.

'*Buenos días*—' he began, but got no farther before I interrupted him.

'Store it, kiddo,' I said. 'We've got no time for pleasantries. Marchand's been located over in Oliva.' I tempered my abruptness with a quick smile and a nod, and he whistled, spun around, and joined us.

'Are you going to take him in or do the talking there?' Carl queried me.

'It all depends on what goes down. If he's a willing little

boy and gives us all the answers, that's one thing. If he won't co-operate and tell us what we want to know, we'll yank him right into the station.'

'Of course, if he answers and we like the words he says, we'll be taking him in anyway,' Kent contributed. 'No matter what, I think this kid is going for a car ride.'

I looked at him and wondered if Rena was still hounding him to quit. But who could really blame her? Ours was one of the most stressful professions in the world, and with Kent's family history, she must have felt he was taking undue risks a little bit too far.

I felt sorry for the two of them. I understood her worry, but I also understood his unrelenting passion for his work. And so the threat would weave itself into their lives and lie there constantly, and she'd continue worrying while he'd go on taking risks and hoping luck would run his way.

I accelerated as I reached the city limits, and soon we were barrelling down the open road that ran across the farmland, leaving puffs of dust trailing in the wind behind us. We reached Oliva as the morning sun began to heat the fields and touch the crops with golden brightness.

The narrow street wasn't hard to find. A plain-clothes sheriff's deputy was standing near the end and pointed out the stucco house half-way down the block. Unlike March-and's home over in Jacinto, this structure stood slightly distant from its neighbors, several scraggly pines marking one side of its boundaries.

Again I sent Kent around the back, where he joined the deputies who watched the rear. Carl and I knocked quietly on the door and waited till we heard approaching steps. A skinny, bony woman with bird-bright eyes and rounded shoulders peered out and raised her eyebrows questioningly.

'Who's in 2B?' I asked her curtly.

'Fellow by the name of Billy Curtain and some pal of his.'

She was smarter than the landlord in Jacinto. She knew better than to try to stall us.

'San Madera PD. We need to see the pal, and we'd sure appreciate it if you didn't give him any warning.'

She shrugged her curving shoulders and let us come inside. 'No never-mind to me,' she murmured as she pointed up the stairs.

We moved stealthily from step to step, our backs against the wall, our hands hovering near our weapons. We saw no one in the hallway, no one going in or coming out of rooms.

We paused before 2B, and as we held our breath and listened, we heard a shuffling sound inside, then a little croaking laugh. I nodded, then began to knock. The laughing stopped. I knocked again, this time a whole lot harder.

'San Madera police, Marchand. We need to talk with you.'

The door burst open and a lanky black man shoved past us, racing down the bare-wood hall, hurtling down the stairs. I turned back and saw Larry Marchand disappear across the sill and drop towards the ground below.

'Goddamn it, no. No! Fuck off, you bastard cops!' I heard the yell as I leaned out of the open window, and watched as they tussled with him in some bushes, then took him into custody.

We turned around and ran downstairs and outside. The fleeing man was nowhere to be seen. Larry Marchand sat against a tree, his face bloody where he'd fallen, his wrists cuffed behind his back.

'We just want to have a little chat, Lawrence,' I told him in my nicest tone. 'No reason to make such a nasty stink and tear yourself up that way.'

I crouched down beside him and looked into his eyes. They weren't flirting with me now. Contempt and seething hatred had replaced the lighter feelings.

'Let's go sit over here,' I motioned toward a dilapidated bench, 'while you pull yourself together.'

'Why were you running, son?' Carl came up behind us. 'We just wanted to talk to you a little bit.'

'Hell, no, I wasn't running,' Marchand shot back quickly.

'We waited for you over in Jacinto and you never came back home. Now we find you where you don't belong. What do you call that then?'

'I was catchin' up with Billy, droppin' in to see a friend I hadn't seen since he got out. Findin' out what he was up to. What the fuck's wrong with that? Is there a law?' Jailhouse bravado still played strong outside the prison walls.

'Funny how you took a sudden notion,' Carl continued, 'and how you've been lying pretty low ever since you got here.'

Marchand ran a hand along his chin, then studied the bloodstains on his palm. 'So what's this all about? What's going on anyhow?' A trace of nervousness started to appear.

'We know you met Connie Hammond in the woods that Thursday night. We found the note – the sweet memento on light pink paper that you buried in your drawer.'

A look of fear spread quickly across his face as his eyes

flicked from me to Dan to Carl. A look of fear, and something else as well. 'I didn't meet her. There was no note. I don't know what the hell you're talkin' about. You're tryin' to pin something on me I didn't do.' He wet his lips and twisted as if he was sitting on tacks. The bravado was fading fast away.

'Tell us about the necklace.'

'What necklace? I don't know nuthin' about no necklace.'

'The necklace you pawned for pennies in the hockshop in Jacinto. The necklace Connie Hammond wore around her throat the night you met and murdered her.'

'My God, I don't know what you're talkin' about. She was nothing to me any more. Why would I want to hurt her, let alone murder her?'

'Because she dumped you and she showed you up,' I told him with finality, 'and you couldn't stand it, so your rage and anger made you take her life.'

'Fuck you . . .' he protested, then his voice trailed off.

'We've got the records on the pawn, buddy. Your driver's license, your picture ID.'

'For Christ's sake, no. It wasn't me.' He began to whimper, then to sob. 'I swear to God I never went near her Thursday night.'

'So who can vouch for that?' I asked. 'Have you got an alibi? Come on, Larry, spit out some names, give us some-one to talk to – and I don't mean one of your lying say-it's-so jailhouse cronies who'll tell us you were lapping up the soaps with them.'

Silence fell across the yard as the heat began to rise. The deputies stood motionless, arms tight in front of them, wait-ing to hear Marchand's words.

'No alibi,' he told me weakly, 'no one to back me up. But I didn't kill her. I didn't go near the cow that night or any time in the past few weeks.'

'Facts are saying otherwise, Larry, and there's something else you ought to know. Someone is telling us they saw you with the murder weapon in your hands the morning after Connie Hammond died. A very positive witness, indeed. I'd even go so far as to say you couldn't shake this person's story. Care to tell us all about it?'

'I never saw the gun. I never touched it afterwards. What – is – going – on?' His face contorted till it was badly out of shape and his eyes grew large and wild. 'I don't know what the hell is going on here.'

'We're going for a ride,' I told him as I reached across and took his arm. 'That's one thing that's going on. I'm taking you in for questioning in connection with the shooting death of Connie Hammond. Perhaps a little time in an old familiar jail cell will present you with a new perspective and help to loosen up those vocal chords.'

Kent brought the car around, and Carl and I began to lead him toward it. Walking in a stumbling fashion, his head down and eyes upon the ground, Larry Marchand moved unprotesting between the two of us, and bent to enter the back seat. I spread my open palm across his skull, to protect it from a strike against the doorframe, then climbed in beside him. Kent and Mungers got up front and the four of us rode in silence back to San Madera.

I'd let him sit and stew awhile, see if his new surroundings worked the wonders I was hoping for. I wasn't at all convinced he'd killed Connie with premeditation, nor even certain that he'd killed her at all – but he owed us some explanations for the note, the necklace and the weapon he'd been fondling.

I didn't have to charge him with anything just yet, so I'd try to wait him out, hoping he'd break down before I had to throw him out the door.

And then a bit of luck slid my way and made it all a little easier. Another routine computer check on Larry Marchand showed he'd been named as suspect in a simple assault case in the adjoining county – a summons that had just evolved into a warrant for non-appearance at a court date.

I phoned Merced County Sheriff's and explained the situation, and they said they'd take their good sweet time in getting there to pick him up, maybe all the way till late tomorrow. This meant we could now legally hold Mr Marchand while he helped us sort things out about the murder.

I started toward Carl's desk, to ask him what he'd meant about the diary, but I saw he was talking to a witness in a recent felony assault so I passed on by. I'd catch him up some other time about it.

I didn't need to know any more about the wretched early life of Mabel Branscombe, but a compelling urge made me want to learn more details of the murder–suicide more than forty years ago. I was drawn to it irresistibly and I knew I'd better satisfy my curiosity now and get it over with, or it would torment and gnaw at me until I did.

I walked several blocks to the city library and asked for the microfilm from the early fifties.

'Microfilm, indeed,' the old librarian snorted. 'We've only got the past decade set up that way. Budget cuts and such keep us running at poverty level, in case you haven't heard. If you want papers that far back, you'll have to go down to the basement and dig out the actual copies themselves.'

She checked my ID, then gave me the key to the dusty, silent vaults. I flicked on a light, went down some metal stairs, and found myself standing in a narrow room with tall steel shelving flanking either side of a narrow hallway.

I was all alone, but somehow the solitude was comforting. I'd always liked the serenity of libraries. Long ago, in fact, in the early days of my youth, I'd worked briefly at a branch of this very same one.

Moving forward in the coolness of the basement air, I began to scan the shelves for dates. I had only a little bit to work with – the fact that Mabel was now sixty-two and had been eighteen or so at the time of the murder–suicide. I could figure out the probable year the killings had occurred, but not the month or even the season. I'd start at January, I decided, and quickly scan all the front pages from then on. At least I wouldn't have to thumb through the entirety of each edition – this story would not be hidden in the inside columns.

I pulled the first set of yellowed papers down from where they lay – had probably lain for many months – and carried them to a long table to one side where I could spread them out.

I started slowly, turning the pages carefully and squinting studiously at each headline, but soon, as the bold type yielded nothing, I speeded up the process, anxious to find what I was looking for. January, February, March zipped by. I was starting to despair and wonder if I had the wrong year after all. And then I flipped a page and it leapt out at me: FARMER SLAUGHTERS WIFE, SHOOTS SELF, ON LONELY FOOT-HILL SPREAD.

I caught my breath and began reading avidly. I was no longer the detached and seasoned homicide detective; I was just an average citizen filled with hunger for sensational details.

I could've gone straight to our own files, though a case this old probably would've been buried even deeper than in the library – but, for some reason I found difficult to fathom, I'd wanted to read it in the wondrously descriptive form of creative writing, not in the stark, stripped-down, unemotional jargon of police reportage.

The story went pretty much as Aunt Joan had told it to me: Jason Branscombe had been seen in town that morning buying fertilizer for spring planting, and had seemed much the same as always – abrupt, rude, sourfaced and complaining.

He'd then gone home, and sometime late that evening had slashed his wife of twenty years, then turned a shotgun on himself. The call came into the sheriff's department early the next morning from the person who had found the bodies – the couple's daughter, Mabel Branscombe.

I stopped short. The following morning? I didn't get it. Had the children been asleep and failed to hear the shot? Had they been away from home after all and not inside the house as Joan had said? I began to skip ahead, looking for a paragraph that would explain the mystery to me. And then I saw it and began to read, my eyes opening wide in horror and in disbelief.

'Due to Tuesday's unexpected snowstorm in the foothills, the phone lines to the Branscombe farm were down from late that afternoon till early Wednesday morning, preventing Miss Branscombe from notifying authorities until nearly twelve hours after her grisly discovery at eight p.m. Because of the snow's depth and the high winds which piled it into even higher drifts, the daughter was unable to leave the farmhouse to seek help on foot.'

'Besides,' Mabel had explained to the reporter, 'my little brother was in my charge and I couldn't leave him there by himself with our mother and father.'

I sat back, feeling punched. So she'd been alone with the bloody bodies for an entire night, from the time the dark came down around them until the sun rose the next morning. She'd been trapped in that house of stinking death with no possible escape.

What had she been thinking all that time? What had she been feeling? Had she tried to keep Kenneth from the awful scenes? Had she stayed away herself, following the initial discovery, or crept back from time to time to gaze in numbing disbelief at her mother's severed head or her father's blasted body?

I shuddered as I raised my eyes and stared in front of me. I could imagine no more hideous torment, no more agonizing situation, than the one described on the pages of this paper. How had Mabel Branscombe kept her sanity through that long, cold April night? Why had she not gone totally insane, perhaps running from the smell of bloody death and plunging to her own end in some snowdrift because her madness had removed all reason? I felt so sorry for this woman, so very sorry.

I replaced the papers and returned the key to the librarian. I felt hollow, as if somehow the happening had been mine as well. I walked from the building with the mental image pounding through my mind – the silent dark, the mutilated bodies, the children trapped with the horror until dawn. Shaking my head as if to clear the vision from me, I began to drive.

Again, the car swept up the winding driveway to the isolated farmhouse. Again, I saw Mabel Branscombe standing near the chicken pen, a Plymouth Rock cradled in her arms.

I got out, waved and went to her. 'I just came by to tell you we've picked up Lawrence Marchand. I can make no promises but I think I owe you that news at least.'

My mouth voiced the message I'd come here to give her, but my eyes were busy searching her expression to see if I could spot a vestige of the effects of that grisly experience so many years ago. I saw nothing unusual, only a normal, average person saddened, understandably, by the fact her brother was in custody.

'Thank God, Katharine. Now you'll find out the truth and Kenneth can come home. I've taken care of him all my life and it kills me that he's in that jail, not here where he belongs. Oh, that boy, I'm not a bit surprised. He was one of those I told you about who tried to hurt the little animals. I was just about to fire him when the girl got murdered. Did you find anything on him? The note? Anything?' She waited eagerly for my reply.

'You know I can't discuss evidence with you, Miss Branscombe. Whatever we have or don't have, we'll get it all sorted out, don't worry.'

'I know you will,' she told me earnestly. 'I'll just wait to hear from you.'

I couldn't help but look at her and feel a wash of pity as I thought about the rotten hand that life had dealt her. She was another victim I was powerless to help. But perhaps this time I could offer comfort. Again I longed to hold her, again I kept my arms beside me and walked away.

I swung back toward the station, to see if the flavor of the jailhouse had caused my latest prisoner to have a change of heart. I found him stretched out upon his cot, eyes closed, arms folded and lying on his chest.

'I've got enough to hold you on the murder charge,' I informed him bluntly. 'The note setting up the meeting, the pawn shop info, the wit who saw you with the gun. I'm just trying to help you make it easy on yourself. Talk to me before I have to book you and I'll consider that co-operation with authorities.'

Of course I was only bluffing. The DA wouldn't file a capital murder case based just on a pawn slip and a piece of pale pink paper. Despite what I'd hinted earlier to Marchand, I could hardly expect the DA to consider Mabel Branscombe, whose own brother now stood charged with the crime, a reliable and impartial witness.

Larry only glared at me, but then, just as I began to turn away, he rose from the cot and started coming toward me.

'Hold on a minute.' I paused and waited. 'No, nuthin'. Never mind.' And he went back and lay down, this time prone with his head turned toward the wall.

I shrugged. If that was the way he wanted to play it, then so be it, though I admit I felt a tug of disappointment.

I walked back upstairs. Carl was nowhere to be seen so I opened his top drawer and pulled out the purple diary, thinking maybe I could make out what he'd been talking about.

I thumbed through it with curiosity but was unable to pick up on anything unusual, at least at a casual glance. It seemed just like any other farmer's diary to me – recording the planting dates for beans and grapes, the arrival of a new calf or foal – except for the entry near the end that had drawn our attention to it in the first place. I'd put it down and wait until tomorrow, when he could show me for himself the part that bothered him.

I decided to call it a day and go on home, then take Tommy out for dinner. Maybe Mrs Miller could join us and we'd all catch a fat-and-juicy at the local burger shop.

Tommy was rolling on the grass with Molly when I pulled up and asked him what he thought of my idea. 'Hey, yeah!' he whooped gleefully. 'Let's go!'

As he led the dog inside the house, he turned to me, his face suddenly serious. 'Hey, Mom, I want to ask you something. You know that lady we saw the other day? The one who knew my grandma?'

'Yes,' I answered, inexplicably uneasy, wondering what was coming next.

'Are we going to go back there again? Because I'd really like to.'

'Maybe, maybe not. I haven't given it much thought.'

'Well, I hope we do. That was fun and she was really nice. And she actually knew my grandmother and all. Hey, do you think maybe she'd let me call her grandma, kind of like a substitute, you know . . .?'

'I don't think that's a very good idea, Tommy,' I'd answered abruptly and was surprised at the curtness in my voice. 'She's *not* your grandmother or a substitute for her. She's nothing to either one of us. In fact, we hardly know her.'

He gave a little shrug, and a pang of guilt moved through me as I saw dejection settle on his face. I felt as if I'd snatched a longed-for gift away from him.

'Come on,' I told him gently as I ruffled his hair, 'lock up that dog and let's go eat. I'm starving!'

I was dreaming, and I watched, detached, as the shifting images rolled over me like waves. Women's faces, faint and hazy, appeared like theatrical masks then disappeared, only to come around again.

And then a face moved forward that was stronger, more defined than all the rest – the face of my mother. I began to dream that she was braiding my brown hair, the way she used to in those distant summer days when the heat caused it to lay heavy on my neck. I saw her twist the rubber bands around the ends and then tie on two gaily-colored ribbons.

The kaleidoscope kept shifting, presenting me with different scenes – and now we were going for an ice cream cone, walking down the sidewalk holding hands. 'I love you, Katie,' I heard her say to me. 'You're my little girl and I love you very much.' I felt her fingers gently brush my cheek as she bent to kiss me.

And then her image was fading fast, and the smile I knew so well disappeared from view.

Suddenly a different face replaced that of Chrissie – the earnest, honest countenance of Mabel Branscombe. I saw the same kind expression in her eyes, felt the same gentleness as she laid her hand upon my arm. And then she too became nebulous, unformed and drifting far away – and now my dream was empty.

I tossed and turned and broke out in a drenching sweat, floating in and out of sleep as these images tormented me. I felt a powerful force building deep within me, rushing towards a sure crescendo.

'Mama!' I screamed aloud, wide awake and sitting suddenly upright, tears flooding from my eyes and down my cheeks. 'Mama, mama, please don't leave me!'

Chapter Twelve

Carl was thumbing through the sports pages, muttering darkly to himself. I'd spotted him in records just a short time earlier, chatting with that 'little girl' Sandy, and he'd seemed happy enough then.

'What's wrong?' I asked, concerned something might've jeopardized our case.

'Hunter's lost it, Kate – going from bad to worse on a daily basis.'

'Lost what?' I asked, thinking Hunter was some officer of ours who'd misplaced a crucial bit of evidence.

'The ability to pitch. He's not had a lousy record like this in several years. Damn it, the Braves won't take the Series this time either. They'll be lucky if they even win the pennant!'

I relaxed. 'Carl, about that diary. I looked through it yesterday – not real close but paging through – and I couldn't see anything disturbing.'

'Well, it may not be much, but there're several things that just don't jive. For instance, look at this.' He picked up the little book and started flicking through it. The entries had not been made on a daily basis – I'd noticed that before – but had been written, it seemed, only when the writer had something specific to talk about.

'Here we go,' Carl announced, 'listen to this: "We attended Rachel's wedding this afternoon. I wore my new blue coat and hat," and then here: "The picnic was a big success. Maybe I'll get up the nerve someday to wear a suit like some of the others did." ' He looked at me quizzically. 'Don't you think that's odd? I mean, a man doesn't ordinarily worry about his new hat or talk about his suit.'

I frowned. The phrasing *did* seem strange, out of kilter with Kenneth Branscombe's other entries. 'Maybe he's a snappy dresser,' I offered half-heartedly. 'Were there any other weird notations?'

'Nothing, and nothing else that points towards our murder victim either, though that one page we've got should certainly do the trick.'

'I can't explain it,' I said, 'but I'll sure keep it in my mind. Maybe the explanation is so obvious it'll leap right out and hit one of us between the eyes.' I paused as I thought of something. 'Has Dan given it a try? Why don't you let him read it, maybe we'll get a different point of view.'

'Good idea,' Carl agreed. 'I'll hand it over to him when he comes back from court. I won't mention what our problem is, just let him read it fresh and see if he picks up on it.'

I glanced at my watch. Apparently my ploy hadn't worked and I'd have to release Larry Marchand within the next few hours. I felt a surge of pure frustration, and when the phone rang I snatched it from its cradle.

'Hiya cutie, you've got someone here who wants to see you.'

It was Don, the jailer. We went way back, to the day when I'd dragged in drunks while I was on patrol.

'And who might that be?' I asked, hardly daring to hope.

'That young lad you brought in yesterday, one Lawrence W. Marchand, booking number 0864—'

'I know who you're talking about,' I interrupted him. 'We'll be right down, and thank you, Donald!'

I tapped Mungers shoulder. 'The jailee wants to see us,' I informed him, raising my eyebrows.

'Maybe he wants to complain about the food,' Carl shot back as he rose to join me. We went downstairs, wondering what we were going to hear.

Marchand was sitting on the edge of his cot, his feet shuffling back and forth in front of him. His head jerked up at the sound of our footsteps, and he stared at us, eyes narrowing into slits.

'I want to talk with you,' he said.

'Sure you don't want your lawyer present?' I asked him.

'Fuck no, I'd say the same sorry thing whether he's with me or not. But I sure would like a smoke.'

'Okay,' I answered, anxious to oblige him, 'let's all move down the hall to where we three can be alone and speak in privacy.'

Don unlocked the cell and we escorted Marchand to a closet-sized room usually reserved for arrestees and their counsel.

He slung himself hard into the wooden chair and banged his fist down on the table. I could see he was in a state of mental turmoil, and I was certain I was going to get a full confession. I reached into my bag for a pack of cigarettes I kept there for just such a purpose.

Ordinarily, in interrogation, we'd keep the edge on the suspect by refusing to allow him to relax his nervous tension; but each case is different and this time I knew Marchand was eager to spill it all so I wanted him to be at ease.

'I didn't kill Connie Hammond and I can prove it,' he blurted out as soon as he'd lit up and blown the smoke away.

'You've suddenly found yourself an alibi?' I asked. 'Because that's about what it will take. A cast-iron alibi, at that.'

'Yeah, I found one.' He gave me a peculiar look, not seeming particularly happy, which I thought strange for a person getting ready to walk right out of a heap of trouble. 'Actually, I've had it all along.'

'So tell us about it, then.' I switched on the tape recorder.

Marchand cleared his throat nervously and began to tap his fingers on the table. 'Aw shit,' he moaned, 'I don't really wanna do this.'

We waited, saying nothing. Then he opened up his mouth and let it all burst out.

'Thursday night? You say Thursday night? Around eight or nine o'clock? Maybe even later? Oh, man, I was nowhere near those woods on Thursday night. I was on the road to Fresno knocking off some nothing convenience store!'

Carl and I swiftly exchanged glances. Whatever we'd expected to hear it hadn't been this. 'Do you remember the exact location?'

'Nah, but it was gettin' pretty close to town. You could see the city lights. You gotta know about it, though. The old man wouldn't hand it over so me and my buddy had to rough him up a bit.'

Marchand cast his eyes down toward the floor.

I remembered now. A hold-up in a Mom-and-Pop store just outside of Fresno. I'd heard it on the news that Friday as I was driving to the Hammond house to tell her parents she was dead. Two male whites, late teens to early twenties, had pulled a knife on the seventy-year-old owner. Then, when he'd failed to hand over the cash as requested, the taller of the two had whipped him with his fists. He'd been rushed to Mercy Hospital where, hours later, his broken facial bones had finally been joined back together.

'Which buddy? Billy Curtain?' I asked.

'Nah. Fella name of Germaine who rooms near me in Jacinto. We did time together at Chino.' Chino was a state prison thirty miles or so east of Los Angeles.

'And who beat up the old man, you or your friend?'

He licked his lips, looking sly, trying to decide whether to confess or not.

'Aw, hell, I did. He'll make me anyway when you put me in the line-up. Crazy old grandpa. If he'd just given me the money like I asked him, I'd never a' had to touch him.'

I looked at him in absolute disgust, glad he was going to get what he deserved.

'There're a couple of loose ends, son,' Carl told him. 'What about the note we found in your drawer, what about the necklace pawned by you, what about the person who saw you with the gun following the murder? Maybe you have an alibi for the time of the killing, but that still doesn't explain these other factors.'

Marchand screwed his face up tight. 'I don't know nuthin' about no note or necklace, I swear I don't.' His eyes stared at me, filled with pleading. 'You say they showed my ID. Well, it went missing several weeks ago.'

'I'm surprised you even noticed,' I told him, sticking in the needle, 'you have such a nice collection lying around to choose from.'

I studied him and wondered what a girl like Connie Hammond could've seen in him. Perhaps it was because they were so opposite, from such different worlds. Or perhaps it was the aura of tawdry danger he gave off. Some very moral and simple girls feel an irresistible attraction for a guy who's always living on the edge.

'Listen, Larry.' Carl edged forward on his chair. 'It won't go against you if you tell us you were at the scene. In fact, it might even help us and we'd take that fact into consideration. Maybe you came across the body much later on that night and took the necklace from it. Maybe you got the note and couldn't keep the date but went there anyway, some time after the robbery, and found her dead.'

'It wasn't like that!' he yelled out. 'I went straight back to my room after knockin' off that store and not to no fuckin' woods!'

'Were you at the Branscombe farm any time that Friday?'

He looked from Carl to me and back again, searching for a trap. 'I was there, yes, but not for long. Why?'

'Did you see Branscombe's .32?'

'No, I never saw it. I didn't even go inside the house, just fed the horses and left.'

Merced would have to wait awhile on that warrant business. I phoned up Fresno County sheriff's department and told them we were holding a prisoner they might like to talk to. They arrived within the hour, bringing with them a video surveillance tape from the convenience store.

There, in glorious black-and-white, was the side view of a twenty-year-old beating up a helpless, frail old man. If you knew who you were looking for, you could tell it was Larry Marchand. The time, shown in the lower left-hand corner, from when the pair first entered the store until they did their dirty work and left, ran from eight-fifty till nearly nine o'clock. Our boy couldn't have been in the clearing off the Canfield road when Connie Hammond was shot to death.

'Take him away,' I told the deputy, 'he's all yours. We have no use for him any longer.'

Larry Marchand had talked his way right into a return visit to the slammer, but by this act he'd avoided a far greater evil – he'd escaped unnatural death by a California execution.

'So what do you make of that?' I asked Mungers when we'd both gone back upstairs. 'Can you sort it out?'

'Yeah, I can easily sort it out. The little bastard's lying. He got the note, he went to the woods late that night, he found that poor girl's body lying there and was cold enough to take her little necklace just to make himself a few bucks. And then the next day, not knowing it was the gun that killed her, he was admiring Branscombe's .32, maybe with the thought he'd help himself to it somewhere down the line.'

'So why weren't his prints on it then?'

'I'd say it was automatic – the developed cunning of the criminal mind. Even if he'd done nothing wrong, Marchand probably didn't want his fingers tied to any gun, so he wiped them off before putting it away.'

I agreed with everything Carl said. It'd looked so promising in the beginning – another viable suspect besides Kenneth Branscombe – but there was no denying the proof offered by that videotape. Marchand wasn't lying about not having murdered Connie, but he *was* lying about all the rest, just to keep his nose completely clean and stay as far away as possible from any connection with our case.

Carl was staring at me curiously. 'I saw you turning into the Branscombe drive on Saturday,' he told me slowly. 'Sandy and I were taking a little ride and I saw your car going in there. I think your son was with you too. Was anything going on that I should know about?'

I started. I could feel his eyes locked on me, and a wave of unwarranted guilt coursed through me. I felt as if I'd been caught in the act of something awful when in fact I'd done nothing wrong.

'Not at all. We were riding past on our way to my Aunt Joan's and I decided to stop by, just on the off-chance she might drop something that would strengthen our case against Kenneth.'

'And did she?'

'No,' I answered him. 'Nothing came of it or I'd have told you, but I still think it was worth a try.' I paused, then, 'Carl, do you know about their parents?'

He shook his head and waited, and I began to tell him all

I'd learned from Joan and from the papers. When I finally finished, he gave a long, low whistle. 'Does the tendency to murder run in a family?' he wondered out loud. 'I don't really think so, but I do think that one has had more than its share of tragedy.'

I left him working on the details of Branscombe's preliminary hearing and walked across the room to a telephone sitting on an unused desk. For some reason, I felt a little odd about the possibility of Carl overhearing the call I was about to make.

I dialed the number, looking around and tapping my foot impatiently while waiting for an answer. Finally there was the sound of the receiver being picked up and then a tentative, 'Hello?'

'Miss Branscombe?' I began. 'Katharine Harrod here. I'm afraid I have some bad news for you. We've had to let Larry Marchand go. He's got an indisputable alibi for the time of Connie's murder. I felt it was only common courtesy to let you know he's no longer considered a suspect in this case.'

I heard the sharp intake of breath and an involuntary moan, and I could feel my pity for this woman rising as she watched the door close ever tighter on her brother. First her mother and father, now the sibling she'd cared for all her life – one by one, they were taken from her.

'This can't be,' she finally said, speaking in an anguished voice I hardly recognized. 'Don't you see? His alibi must be made up. Of course he'd be clever enough to have had one all ready in case he needed it. I gave him that note, I saw him with the gun, and I heard you found he'd pawned some jewelry that the girl was wearing when she died. You know he was the one who shot her, not my brother!'

'I'm sorry, Miss Branscombe. The alibi was not made up. It's as solid as they come.'

'You mean Kenny isn't coming home?'

'I'm sorry. The preliminary hearing will be held tomorrow as scheduled.'

She began to sob and I heard the receiver gently returning to its cradle. I hung up, saddened by the turns taken by some people's lives and knowing I was powerless to change them. Then I frowned. What was that she'd said? She'd heard about the jewelry? I'd never cease to be amazed at the way the word gets out and how quickly it travels once it does.

The preliminary hearing was just about as cut and dried as it could be. Kenneth Branscombe sat in a neat twill suit, his farmer's hands folded tight in front of him, and listened while the district attorney laid out the facts about his jealousy, the slap across the face, the murder weapon that he owned, the fingerprint found on it. Confident we'd given enough to bind him over to trial, and not wanting to tip our total hand, we'd decided to save our eyewitness, Stuart Greenwell, for the main event itself.

The defense could offer little in the way of solid evidence to rebut the prosecution's case, and before the day was out, Kenneth Branscombe heard the judge order him to stand trial in Superior Court, County of San Madera, for the shooting death of Connie Hammond.

A slight commotion on the far side of the courtroom attracted my attention when the gavel was slammed down, and I raised my head in time to see Mabel Branscombe fall forward in a faint and nearly tumble to the floor before others sitting near her put their arms around her and supported her till she recovered.

Kenneth Branscombe, apparently unaware of his sister's predicament, was led dumbly from the courtroom by two deputies, eyes straight ahead, a dazed expression on his face.

I watched him disappear beyond the doorway, and I watched as Mabel gathered up her things and made a lonely exit from the courtroom that had just sealed her brother's fate.

CHAPTER THIRTEEN

I saw her heading down the street, moving with her usual long and flowing strides.

'Wait up, Karen,' I called, 'I'm going that way too.'

She turned around, and when she saw me a mischievous smile began to play along her lips. She started toward me, full of verve, and I wondered what had put her in this invigorated state. It didn't take me long to find out.

'He's grand, you know,' she told me, a delicious twinkle in her eyes. 'You were all wrong about him – I'm so very glad I didn't take your advice.'

I groaned. Steve Darrow had added yet another to his list, though Karen was certainly far above the usual run of beautiful but dumb bunnies. 'I'll check you out a month from now and see how you feel then,' I told her. 'I'm too old and jaded to believe that he can change.'

I paused, wondering whether I'd be going too far if I told her any more, then decided the hell with it. She was a good friend, after all. 'He used to work for me, you know.'

'You told me so the other night.'

'Well, he isn't working for me any longer. He was

temporarily transferred to another table, as a wrist-slap for an inappropriate action. Something wrong he did while on duty.'

'To you?' Karen had stopped walking and was staring hard at me, hooked on every word I said. I'd gotten her curiosity up good.

'No, not to me, to the sister of a victim in an assault case. He was supposed to be interviewing her and he put the make on her instead, and not in a real subtle way either.

'She didn't buy his charm – and neither did her husband, who happened to be coming down the hall. The two of them filed a complaint against him and that, along with several prior citizen complaints for rudeness, got him re-assigned for conduct unbecoming an officer.'

She relaxed. My words hadn't fazed her one little bit. 'Silly bitch. How was he to know she was married? Besides, when is it a crime to make a pass?'

'The time, the place, the manner were all wrong,' I pointed out. 'He was on official business and he got out of line. He's rough and he's abrasive and he makes his own rules.'

She shrugged. 'You've got your regulations, I know – but frankly I'm not certain what he did was so very wrong. Not wrong enough to make such a fuss about, anyway.'

It was hopeless. Karen was going to see only what she wanted to see and nothing else. He'd hooked her, just like all the others, and she'd have to get her own personalized face-slap before she saw Darrow for what he really was.

I sighed as I thought about the hurt to come, but knew that nothing more I could say would change the course her life was taking. She'd have to learn it all herself.

'Look,' she said, a little nervously, 'I was going to call you later. I don't suppose you'd be interested in a double-date tonight?'

'With you and Steve? No, Karen, no way. I do not socialize with Darrow. Besides, I'm not one bit interested in the opposite sex.'

'I thought you'd say that,' she told me, crestfallen. 'But see, it's like this. You'd be doing me a real favor if you said yes. My cousin's just come into town on business and I need to entertain him, but I've already got a date with Steve and I want to keep it. I'm really in a bind, Kate. This all came up unexpectedly.'

I shook my head firmly. 'Sorry, Karen. Not interested.'

But she wouldn't let it go. 'Don't look on it as a date then, just look on it as helping out a friend – which it is. Please, Kate, do me this favor. I don't have anyone else I can ask.' Her usually composed face looked strained and nervous and her raw desire to be with Steve that night was plainly visible.

'How old is he?' I asked, and then I could've kicked myself.

'Ah.' She saw a ray of hope. 'He's in his early forties and he's been married and divorced. Actually, I haven't seen him in several years. He called out of the blue and said he was spending the night in San Madera. We're having dinner together but it's afterwards I'm worried about. I can't just dump him, and you say you won't be in the same company as Steve . . .'

Oh, what the heck, I thought. Maybe it would be fun. And do me some good. Get me out of the house a little. I wasn't doing anything tonight anyway. Jon had taken Tommy to a Cub Scout picnic at the park this afternoon and they were going to catch a movie together in the evening.

'All right, kiddo, I'll help you out this once,' I told her, though very reluctantly. 'Have him pick me up at eight.'

'You're a pal.' She grinned and slapped me on the shoulder, then moved on down the street in those long and flowing strides.

Her voice trembled as she spoke.

'I didn't believe it would happen,' Mabel Branscombe said, her words coming in whispers on the phone. 'I didn't believe the judge would keep my brother locked up. I thought she'd let him go.'

'There was ample evidence, Miss Branscombe,' I told her. 'The judge could've come to no other decision.'

'Oh, Katharine,' she moaned, and I pictured the gentle little woman gripped with agony, 'I don't blame *you*, but it's wrong, wrong!' I heard her cough and then begin to cry in little gasps that sounded almost like hiccups.

'Can anyone stay with you?' I asked, concerned. 'Any of the women from your church? I don't think you should be alone right now.'

'No, Katharine, I don't need anyone, only Kenny. Will they take care of him? Will he be all right?'

'The best of care, Miss Branscombe, I assure you.'

'That's better then, a little better,' she replied. 'But something's got to be done to get him free. You know, Katharine—' and the way she said it reminded me of a certain long-ago lilt in my mother's voice – 'I find the pain is sometimes greatest just before it ends, so maybe something good will happen soon. Because my brother and I are feeling an awful pain right now.'

My compassion wouldn't let me tell her lies that would pump up her hopes then only bring disappointment, so I brought the sad conversation to a close and hung up thinking how many lives are forever broken by the doing of one savage act.

Misgivings flooded me as I crossed the hall. Why was I doing this? I thought. I didn't owe Karen that much. A good long soak in the tub or tying on those skates and flying with the wind would've been the perfect way to spend this evening.

My heart sank even further when I opened up the door. He was standing there, a hearty grin across his face and eager-beaver eyes staring at me brightly, as if he were just about to pounce. He was crowding in so close he seemed to dominate the doorway and I took an involuntary step back.

'Katharine Harrod? Jimmy Rogers at your disposal. Glad you could power me around a little bit this evening, maybe show me a bit of your ol' town.'

Where had this guy learned to talk? His phraseology seemed slightly strange to me.

'Yes, I'm Katharine, Karen's friend. She was worried about leaving you on your own this evening so she thought maybe I could fill in the gap.' I found myself wanting to get it straight right away that I wasn't looking forward to some big date but was instead approaching this event as a substitute hostess performing a perfunctory duty for someone else.

'Yeah, she had to see her guy and I don't think she wanted me along.' Jimmy gave a big wink as he said this. I was waiting for the leer.

'Look, it's nearly dark,' I told him, 'but we can still drive around and I'll show you some of San Madera since this is your first time in town.'

'Fine with me,' Rogers answered, and took my arm to help me down the steps. I discreetly disengaged myself and navigated on my own; I found I didn't want the physical contact. 'Maybe then we can stop somewhere for a drink.'

'Maybe,' I responded, 'but I can't be out too long. I'm a single parent and my little boy will be coming home soon.'

Ordinarily I'd never have tried to cut a date short before it even started – or I didn't think I would have. It'd been so long since I'd been in the game, how could I really know how I'd act? But it seemed to me in this case that I was already hastening the end. Oh well, he seemed nice enough anyway, even if slightly oafish, so I'd get through it.

'Why don't you take the wheel, Katie,' he said, motioning toward a drab gray car. 'You know the route better than I do.'

I saw him pop a stick of gum in his mouth as he jumped into the passenger seat while I walked around the front. I was glad. I'd noticed a slightly stale odor when he'd blasted his hello.

'What's your business, Jimmy?' I asked, making conversation. 'What brings you into town?'

'Janitorial supplies. I'm a salesman. Just got this new territory a month ago. I'll probably be popping in here on a pretty regular basis.'

I noticed his head swing toward me, and he shifted sideways.

'What types of businesses do you service?' I asked the words automatically while I negotiated a left-hand turn.

'Anything big,' he answered proudly. 'The little guys buy their own. You know that new office building over near Alvarado? Well, we got a contract for that, for instance. Keep 'em happy with the latest solvents and purgers to take care of their sanitation needs, as well as whatever their maintenance staff has to have to keep the place neat and clean.'

'I've never known anyone in your line of work before,' I said, and I hadn't.

'Oh, it's pretty neat. Ever been in one of those big buildings when the plumbing backs up, Katharine? Sure you have! What a stinking and sloppy mess that can be. Sometimes the crap comes flowing right across the washroom floor. Well, how can a place do good business in a bind like that? Answer is, they can't. Not very user-friendly, as they say.' Here he gave a hearty laugh. 'So we have high-powered, cutting-edge chemicals you feed down those babies on a regular basis and your chance of that ever happening to you is cut to nil.'

'Fascinating,' I murmured as we drove close to the little park.

I pointed out the hanging tree and told him some of the history, then drove him downtown and showed him city hall and the other municipal buildings surrounding it. As we swung back toward the West End, we crossed an arched concrete bridge standing above a narrow stream of water.

'That's Wild Rock River,' I told him. 'It's calm now but in the winter it really rages. It flows north to west through the upper part of town, coming out of the High Sierras, and sometimes, when the rains are heavy, it overflows its banks.'

I looked at it now, so placid and pretty, and thought how I loved a city divided by a pleasant stream. It was like a verdant oasis in the center of the concrete.

'Look, Katharine, what I'd really like to see is where you work,' Rogers told me. 'Karen says you're a cop, a pretty big one too. Gee, I've never known a lady cop.'

'The station's a little out of our way,' I told him, 'and lady cops aren't that much different from all the others.'

For some reason, I didn't want to ride him past my place of work and take the chance that my fellow officers would see me with this guy. Probably because there'd be too many questions later I didn't want to deal with. Besides, my work was personal. He didn't need to see where I hung out.

'Okay, how about that drink then?'

I glanced at my watch. It was still early yet and I knew that, in all good conscience, I'd let Karen down if I ended it so soon. The city tour had taken far less time than I'd thought.

'All right,' I said reluctantly. 'There's a nice little place around the corner but I can't stay out too long.'

I pulled into the parking lot behind Twain's, a rather staid low-key lounge, and we went inside.

Jimmy sat across from me, ordered a whiskey and water, then asked what I would like. Vodka-soda, I told the girl.

'I'm from Idaho, Katie. Sort of out in the boonies. That's where company headquarters is. Good industrial park, but not much else. Anyway, we don't have many lady cops there so you're a new trick to me.'

I glanced up quickly, frowning, but he seemed unaware of what he'd said.

'Whaddya do exactly, anyway?'

'I'm the head of homicide for the West End of San Madera,' I told him bluntly. 'I investigate murders.'

'Whooo-eee!' Rogers let out a sound that made the bartender stare across the room. 'That's heavy-duty! Man, you get right into it, don't you? All that blood and gore!'

'I don't look at it that way,' I answered stiffly. 'I look at it as the death of a person who never should've died and the need to speak for that person and apprehend his or her killer.'

'Still . . .' His eager-beaver eyes looked at me brighter than ever. Then he gave an embarrassed little laugh, turned his head a little to one side, and swung it back to me. 'You know, Katharine, maybe you can tell me this. Whaddya do when you arrest a guy? I mean, a *guy*? Do you do that pat-down yourself or what?'

I looked at him sharply and set down my glass, but he seemed to be asking out of honest curiosity, not to lead the talk toward a steamy direction. 'Male officers do that,' I explained. 'If I'm not working with one right then, they can be summoned. That's how it's handled.'

He took a big slurp of whiskey, then gave that funny laugh again. 'I guess some cops can get pretty kinky, huh?' And his voice began to drop lower. 'You know, handcuffs and stuff. I bet some of you guys use some of the gear in your spare time. Especially maybe when a lady cop dates a man and wants to reverse the tables on him. Makes for a bit of excitement, I bet. A bit of old spice thrown in.' Now I saw the leer.

I'd known guys like this before – all the gals in the business knew the type well. The idea of a woman in uniform turned them on mightily and they longed to feel the sexual domination they thought we'd display.

'Look, it's late,' I told him, avoiding the question. This evening was stopping right here. 'I've got to get back, so we'd better pay up.' I took one more sip, then set down the glass and picked up my purse.

'Oh, hey, Katie, I was hoping I'd see a bit more of you. You sure?' The breath showed signs of needing a new stick of gum.

'Absolutely. Tommy's probably home now.'

I took the quickest route back and Rogers stopped at the curb.

'I'll walk up with you,' he said eagerly, starting to get out.

'No, no,' I countered, 'I've got it. Have a good stay, however long you're here for.'

'Just till tomorrow,' he answered, 'but like I said, I'll be back soon. Give me your number and I'll ring you up.'

'This has been nice, Jimmy,' I lied, 'but I don't think so. I'm usually tied up so much with work I don't get out.' And I closed the door and walked quickly to my house.

Learn from this, gal, I told myself as I took out the key. That's what's out there now, fun guys like this. You couldn't even get a nice dull one – though God knows, that would've been boring – you had to end up with a jerk. Next time, stay home instead and run that bath. And I opened the door, kicked off my shoes, and headed gratefully for my room.

CHAPTER FOURTEEN

The bombshell dropped several mornings later. I was sifting through some paperwork, preparing for the trial, when I looked up and saw Mabel Branscombe entering the squad room in an agitated state.

I watched as she came across the floor. By the time she reached my desk, a cloak of composure had swept over her, and when she sat down beside me she was totally in control.

She leaned toward me till her face was almost next to mine, and in a soft, firm voice that only I could hear, she told me, 'I murdered Connie Hammond. Not my brother and not Larry Marchand. I'm the one who shot her and I can prove it to you.'

Despite all my years' experience, my mouth dropped wide open and I stared at her as if she'd gone mad. 'Miss Branscombe, you don't know what you're talking about. You're doing this to try to save your brother and, while that's certainly admirable, it just won't work.'

Actually I don't know why I was so surprised. In most murder cases there are at least several false confessions, so why should this one be any different? Besides, wasn't this the expected pattern she might follow? She'd cared for Kenneth all her life and now that he was in deep trouble she was trying to cover for him and take the heat herself. A noble effort, but of course it would wither in its embryo state and fail before it even started.

'Of course that's why I'm telling you,' she said, 'but it also happens to be true. Can't you see Kenneth wouldn't have it in him to do anything like that? Big sweet baby of a man! I'm the person you are looking for and I would like to tell you all about it.'

'Please do so, then,' I answered, deciding I'd let her go ahead and pretend to spill her soul, to see how far she was willing to take this thing.

But she shook her head violently back and forth. 'No, not here – I don't want to do it here. I don't want anything written down, any tape recorder near me, any other person there but you. I just want to meet somewhere quiet and talk so you can listen and then do what you can do for Ken. But Katharine, it must be you alone.'

I was becoming intrigued now, though still totally skeptical. What was this cloak-and-dagger stuff about some secret location, just the two of us? High melodrama, indeed, probably born from some television daytime drama.

I studied her and thought of this desperate effort by a plain, honest little woman. How did she imagine she could pull it off? And yet the look on her face was one of utter confidence and determination.

'Where do you suggest?' I asked. 'Do you want to meet somewhere this afternoon?'

'No,' she whispered, 'sooner if you can. There's a park

near the city hall. Do you know it? Well, maybe we could walk there now.'

I checked my watch. I had an interrogation coming up in twenty minutes that I could not afford to miss. 'I'm afraid that's no good,' I told her, 'but I could probably be there around noon.'

Maybe she'd change her mind and not show up, I thought, and this whole absurd incident would die away.

But she agreed and left the squad room with a quick goodbye, and I picked up a rap sheet and a pencil and waited for patrol to appear with my ADW suspect. I threw a glance at Carl, who'd just come in and was hanging up his coat, and debated whether or not to run all of this past him, just so he'd have a good laugh.

But then I decided not to. He might get to be a stickler in this drama of absurdity and insist on going along too – toting cuffs, recorder, and scaring Mabel Branscombe half to death. No, I thought, I'll handle this myself.

I left the station shortly before noon, having booked my suspect on suspicion of taking a claw hammer to a neighbor's head during a botched robbery attempt.

I soon reached the little park – nicely shaded, with sunlight moving through the trees, dappling the ground in a rippling effect.

Mabel Branscombe sat alone on a bench near the middle. She wore a cotton dress, neatly buttoned down the front with large white buttons, and sensible low-heeled shoes. Her hands were clasped together and rested in her lap, and her eyes were staring straight ahead.

I took a seat beside her and she acknowledged my

presence with a little nod. Now that the time had come for the details of her 'confession,' she seemed preoccupied and quiet. Perhaps second thoughts had taken over.

She seemed to read my mind, for she turned to me and smiled into my eyes. 'I'm just wondering how to begin, Katharine – just making sure I have all the words in the right order, because I want to make myself extraordinarily clear. I don't want to leave anything out because I want you to understand what I did and why I did it.'

This is going to be one elaborate yarn, I thought, and found myself wanting to tell her kindly to spare herself the effort and go on home. But then that special unspoken bond I felt with her tugged at me, and I decided to indulge her and hear her out.

'I want to go back a long, long way, Katharine, to the time I started raising Kenny. It wasn't just after our parents died, when the courts gave him to me, it was long before that. Our mother was a dear sweet soul but often weak and sickly. Our father was a good enough man but always in the fields. It was left to me most of the time to look after my little brother.

'I think I did a job I can be proud of in bringing him up, in seeing that he went the right way and never wanted for anything. It was a struggle, but one that I was glad to make. He waited a long while to marry but then he met Alice, a wonderfully refined young woman in my church group. They wed, as I told you, and lived with me until she died of cancer.'

I sat and listened to her as she led me through her life, wondering at her description of her father as 'good enough'. I would not let on that I knew about the awful happenings of that April evening long ago – it would serve no useful purpose, except to destroy the protective front she'd invented and put up for other people.

'After she was gone, Kenneth was lonely for a time, but then that passed, or so I thought, and the two of us existed as we had before – alone together, finding what we needed in each other. It was a calm and peaceful existence, the animals and us and all the quiet and solitude.'

Suddenly she straightened up and seemed to stamp one foot upon the ground. 'But then that girl came into his life, that dumb clunky girl who was young enough to be his daughter. I lied to you when I told you he didn't care because I was so ashamed. I lied to you and to everybody else, because it was so disgusting that he would make such a fool out of himself. My beloved brother was infatuated, mooning all around. I couldn't bear to see it, but he wouldn't listen to me when I tried to talk to him about it.'

She turned to me and pain was in her eyes. I had no doubt that what I was hearing was the truth, but this was not a confession of murder – this was the sad anguish of a sister who loves her brother deeply and wants to save him from himself.

'I'm a respected woman, Katharine – both Kenneth and I are respected people. We've overcome such odds to get where we are in life. And then everyone was laughing at us – the women in my church group, the people in the town. I couldn't stand it. His sickness was getting worse and worse, and I was afraid he was going to talk of marrying her. Oh, not that she'd have anything of him – I think she just strung him along like girls will do – but that's how far gone he was and he was bringing down the two of us and couldn't see it.'

I felt someone had to stand up for the dead girl. 'If it makes any difference, Miss Branscombe,' I told her, laying my hand upon her knee, 'I've uncovered no evidence to show that Connie Hammond even knew your brother cared for her. I sincerely doubt that she teased him or led him on in any way.'

'I have my own opinion on that,' she told me firmly, then continued with her story. 'I knew I had to do something to end it all and I started planning how to get rid of her. I knew that her death was the only thing that would keep Kenneth away from her. I was laying it all out in my mind and then that awful outburst took place at the field, in front of every-body – the time he lost his temper and slapped her in the face. I knew then I had to move fast, before maybe he *did* go over the edge and murder her himself.'

I began to shift on the bench as a feeling of unease crept over me. This was sounding all too real. What had started as a recital of a sister's disapproval of her brother's doings was now turning to a tale of a much more serious nature. She must've practised this scene well, for her sincerity was faultless.

'Miss Branscombe,' I asked, suddenly very wary, 'please let me get this taped, or at least have my partner meet me here. For your own protection, really.'

'No!' she yelled. 'This is just for you and you alone. I will deny this if you ever throw it up to me. Now please let me continue, Katharine.'

I settled back, a sickness churning at my stomach. This

can not be, I thought. This woman just has a vivid imagination and will not be able to sustain the pretence very long. Soon the entire fabric of her invention will crumble all around her.

'I knew about Larry and Connie, and I knew about his arrest record. I also knew that if the girl were found dead, the police would soon come to my brother because of all the gossip about him and because they'd learn he'd slapped her. That couldn't be avoided. I even helped him get arrested – I left the gun out so he'd print it – because I knew I could frame Larry and my brother would be cleared. That's why I kept him coming around after Kenneth fired him – because I wanted to keep a track on him and to have him handy.'

She paused and looked at me regretfully. 'But it didn't work that way, and I don't to this day know why. I didn't think the boy would have an alibi for that night – even if he had, I believed you'd release my brother once you got interested in the other one. And I thought the law was that once arrested and released he couldn't be picked up again. That's why it was important that you get Kenneth first, not be pointed straight to Larry Marchand.' She looked at me in bewilderment. 'Isn't that right? Tell me what went wrong!'

'It's not right, Miss Branscombe. It has nothing to do with your brother's circumstances. You're thinking of double jeopardy, where a person can not be *tried* twice for the same crime, not picked up and charged.'

'I was sure, I was so certain . . .' She faltered and was silent for a moment. 'That is all the more reason why I have to tell you the truth now,' she said. 'It still would've worked if that awful boy hadn't had an alibi. I do believe you

233

would've come to think he was the one who did it, and I'd never have to be telling you this tale.'

She swallowed hard, and continued. 'I'd kept a note Larry had written to Connie much earlier in the summer – one he'd discarded in my trash can. It was asking her to meet him in those woods one night. Apparently that's where they always used to go. I made a point of seeing her in town that Thursday and gave it to her, and then I got her to write him one back. I went to the woods that night myself, and she was waiting there but she didn't see me in the bushes. I saw her turn toward me and I shot her in the head, then I took the necklace from around her neck.'

I was mesmerized, listening in disbelief. The ring of truth would begin to toll throughout her words, and then the sheer absurdity of the whole confession would enter and replace it.

Mabel Branscombe began to cry. 'I didn't want to do it. I wish it had never come to that – but I had to. It was the only thing to do to save him from destroying himself and us, to keep us from being laughing stocks or worse. She was a bad conniving girl, no matter what you say, and she liked to toy with his affections and then giggle about it with her friends behind his back.'

She dabbed her eyes, regaining her composure. 'I took the gun back home and wiped it clean, then left it in plain sight so Kenneth would pick it up and put it away. Which he did, leaving the fingerprint on it that I wanted you to find. As I said, I knew you would come for him anyway, but I wanted to make it faster, to get things moving, so that he could be in and out in a hurry. I pawned the necklace and I placed the note from Connie in Larry's bureau drawer, and then I waited.'

The more she talked, the more relaxed I became, and I felt my wariness recede. This was simply a tall tale after all.

'You arrested Kenneth,' she continued, 'I pointed you to Larry and the evidence, and I was happy. Everything was going just as planned. But then it all started to fall apart because apparently I misunderstood, I'd had the wrong information. And now I'm here telling you the *real* truth, so you'll let him go.'

I shook my head in sadness at what I was going to have to tell her. 'Miss Branscombe, your willingness to sacrifice yourself for your brother is one of the most selfless displays I have ever seen. But I do not believe you, and I can not let Kenneth go. For one thing, there is no way you could've walked into Marchand's rooming house and planted the note the way you say you did. For another, the pawn shop owner told us someone using Marchand's ID *and closely resembling him* hocked the necklace.'

'No,' she cried, 'no, you're wrong. I *did* get into that room, and I got another boy to pawn the jewelry – another boy who used to work for me. He didn't know what it was all about. I made up some story and gave him a little money, and he did it!'

'Miss Branscombe, please, let me take you home. You've tried your best but it just does not make sense. This is not working out the way you thought it would.'

Frustration must have torn her inside, for the signs of it were all over her face. She picked in agitation at a button on her dress and began to cry as she had done earlier.

'Katharine, Katharine, please believe me. I'm telling you the truth!'

'And what if you are?' I asked. 'Let's just pretend for a moment that you are. You won't let me record this conversation, you won't let me have another detective present, you say you will deny it all if I ever try to reveal it. What in heaven's name do you think would happen if I *did* believe you?'

'Why, then you'd have to let him go and try to get some proof on me – some proof you could find, now that I've given you the knowledge, but proof without my help. It would be up to you, but in the meantime you'd have to release Kenneth because now you know he didn't do it.'

'I'm sorry, my dear,' I told her. 'I'm truly sorry. Once again, it doesn't work that way, that isn't how it is.'

She put her head down and began to sob in earnest, her body swaying back and forth, long, low moans coming from her throat. Despite my best intentions, my resolve to stay physically distanced from her, my heart decided for me and I took her in my arms. I held her there, and I felt the wracking pain that consumed this loyal woman.

I would probably never have told him if he hadn't asked.

'What's going on, Kate?' Carl queried me when I got back. 'You've got a real funny expression on your face.'

'I do?' I asked, caught totally unawares. I'd been running the past hour's conversation with all its oddities through my mind, and I guess my concern for Mabel Branscombe was mirrored for all to see. Yet I hesitated. 'I've been reviewing the case against Harvey,' I responded, referring to the ADW suspect I'd booked earlier, 'to make sure we have enough to get it filed and make it stick in court.'

'No, I don't think that's it,' said Carl. 'Come on, talk. What've you been up to?'

Kent was hovering in the background, his all-American-boy look as bright as ever, and when he heard the question he pulled up a chair and sat.

'I just had a real funny experience,' I told them both, deciding to pass it on after all. 'Mabel Branscombe demanded a *tête-à-tête* with me, to confess to the murder of Connie Hammond.'

'Jesus H.,' exclaimed Carl, 'most times we don't have enough suspects, now we've got them coming at us from all sides. Was there anything to it, need I ask?' He looked down while he flicked ash off his trousers.

'She's doing it to try to sacrifice herself for Kenneth,' I explained, and proceeded to repeat the whole sad story Mabel Branscombe had given me. When I'd finished, I waited for the usual lifted eyebrows. Instead I saw two serious faces with distant eyes.

'You know,' Kent began, 'it could've happened just that way.'

'Right, it could have,' I retorted. 'Just like some service person to the farm could've lifted the weapon, shot the girl, then wiped it clean and put it back. *Of course* there could be another murderer than Kenneth Branscombe, but is it very likely, based on the evidence we've got and the knowledge we possess? Surely you're not serious?' I made a mock face of astonishment.

'No, wait, Kate,' Carl joined in. 'Just consider the

scenario for a moment. Like Dan says, it's a possible. Think of the woman's feelings for her brother.'

'Exactly,' I answered quickly. 'And that's just why she'd lie for him too, and say she did it. C'mon! You are seriously going to mess up the worthwhile case we've got with some other cockeyed theory?'

'All I said was it *could've* happened that way but – no, I'm not messing up anything. I know deep down the man's the murderer.'

'Well, if either of you still isn't convinced, this should do it for you.' I'd failed to detail the alleged planting of the note and pawning of the necklace, so I did it now. 'She actually expected me to believe she could sneak unnoticed into that rooming house, go up the stairs, and into that room. And that she could talk some mysterious boy stranger into hocking that jewelry.'

I saw Carl's eyes narrow and sweep up to search my face. What was wrong, I wondered?

'Did you reveal evidence to Mabel Branscombe?' he asked me accusingly.

'Of course not. What're you talking about?'

Dan sat there next to him, nodding his head up and down.

'How did she know any jewelry was pawned?' Carl asked quietly.

I wet my lips and frowned.

'She knew, somehow. She mentioned it one time before – the day I called her to tell her we couldn't charge Marchand with the murder – and I assumed the word had gotten out, as it so often does. Perhaps from the broker, perhaps from Connie's parents, maybe from someone who saw us going in the store and nosed around. In fact, I remember now that she told me on the phone that she'd heard about it somewhere.'

'Kate, you can't *assume* anything,' Carl said carefully, in an even tone, 'but who am I to tell you that? And what's this about informing her we'd released Larry Marchand?'

'I did it as a common courtesy,' I told him, 'because she was the one who put us on to him, in case you've forgotten.' My tone was slightly sharp – a tone I seldom used with Carl. We sat in silence for a moment, each waiting for the other one to make a move.

'So what are you saying?' I asked finally. 'That her knowledge of the pawn means she did the crime?'

'Not at all,' Carl answered, 'but I think we'd be awfully derelict if we didn't follow up on that and ask her where she got her information.'

I mulled this over in my mind. 'Don't you think she's got enough grief, without our starting to harass her?'

'I don't think that's the point here, Kate. And besides, you've at least got to do a 1.44 on her "confession" to you.' He was referring to the short lined sheet on which we informally note down all occurrences connected to an investigation.

'Well, yes, I guess I'll have to,' I replied, though I really hadn't planned on it. I did not consider this futile stab of Mabel Branscombe's a valid part of the Connie Hammond murder case.

'C'mon, Kate, what's wrong with you? You're not usually like this, foot-dragging on a lead. What're you holding back for?'

'I'm not,' I protested. 'I'm just wondering whether there's any sort of lead to follow.'

'Well, are you coming with us?' Carl asked. 'I think we'd better ride out there and have a talk with her, just to dot the i's and cross the t's if nothing else.'

'Look,' I said, suddenly contrite, 'I'm sorry I'm giving you such a hard time on this. Perhaps you're right. It certainly wouldn't hurt. And of course I'll do the 1.44. I don't know where my mind was.'

'C'mon then, let's go.' Mungers got up and grabbed his coat and Kent began to follow.

'No, you two go on without me. It won't take the three of us, and I've got a lot of catching up to do on the trial preparation.' If they wanted to go ahead and badger Mabel Branscombe, I didn't have to watch. They could get it all sorted out to their satisfaction, then report their findings back to me.

Carl nodded quietly, then shot me a funny glance as he started away. My reluctance to proceed clearly puzzled him, yet in all honesty I did not believe my personal feelings for Kenneth Branscombe's sister were what prevented me from questioning her further. I genuinely did not see the need.

I plunged into the pile of papers relating to the trial and worked steadily for an hour, sipping at my coffee even though it'd grown cold. At nearly four o'clock I decided to wrap it up and go on home.

Just as I got up to leave, I saw Dan and Carl coming through the door. I barely glanced at them. Instead, all my attention focused on the person walking in front of them. It was Mabel Branscombe, and she was wearing handcuffs.

I started toward them, questions all across my face. Carl put up his hand as if to say 'Hold on', and then pulled me to one side.

'She knows too much that no one could know unless they were at the murder scene or had detailed knowledge of the murder,' he said. 'I'm not saying that she did it, much as she may want us to believe that, but I am saying that something's going on here that needs sorting out, and I'd like to hold her till we can do that sorting.'

'What does she know, for instance?' I asked as I glanced at Mabel, standing silent and remote as she waited for the next step. She caught my eye and nodded, as if to say, 'I told you that I did it.'

'She could describe the position of the body – how the girl lay face down with her arm slung out in front of her – and she could describe the necklace to a T. She also gives what *we* think is a plausible explanation for how that jewelry got pawned.'

'What are you going to hold her on till you do your sorting out?' I still found it difficult to believe all of this was happening.

'I'd like to book her on theft of the necklace, if you'll sign the approval slip—' he looked at me questioningly – 'with the idea of possibly naming her an accessory, at the very least, if we find enough evidence in our investigation.'

My stomach heaved and sickened. I could not easily accept the turn that events had taken. And yet I trusted Dan and Carl – especially Mungers. He was too good a detective not to know probable cause when it existed. Perhaps, after all, my feelings *had* blinded me to what might turn out to be the truth. For the first time I had seriously to consider the

possibility that Mabel Branscombe might've murdered
Connie or, at least, aided and abetted Kenneth in trying to
cover up his guilt.

'She'll make bail on the theft charge as soon as you can
wink,' I said. 'You can't even get her for grand, only petty.'

'No, she won't,' Dan answered as he scratched a spot
behind his ear. 'She wants to be here in jail. That's where
she's been trying all day to get us to put her. Before we left
the farm, she even asked if she could make arrangements for
the animals, and then calmly did just that.'

I walked over to where Kent was sitting with the prisoner
and looked down at the worn hands cuffed together and
lying quietly in her lap. I saw the honest eyes, the gray hair
pulled back into a bun, the peaceful smile that played around
her mouth. I saw my mother.

I felt a powerful tide of rising sorrow, but I knew what I
must do. I had to push personal considerations aside, hard
and far, and act like the professional I was with dignity and
strength.

I sat down beside her. 'Miss Branscombe, why did you
change your mind? This morning you wouldn't go on record
with your confession, and now you have. You wouldn't let
me bring in another detective, yet you willingly talked to
Kent and Mungers.'

'Because I could see there was no other way,' she
explained, clasping and unclasping her hands within the
cuffs' confines. 'I wanted you to have the knowledge
because I thought that alone would free my brother, but it
didn't. When I left you in the park, I went home and prayed. I
knew nothing was left but for me to turn myself in, and I was

just about to call you when these two gentlemen arrived.'

'Please tell me in detail about the planting of the note and the pawning of the jewelry.'

Her words rushed out, as if she were only too eager to convict herself. Which, of course, she was. It was as if our conversation in the park was still in full, uninterrupted flow. 'I'd learned the habits of that old landlord of the boy,' she told me. 'I knew he walked out between nine and nine-thirty every morning to get a paper. I drove to Jacinto that Friday, early, and I watched from across the street and waited for my chance. I'd left Larry at the farm – he'd dropped by to do some chores after Kenneth went to work – so I knew his room would be empty.'

She paused and I handed her a glass of water. She took several little sips and then continued. 'I saw the old man come out the door at nine-fifteen. I walked across the street, up on the porch, and through the screen. I didn't see a soul. If anyone had found me, I'd have said I'd knocked and no one answered, and that I was someone's aunt come to visit.

'I knew where Larry's room was, for I'd talked with him about the rooming house so I could learn its location. I tiptoed up the stairs and down the hall. Everything was quiet. Everyone must have been either out or sleeping. It was almost too easy.

'The door wasn't even locked, and I slipped in and stuck the note in a wallet, then shoved it beneath a pile of clothes in the bureau drawer – way down deep where I felt sure he wouldn't run across it himself. And then – the good Lord must have been watching out for me – I accidentally ran across Larry's driver's license. It was like a godsend; it would make pawning the necklace so much easier.'

'It would make pawning the necklace *possible*,' I corrected her. 'The law requires you to show picture ID before a pawnshop owner will accept your merchandise.'

'Oh,' she said in a tone of bewilderment, 'I didn't know that either. I just thought you could walk in and get rid of it, no questions asked. Then it's luckier than I thought that I found the license.'

She finished the water and I refilled the glass. I sat down again while Kent and Mungers stood beside me.

'How did you make that work, Miss Branscombe? The hocking of the jewelry?'

'I told you earlier but you wouldn't listen. There was another boy, a boy named Harold something or other, who looked an awful lot like Larry. The same age, build, coloring, that is – enough to pass himself off. I told him I was playing a little joke on someone, and that I needed him to hock the necklace because I wanted a certain girl I knew to think her no-good boyfriend had done it. I offered him ten dollars, told him to say his name was Larry Marchand and gave him Larry's ID, and he gladly did the job.'

'Who is this boy, Miss Branscombe? What's his full name and where can we find him?'

'I never knew his name and I haven't seen him since that day. He just called me to say he'd done what I wanted, then he disappeared. They come and go, these boys . . .' Her voice began to trail away.

I frowned. 'What boys?' I asked. 'You say "these boys" as if there were a lot of them. Are they some group or something?'

'Not exactly,' she explained, 'but they do all come through my church circle. Boys just out of prison or down on their luck in some other way. The church finds them little jobs to do to earn their keep. That's where we get most of our young help around the farm and how we first found Larry Marchand.'

'Did this boy know Larry? Didn't he wonder where you got the ID?'

'As far as I know, they never met. And no, he didn't seem to wonder. I don't think Harold had been in prison. He seemed a very naive sort who didn't think too far ahead and just liked to please, and he seemed very happy to get that little job.'

'But Harold is gone now? He can't back up your story?'

'I wouldn't know where to find him, Katharine. I'm telling you the truth.'

At the sound of my first name, Carl threw a glance from her to me. He was noting the familiarity and wondering at its roots.

'Detective Harrod. I'd appreciate your addressing me as Detective Harrod, please.' That should satisfy him, I thought, and forestall any awkward questioning.

She nodded in agreement, apparently accepting the differences that had come between us.

'Miss Branscombe,' I asked, speaking slowly and distinctly, 'why did you plant the note and pawn the necklace?'

'I told you,' she said patiently. 'To frame Larry Marchand so he'd be charged with Connie's murder and Kenneth would go free.'

I motioned to Dan and Carl, and we moved a little bit

aside, away from the prisoner's hearing. 'I don't believe, at this point anyway, that she did the crime, but I *do* believe she's somehow involved in it – either as a cover-up for Kenneth because *he* arranged the planting and the pawning, or because she did those things herself, trying to throw the blame off him for murder. Either way, I think we have enough right now to book her for the frame along with the theft.'

'Good girl, Katharine.' Carl clapped me on the shoulder. 'I hoped you'd see it that way once you really listened to her story.'

I turned to Mabel Branscombe and spoke solemnly. 'I do not accept that you murdered that young girl; your brother did that. But I *do* now believe that you have interfered with this case, either by planting evidence in the hope your brother would be cleared or by covering up the fact that he planted it himself. I believe you had sure knowledge of the crime and of your brother's involvement in it and concealed that knowledge from us. Mabel Branscombe, we are holding you for your involvement in the shooting death of Connie Hammond.'

'Kenneth isn't going free?' Wide frightened eyes fixed on mine. 'Kenneth isn't going free and I'm going to go to jail as well, but not for murder? Is this what you're saying to me now?'

'Yes, it is, Miss Branscombe. I'm sorry, but it is. You've committed a very serious crime.'

She brought her hands up to her face and tried as best she could, despite the cuffs, to bury her head in them. A loud keening sounded through her lips. 'Oh, my God,' she cried.

'Oh, my God, what have I done? The hope is gone – there is no hope!'

The three of us were taking a break after booking Mabel Branscombe. We'd walked down to Marty's for a cup of coffee and taken a back booth where we wouldn't be disturbed.

'All right, let's bat it all around,' I said. 'What's really going on here?'

'I can think of several different scenarios,' Dan began, then paused while the waitress set the cups down. 'Branscombe did the crime he's charged with and Mabel did the little jobs over in Jacinto, thinking that she'd help him out. Or he pawned and planted that stuff himself. Maybe she followed him to the woods, suspicious of what he was up to, and that's how she knows about the position of the body.

'Or he could've broken down and told her. She seems to hold the upper hand in that family and she might've wormed it out of him. I suspect he was pretty damn upset after the killing was actually over, and she might have played on his emotional state to get him to confess.'

He stirred sugar slowly with his spoon, then added drops of cream. 'But, you see, you can turn it around the other way too. Mabel *did* do the murder because of jealousy and hatred, and also did the pawning and planting, just as she says. Perhaps when Greenwell saw Kenneth at the woods, he was actually there following Mabel to see what she was up to. And of course he isn't about to give up his own sister to the cops, even under penalty of death. At least not now, not yet.'

Carl nodded thoughtfully as he listened. 'I think everything you've said is possible,' he volunteered. 'What I *am* absolutely sure of is that the two of them did not conspire to do the crime. They had different motives that would not enable them to come together to murder her. One of them did it, yes, with the other as a witness or accessory, but which one? Now I really *am* starting to wonder.'

'I disagree about only one thing you've said,' I interjected, surprised to hear myself taking this tack. 'I do not believe that both of them were necessarily involved in the crime.

'If Kenneth killed the girl, as I still believe, I can see Mabel trying to do the frame and cover up for him. She's quicker upstairs, I think.' I pointed to my head. 'And besides, she was the one who knew the boys and could cultivate them. It'd also have been easier for her to slip in and out of that rooming house unnoticed.

'On the other hand, if Mabel killed the girl, she probably acted alone – the murder, the planting, the pawning. It's true Kenneth could've witnessed the shooting, but it's equally true he could've gone into those woods and come out again without ever knowing what had happened in the clearing. He could've lost track of Mabel in the darkness, turned around and gone back to the truck. No one saw what time he left, after all.'

The other two pondered what I'd said.

'Damn right,' Carl exclaimed. 'The poor bastard could be sitting in that cell right now without a clue what's hit him, having no idea at all who really shot his sweetie. If his hands are totally clean, he wouldn't know about the frame unless

Mabel told him, which I doubt, so he wouldn't even begin to suspect her.'

'Don't get carried away, though,' I cautioned him. 'Always remember the Big Three – motive, means and opportunity. He's got them all. And to single him out a little better, to point the finger at him a little more directly, there're witnesses to the crack across the face and to his presence in the woods, and there is a thumbprint on the gun that killed her.

'You might say, "Well, Mabel Branscombe has the Big Three too." Right, she does, but remember this: here is a woman who has raised this boy since childhood, who sacrificed her own desire to ensure he had a chance at life.

'Wouldn't it make perfect sense – isn't this exactly what she *would* do – for her to try to take the blame? Definitely in character, I would say. Is her temperament such that she would kill a teenage girl just because she thought her brother cared for her? That's a pretty drastic step, and I'm not sure we've seen a part of Mabel Branscombe that could do this. The other, yes – the sacrificing of herself – but maybe not the killing.'

'There's something else, too,' Kent began as we sipped our refills. 'We've got nothing to tie her to the scene – after all, she could've learned about the position of the arm from him – but we *do* have someone who can place *him* there.'

'Stuart Greenwell,' I murmured. 'Thank God for him. Without the eyewitness, a slap and a print on your own weapon wouldn't go too far.'

'So, boss, what's the drill?' asked Carl.

'The drill is that we're going to nose around in Mabel

Branscombe's life to try to find out more about her – try to determine if she is capable of murder and if maybe she could be the one who pulled the trigger. In the meantime, the case against her brother moves toward trial. Nothing's changed in that respect.'

We paid the bill and left, scattering to begin our different jobs.

CHAPTER FIFTEEN

The answer to a victim's death lies within their life. This is true of nearly every murder investigation except random killings. Certainly, if Connie Hammond had died by either Branscombe's hand, this truism still stood. Her actions while alive, though not consciously provocative, were surely what had caused her death.

And just as true is the fact that the reason someone murders lies within *their* life. So once you get a suspect, you begin to dig, to explore, to uncover hidden corners of their past, to help you get at character, experiences, and bent of mind – anything that might've shaped him or her into a person coldly capable of killing someone else.

Mabel Branscombe was a suspect now – not in the way her brother was, formally charged with the crime – but a suspect none the less. There was little doubt that the three of us were admitting the strong possibility that she might one day stand in Kenneth's place – and so we had to get to know her.

I'd already absorbed and passed along the violent horror of her youth – a horror that had surely made such a powerful impact on her that it would affect her outlook and her actions every day of her life. Now I had to find out other things about her – sides of her, if they existed, that I'd never seen.

I decided I'd take another ride to Joan's – this time without my son – to see if she could fill in some missing details. And tell me what religion the two Branscombes followed. From the numerous mentions made by Mabel, I'd come to realize the church played a very active role in their daily lives, and I was confident I could find many there who knew them well and could help me round out the picture of this woman sitting in my jail.

Reluctantly I phoned Tommy. 'Honey, I've got bad news – I have to work a little late tonight. I'm really sorry.'

'Aw, Mom.' The disappointment in his voice was all too plain and it nearly broke my heart.

'Tell you what. I'm going to hustle just as fast as I possibly can. I bet I can be there in time for us to make the seven-thirty show.'

'You can?' I could picture his eyes growing bright and his eyebrows rising on his forehead.

'You betcha. You and Mrs Miller go on ahead and eat without me, but be ready to go out when I arrive.'

The summer heat was starting to fade, to disappear until another year, and the cooler feel of fall began to wrap itself around me as I headed for the car. Already, some leaves had lost the brightness of their green and were beginning to hang limp, soon to drift slowly down and blow away. I pulled my coat around me and held it tight against my chest.

Aunt Joan was eating a solitary supper when I arrived, sitting at the thick pine kitchen table, thumbing through equine magazines while she chewed.

'Don't mind me, Kate, just come on in and pull up a chair. How about some chicken for yourself? There's plenty over there.' She motioned toward a roasting pan sitting on the stove.

I studied her a moment. We got on so much better now that I was older, I reflected, because our positions were now different in regard to one another. I had grown up, so she no longer had to raise me. And because of that, I didn't have to hear the sharpness of her tone when I displeased her, I didn't have to feel that she was holding back her warmth and love. My validation as a human being no longer came from her.

'Joan, I went to the library and looked up the Branscombe killings. I had no idea it was so bad. Where did Mabel and Kenneth go after that? Surely they didn't stay on the farm.'

'No,' she answered, 'not as I remember. I believe she sold it just as soon as possible and bought the place where they live now. She was always well-organized, I can say that for her, and somehow they eked out a living till Kenneth could grow up and pull his weight around the spread.'

'And he never married? Not till he was somewhere in his thirties?'

She frowned. 'Remember, I lost touch with them shortly after the murder–suicide. That's when they moved closer into town. I think there was some talk when he was eighteen or so about some girl he was getting serious with, but nothing ever came of that, I don't know why.'

'But then he married someone in his church when he was much, much older. Is that the way you heard it?'

'Yes,' said Joan, 'you've got it right. I guess Ken was

thirty-two or -three and she was just about the same age. Poor thing, she died too. Of cancer.'

'Why do you say "too"?' I asked.

'Because I just remembered as I talked that the first girl – the one when he was only in his teens – passed away from some sort of sickness. Or accident, I don't remember which. It's all so hazy and so long ago. Anyway, the chap certainly wasn't lucky in love, was he?'

She paused and reflected for a moment. 'And *now* look what's happened to him – another one down! His bad luck just continues to run, even if he killed this one himself!'

'What was Mabel like when you knew her, Joan? You said you were all friends, but did you really like her?'

'Aw, Kate, you know yourself how it is when you live out on a farm. Kids your age are few and far between, so you take what you can get and gladly. But, yes, I *did* like Mabel Branscombe, I liked them both. Oh sure, she had her faults. She could be awfully bossy, and when she made her mind up she wasn't easily swayed – determined and hard-headed as they come – but still I liked her.'

Joan raised her eyes and looked into the distance, a warm and sweet expression coming to her face. 'There's one thing I'll always remember about Mabel,' she told me fondly, 'the way she loved the animals. She could not bear to see anyone do anything she perceived as cruelty to them, even in the slightest degree. When her father sent them for slaughter it almost killed her. I never saw a softer, kinder heart.'

The phone was ringing as I came walking through the door. Mrs Miller handed it to me, saying, 'It's Aunt Joan.'

'Joan, hi. What's going on?'

'I remembered something after you drove away. If you're interested in knowing more about the Branscombes in their younger days, then Sally Draper would be the one to talk to. She was Mabel's best friend and was with her all the time. Even went to the same church – probably still does. She's a widow now, last name of Burnham, and she lives in town real close to you, just where your street nears the city limits.'

I jotted down the information, thanked her, and hung up.

'Come on, kiddo,' I called out to Tommy, 'let's go see that movie.' I'd pick up some popcorn on my way down the aisle. I'd never gotten to the roasted chicken.

I found the phone number and told her I'd like to come by and talk with her about her friend Mabel Branscombe. A cool pause followed.

'Of course you may come, Detective, but I'll tell you frankly I'm not much in the mood to talk with you. We heard you'd put Mabel in jail and I don't feel very kindly toward the police right now. You couldn't have made a worse mistake.'

'I understand your attitude,' I told her, 'but I'd appreciate it if you'd let me come.'

We agreed to meet in an hour, and I spent the time obtaining names and numbers of other ladies in the women's circle of the San Madera Baptist Church.

Sally Burnham lived in a small stone cottage – more English Cotswolds in design than anything Californian – that I'd often admired as I drove past. The picket fence, the

255

rambling flowers just bordering on the edge of wild, carried out the theme.

A winding path of golden pebbles led to a forest-green front door, and I reached for the brightly-polished knocker and gave three taps.

Through an open window, I heard a slight rustling from within and, in a moment, the door swung open and a tall thin woman with startling blue eyes stared out at me.

'Detective Harrod? Please come in.'

I entered the small square hallway, enchanted with the doll-like dimensions of this house.

'May I say how much I admire your little cottage,' I began. 'It's just delightful.'

She made a tiny sound I can only describe as a grunt. 'You don't have to try flattery with me, Miss,' she told me, not in a nasty way but just as a matter of fact.

'Look, Mrs Burnham,' I began, 'let's sit down and talk for just a moment. There're some things I think you ought to know. Just hear me out.'

She led me to a small veranda in the back, set in the L-shaped space between two angles of the house. A soft breeze wafted over us as we settled ourselves around a round glass table set on white iron legs.

'First of all, Mabel Branscombe came to us and confessed that she murdered Connie Hammond. I'm not revealing any secrets – that was on the morning news. Somehow leaks get out. If we'd taken her at her word, we'd be holding her on a far stiffer charge than we are now and she'd be in much deeper trouble.

'As it is, enough evidence exists to believe your friend

may have some involvement with the crime, so we are holding her on a lesser charge till we can get this sorted out. And that is where you come in. I want you to help me with the sorting.'

'Well I never.' Sally Burnham seemed truly taken aback. 'Do you mean to tell me she came to you and said she'd killed the girl, not told you because you – how do they say? – "leaned" on her?'

'That's right,' I answered. 'That's exactly how it happened.'

She leaned forward and looked at me excitedly. 'But don't you see? That's just what Mabel would do. She's shielding Kenny, always has, and that's just what she's doing now. It's so typical of her.' She paused a moment, then said, 'Do you know about their parents? About the tragedy?'

I nodded.

'Ever since then – no, even before – she's been so protective of her brother. She raised that boy better than if she'd been his mother, always looking out for him, always seeing that he got the best. She spoiled him a bit, though – he always came first, in every way.'

'And how did Kenneth feel toward her?' I asked. 'Was he aware of her sacrificing and grateful for her caring?'

'I think he took it all for granted,' Mrs Burnham answered. 'Sometimes I think he even felt she interfered too much in his life. Kenny is a good man, Detective – and I say that despite what he's accused of – but sometimes he can be a little unappreciative of what he's got. Resentful, even.'

And no wonder, I thought. I'd start to feel a little smothered myself if a person tried the mother hen act with me. It would get old and cloying very fast. 'Perhaps it would've been different if he'd married his childhood sweetheart,' I ventured.

'Do you mean Jodie Simons? Oh, you know about that too. Well, yes, it could've been. I think, though, it might eventually have caused a rift between Ken and Mabel. You see, Jodie was a strong-willed girl, a girl with a mind of her own, and she and Mabel would lock horns occasionally even during the courtship. Mabel liked to call the tune, but so did she.

'A shame, though, just a shame. Perhaps they would've worked out their differences and everything would've settled down in the long run. At least the Branscombes wouldn't be having the trouble they're having now, would they?'

'How did the girl die?' I asked.

'She was a great one for walking, Detective Harrod, and she was hiking in the woods one day, came to the edge of a narrow gorge, apparently lost her footing, and plunged over. They found her the following morning, lying on some rocks in a little stream thirty feet below, her neck broken.'

Sally Burnham offered me some tea, having warmed up to me considerably in the course of the conversation, but I declined and got up to go. I'd not learned much, I thought, but what I was doing now was just gathering up the pieces. Later on I'd fit them all together.

'Take care of Mabel,' she told me seriously as I left. 'Get it sorted out soon so she can go on home.'

I gave a nod but no false promises.

Carl called me over when I reached the squad room.

'Branscombe knows his sister's been locked up,' he said. 'Interesting reaction.'

'What was that?' I asked.

'Well, exactly nothing. I mean, the guy just sat there with his mouth shut. Figure it this way. If he did the crime, as we believe, and he knows she didn't, he should be jumping up and down yelling she had nothing to do with anything. But, of course, if he *does* do that, he's giving himself away. Apparently he's a lot less altruistic than his sister, a whole lot more protective of his own hide.

'But suppose he didn't do it. Now, he must've been wondering all along if Mabel fired the shot because who else, as far as he knows, had access to the weapon? He doesn't know the Marchand kid was still coming around the farm.

'So now here's Mabel in jail and he's been wondering all the while if she's the one who killed his honey, but now he *is* going to play the gentleman – he's not going to point the finger at his sister, even if she shot the one he loved. So he just sits there and says nothing.'

'Interesting,' I said. 'I wonder what he really thinks; I wonder what he really knows. I'd give anything to find out.'

I was walking from the station when I felt a hand tap me on the shoulder. It was Karen Windall and she was looking serious.

'Time for a cuppa, Kate?'

I hesitated. I really wanted to get a good start on talking with the church women, but something in her tone made me say, 'Sure.'

She'd phoned to ask about my 'date', and since he was her

cousin I'd tried to be polite, but this was the first time I'd seen her face-to-face since she'd arranged that awful evening.

'What's wrong kiddo?' I asked. 'You look down.'

'Go ahead and say "I told you so" – I don't care. I got burned, that's what's wrong. Steve Darrow is the most despicable bastard I've ever met. I was a fool. I never believed he could be like this.' Tears welled in eyes that I never thought I'd see cry over men. I covered her hand with mine and gave it a little pat.

'What happened?'

'He stood me up at the last minute. Well, didn't stand me up, but broke a date on some lame story about work. I went out later by myself and there he was, coming out of Crocco's—' a nightspot on the other side of town – 'with some blonde.

'I've seen her around before – Ellen something or other. She's trash. Anyway, I made the mistake of bringing it up with him and he just laughed in my face, told me I wasn't his mother, and walked away. Just like that – gone.'

'Oh, Karen,' I said, 'if it hadn't been Ellen it would've been someone else. After a while, it's just time for Steve to move on. How're you doing?'

'I feel like hell, Kate. I really cared – I still care. I violated all my own principles and fell for the jerk. I thought I was so smart; that it'd never happen to me. I hate the bastard!'

She took a big swig of coffee and wiped the tears from her eyes. 'I wish I had a shot of scotch for this,' she said, and, for the first time, gave a little smile. 'Maybe that'd do the trick.'

'That's a no-no here,' I told her, 'but if you feel like it, come on over later tonight and we'll put our feet up, let our hair down, and talk more girl talk.'

We agreed she'd come by around eight-thirty, unless either of us had to work, and I clapped her on the shoulder as I said goodbye.

'Chin up, Karen. Just remember – he isn't worth it.'

We went our separate ways, and I found myself wondering if I'd ever know love or heartbreak again. Right now I had absolutely no desire to get involved, to throw myself into the chancy dating game so many other single women were drawn to. Especially after the other night. I'd rather stay alone – at least for now – than risk the type of burning Karen had gone through.

I walked back to my car and set out to see Trudy Rideout, another woman in the circle. As far as I'd been able to determine, Mabel Branscombe's social life revolved solely around her church. She seemed to have no friends or acquaintances who were not San Madera Baptists.

A narrow, limiting existence, I would say, but it seemed to satisfy her. She did not seem to me like a woman who yearned for more. Rather, she seemed contented and fulfilled by the pattern of her life, current events excluded.

I found the Rideout woman doing floral arrangements in a little room behind the altar, and I couldn't help but notice the contrast between her and Sally Burnham. It could hardly have been greater. Where the latter was tall and thin, Trudy was a short, rotund woman whose round soft body moved on chunky legs. Her brown eyes looked me over while dancing merrily in her face.

'Mrs Rideout? I called earlier. I'm Detective Harrod.'

'Oh, yes,' she lisped, 'about poor Mabel.' She took a daisy from between her teeth and stuck it in a vase of flowers, behind some roses and a tulip. 'Let me just put this here . . . and here . . . and here . . .' She continued placing flowers in various strategic spots until the vase was filled and arranged to her satisfaction.

'Now!' She wiped her hands down her apron front. 'Let me get a chair and we'll start to talk.'

'How well do you know Mabel?' I began, as we sat comfortably facing one another with snipped-off stems littering the floor around us. I crossed my legs and brushed a petal off my slacks.

'As well as anyone, I should expect,' she answered. 'I've been going to church with her for many years, and I knew her, even if not too well, when we were growing up. Besides, my younger sister was married to Kenneth Branscombe! So that murderer's a brother-in-law of sorts to me!'

My eyes shot up and locked on hers. 'Your sister is the girl who died of cancer?'

'That's right – Alice, God rest her soul. They were married only six or seven years when she passed away. Thank God her suffering didn't last too long.'

Trudy Rideout rose and moved a tulip back a little farther in the base. 'None of this would've happened if she'd lived, just think of that,' she said as she sat down again. 'There'd have been no need for that old fool to get involved with that young girl if Alice had still been here.'

'Maybe, maybe not,' I answered. 'It's hard to tell *what* the future would have been under different circumstances.

What was your sister like?' I pictured a younger version of this woman sitting here in front of me – round, bubbly, extroverted.

'The opposite of me,' she said, as if reading my mind. 'I was always the loud and noisy one while she was quiet and shy and hanging in the background. But we loved each other and got along just fine, even though we were so different.'

'I understand she and Kenneth lived out at the farm while they were married. Didn't they want a place of their own?'

'I really think Alice was happiest that way,' Trudy Rideout answered, 'though it wouldn't have suited me at all. See, she didn't know much about running a house and making decisions, and she was very content to let Karla do that for her. The arrangement suited both of them real fine.'

'Wait a minute,' I said. 'Who is Karla? Did she live in the house too?'

'Oh no, that's not what I mean.' She began to laugh, putting her palms on her bulging stomach as it rose up and down. 'Mabel was called Karla – though that really doesn't suit her, does it?'

'I didn't know that,' I told her. 'Why have I never heard it before?'

'Because no one uses it much any more except me. I still use that name from time to time just out of habit. It's what Mabel called herself when she was young. You know how children are, Detective, always fantasizing. Three or four of us used to get together when we were nine or ten, and we each chose a make-believe name and dressed up and pretended we were grown-ups living in another world. Pure fantasy, of course, but Mabel carried it a little farther than the rest of us. I think sometimes she really believed she *was* this other person. She'd occasionally sign her schoolwork "Karla", and she liked her friends to call her that, even when we weren't pretending. And sometimes I still do.'

'Karla,' I reflected. An exotic, tantalizing name, conjuring up thoughts of sloe-eyed beauties in seductive veils bathed in fine perfume. Had Mabel fantasized she was a glamorous, worldly woman, so very different from the person she really was? And did she still do so? Oh, the games we play when we're lonely people, I thought, surprised by this unexpected window on to the soul of that plain work-worn woman.

'Let me ask you something, Mrs Rideout – strictly your opinion. Knowing Mabel Branscombe's character, how long will she stick to a story if it isn't true?'

'Oooooh, let me see . . .' She pursed her lips. 'How best to put it? I'd say she'll stick to it till the day she dies if she thinks it'll do her any good. It doesn't matter if it *is* doing good or not. As long as she continues to believe it possibly *might*, then she won't give up. She's one very stubborn lady.'

Karla, I thought as I was driving back – a most unusual name to call oneself, even in play.

And then, of course, it struck me, and a chill went down my spine. I could feel the little hairs rising at the nape of my neck and my fingers tightened on the steering wheel.

'K' and the diary. Kenneth and the diary. Karla and the diary.

I pressed hard on the accelerator and spun the car into the lot. I went straight to property and filled out the evidence sign-out sheet, then took the small manila envelope, walked upstairs, and sat down at my desk.

The faded purple diary slid on to my blotter and lay in front of me. I looked at the flyleaf first, where the owner's name, 'K. Branscombe,' was scrolled in careful, flowing script. Next, I flipped to the confusing entries Carl had pointed out: 'I wore my new blue coat and hat.' And then, 'The picnic was a huge success. Maybe I'll get up the nerve someday to wear a suit like some of the others did.'

I began to read from start to finish, noting other references to dress or personal appearance. No, they didn't make much sense if you believed the writer was a man, but if the owner of this diary was a woman they became totally clear. My God, had we picked up the diary of Mabel Branscombe, and not a volume that belonged to Ken? A creeping, underlying hunch told me I might be guessing right.

I turned toward the end, to the page that had caught Dan's attention the day we found the diary. There it was, as chilling in its import as before: 'I can't stand the thought of the two of them together. I've got to do something about it quick, even if it's drastic action.'

I read, and laid the diary down, sickened.

I decided to get a breath of air, figuratively as well as literally. I needed a moment alone, a little space, till my mind calmed down its turmoil.

I walked outside and started up the block, heading for a little path that ran across some grass to a pond where ducks were swimming. I neared the water's edge and sat down upon a bench, watching as a feather floated through the air, idly drifting toward me.

I'd been thinking of Mabel Branscombe up to now as a possible accessory but nothing more. Now the discovery that the diary might belong to her had put a different wrinkle on it all.

Suppose she had written the words instead of Kenneth, written 'even if it's drastic action'. Could 'drastic' mean a killing, a bullet to the head to take Connie Hammond out forever? Or could she be meaning something else, something far less forceful, far less evil? Something far more innocent, in fact, such as chastising Connie or telling her parents?

Ah, I thought, and I felt my stomach slow its churning. Ah, that could indeed be it.

But I wasn't being fair, I couldn't have it both ways. If those words were strong enough to use against Branscombe in his trial, then how could I soft-pedal them with regard to Mabel?

Because, I argued back, because in the case of Kenneth, you have that diary coupled with a bullet and a thumbprint and a witness. Those other factors do not enter in with Mabel.

I was satisfied, or so I thought, and I started walking back to work. I'd go over all of this with Dan and Carl, but not right now. First I wanted to determine who really owned the diary.

If the words *did* turn out to belong to Mabel Branscombe, I was not so sure my partners would agree with me about their innocence. I'd give them my opinion, anyway.

But as I thought about those words again, about their harshness and their threat, I was finally forced to face a truth that had been waiting all along – the truth that they were not innocent, no matter who had written them. They held a darkness that no one could deny.

CHAPTER SIXTEEN

'Mom, why is it wrong to lie and cheat?' Tommy asked as I chased him up the stairs. 'I mean, I know it is, but why?'

'Because the world wouldn't work well if you did that. People have to be able to trust each other or the world would fall apart. That's how He set it up in the first place.'

'Fall apart, you mean like this?' He'd reached the landing and he threw himself on the floor, arms and legs outstretched, shoes flying left and right.

'No, silly, not like that,' I laughed as I bent over him. 'There are rules that make life work, just like your baseball game has. Without them, *it* would fall apart, too. See what I mean?'

'Like if anyone could get up and bat without waiting for his turn? Or run out to center field instead of going around the bases?'

'You got it, kiddo,' I told him. 'Now get on in that bath.' I shook my head and smiled. I loved the questions a nine-year-old can ask.

I walked downstairs to wait for Karen Windall – she was due any minute. I wondered if her spirits had lifted since this afternoon. Probably not – Steve Darrow had a way of leaving a very large impression on the women he attracted, one they found they couldn't easily shake.

I set out the glasses and the ice, then glanced around the living room. The couch was starting to look dumpy and the chairs seemed badly out-of-date. It was ages since I'd taken a good look at my belongings, and I vowed to go through the house one day soon and evaluate everything I owned. Maybe it was time to do some decorating. Maybe now, with Jon gone, there actually couldn't be a better time. I'd give it thought.

The doorbell rang and Karen stepped across the threshold. She didn't look any happier than she had before.

She held up a warning hand. 'I'm not coming to cry in my beer, Kate, let's talk about something else instead. Maybe I can actually get the bastard off my mind for a minute.'

'That's fine with me,' I said. 'There's certainly better topics of conversation.' I mixed her usual scotch and soda and handed her the glass.

'I've changed to scotch and ginger ale,' she told me. 'This is fine for now but if I have another, I'll take it differently.'

I made no comment, but I knew the drink she'd named was Darrow's standby. She must really have it bad, to be copying his tastes.

'So let's talk about your case,' she said, as she settled back and swung her legs across the chair. 'It gets more fascinating by the minute.'

'Tell me, Karen,' I asked her, 'how did that leak reach the papers? The one about Mabel Branscombe confessing to the murder?'

'Beats me.' She shook her head in firm denial. 'When I came in that morning, everyone was talking about it. I don't know where it came from, I swear, but these things always happen. You know that yourself.'

She was right, and we could hardly ever find the culprit. Some little file clerk, some detective talking 'off the record'.

'So, she says she framed Kenneth, along with Larry Marchand, so he'd get arrested, then get freed? That's a class act, very inventive!' Karen tilted back her head and took a long deep swallow. 'If it turns out she's the one who *did* do it, then the poor bastard was set up without malice but the set-up backfired.'

She looked at me with a certain seriousness, and I knew the prying was about to begin. 'How do you really figure it, Kate? Off the record, just between you and me.'

It'd do no harm to give her an honest answer – at least, part way. Besides, it'd do me some good to hear myself talk out loud about the case. Maybe then it'd start to make some sense. 'I believe Kenneth Branscombe killed Connie. I believe Mabel Branscombe is involved in some way, but the extent of that involvement we have not yet determined.'

'She put herself at risk to cover him, went so far as to confess to the murder,' Karen mused. 'Imagine that! What kind of love do you think that must take?'

'A very deep love, I'd imagine,' I responded. 'Remember, she raised him from a child and always put him first, before herself – so this was nothing new for her. Rather noble, I think.'

'Noble? Oh, come on, Kate!' Karen gave a little snort. 'Don't you see what's happened here? She's in love with him and doesn't know it. Maybe she's not consciously aware of her feelings, can't recognize them for what they really are, but I'll bet you what I'm saying is the truth.'

My eyes opened wide. I was shocked. Such a thought had never entered my mind. 'That's ridiculous, Karen. She loves him with a sister's love and that's it. You must've been reading too many lurid scandal sheets. For God's sake, don't start writing like that too.'

'Well, how come she's never married? Have you ever thought of that?' Karen got up and mixed herself a drink.

'Because she was too busy raising Kenneth and running the farm. There simply wasn't time.'

'Lots of women do far more and still don't miss out on marrying. What I say is not so far-fetched. Look around you, sweetie. Stranger things are happening every day.'

'I think it's a perverted thought,' I told her, 'and you're just having fun playing armchair psychiatrist.'

'Maybe, maybe not,' she answered, 'but what I want to know is why this is bothering you in such a big way. It's not as if you know the woman.'

I hadn't realized I'd acted so defensively till Karen pointed it out. My emotions began subsiding.

'Well, carnal lust or not, Kenneth's still the one in your book – is that the way to read it?' Karen watched me closely.

'Absolutely. We're full speed ahead preparing for the trial.'

And there was the part-way honest answer. I couldn't

tell her about the small doubt germinating in my mind – the suspicion that the diary might belong to 'Karla' Branscombe.

I got up the following morning and began to drive to work, then, on second thought, swung the car around and headed out toward Sally Burnham's. I'd stop, I thought, only if I saw her on the grounds. I could always phone her later.

As luck would have it, she was bending over in her garden, tossing out some weeds. I pulled alongside the curb and called out, 'Mrs Burnham, may I talk with you a minute?'

'How is Mabel?' she inquired, as I went to take her hand.

'She's doing well,' I told her. 'I'll be seeing her later on today – shall I say that you were asking after her?'

'Please do. I'd appreciate that very much.'

'Mrs Burnham,' I began, 'why did Mabel Branscombe never marry? Was there no one ever in her life or was there some other reason?'

She pulled her work gloves off and laid them on the grass. 'Well, it just seemed as though Kenny took up all her time. That was not an easy job, you know, raising a child and running a farm too. But I also think Mabel just never found the right one. Some few did come "a courtin' ", but she'd always find some fault with them, always turn them down.'

Mrs Burnham motioned toward two chairs and invited me to sit. 'Part of her trouble, I do believe, was that she had a very strict morality. Oh, not that we all didn't then – we were the original "good girls", Detective Harrod. But Mabel went a step beyond. Very rigid, very narrow. I daresay if a fella started getting fresh with her, she'd have tongue-lashed him off the property and never dated him again.

'I mean, no one wanted to be casual about things, like so many people are today but, after all, you reach a certain point with a person you care for and certain things are bound to happen. It's only natural.'

She glanced sideways at me, probably to see if I was shocked. My expression must've reassured her, for she continued. 'But Mabel wasn't like that. She drew a very firm, straight line and would not waver from it. You ask why she never married? I'd say because no living male could walk that line or live up to her standards, so she preferred to do without.'

'Did she never feel emotion, then?' I asked curiously, remembering the tears I'd seen Mabel Branscombe shed.

'Oh yes, she felt emotion – strongly, too, and showed it – but not of the physical kind. She told me once that she honestly believed people could keep their desires in check with just a little willpower, that it was purposeful weakness that caused foolish young girls to give in.'

I reflected on our talk as I drove on to work. Mabel Branscombe seemed to hold a very high moral standard, one that had enabled her to override temptations of the flesh. Or was it not the moral standard but another reason that had made her so impervious to desire? Had she resisted temptation because she'd barely felt it? Because she'd been cold, frigid, arid, and without much heart?

I ached for something physical to happen, something strong and forceful that would cause me to exert myself and push my strength to its limits. I'd reached that point in the case where I needed to take a break, needed to get away from it all and refresh my mind. And the way I often refreshed my mind was to wear my body out.

'Pack the gear, kiddo, we're going camping,' I yelled as my son came through the door. 'Just the two of us. Remember that little stream in the High Sierras we went to three years ago? The one you fell in when you tried to cross it?'

'You mean when Dad was with us? And I caught a fish?'

'Yep, that's the one. Well, let's head for it and spend two days. How about it?'

'Great! Can Mrs Miller come?'

'Ho, that'd be a funny sight, Mrs Miller camping!' she exclaimed as she came up behind us. 'I'll stay right here, thank you, and put my feet up.'

'How about Molly then, and maybe Chris?' he said, naming his best friend Chris Miller, a great-nephew of our housekeeper.

I could see my son didn't share my idea of family alone together, but that was just fine with me. 'The dog stays – she might get lost – but I'll call Chris' mother.'

The three of us set out in early evening, driving north and then northeast along a winding country road. We passed a lonely shed in an unploughed field, and I remembered the pathetic little body that had lain there in another case I'd handled.

My throat began to tighten and I swung my head away. When I spoke, my voice was husky. 'Who wants a sandwich? Or shall we wait till we get to camp?'

'Now,' the voices chorused, and the boys unpacked the food and poured hot cocoa.

It was nearly eight when we arrived at the campsite. Only three or four other tents were pitched and a blissful quiet hung in the air around us. High above, a full moon cast its light across the evening sky as we breathed in the pungent smoky smell of glowing fires burning low for the long cool night ahead.

We sat around our own campfire, telling ghost stories that scared us half to death – or we pretended that they did. Then we unzipped the sleeping bags and tumbled into bed.

The following morning, as we fried bacon over strips of burning wood, I saw Tommy looking slightly pensive. When Chris wandered off to find more fuel, I went to him and asked him what was wrong.

'Is Dad ever coming back?' he said.

'No, Tommy, he's not.'

'You mean you two aren't getting back together?'

'No, honey, there isn't any chance of that.'

He accepted that, or seemed to, then asked shyly, 'Will there ever be another Dad?'

'How do you mean, honey?'

'I mean, will you get married to another man?'

'That's so far ahead I haven't even thought about it,' I responded softly. 'But no – probably not. Right now, any-way, it's just the two of us.' I hugged him to me.

'And the dog,' he said, and smiled.

'And the dog.'

We fished and hiked and swam and ran races with each other. Chris, who was a taller, bigger boy than Tommy, usually managed to beat us both, though I wasn't always putting forth my best effort.

As day's end neared, I suggested another walk, into deeper woods and meadows. The boys readily agreed and began to march along, singing as they went.

Sometimes I stayed with them, sometimes I ran on ahead, sometimes I diverted and climbed a mammoth boulder or scrambled up the steep side of a hill. My calves and thighs were aching and my breath was drawing deep to supply my lungs' demands. I breathed in the freshness of the air, the sweet clean goodness of the unspoiled mountains and flowing streams. I felt exhilaration, and I smiled and raised my hands wide above my head, as if in victory.

We returned to camp and cooked the several fish we'd caught. Then, too tired to tell more tales, we crawled inside our sleeping bags and slept.

The following morning we broke camp and, amid the sound of happy chatter, headed home. Every bone was weary, every muscle ached. I was totally tired out. But I was refreshed.

The Reverend Hubert Darwell received me in his study, which reminded me of one you'd see in a quaint English parsonage. It was more like a High Episcopalian manse than the home of a San Madera Baptist.

The cosy little room had bookshelves for two walls, filled with volumes bound in deep green and maroon. A faded Persian rug was laid atop a floor of wood that glowed richly with a warm patina. Behind the desk was an enormous leather armchair, obviously well worn because it boasted bumps and hollows gained only by use. A small Tiffany-type lamp stood gracefully on a corner of the dark oak desk, presiding over notes and other papers scattered across the top.

The Reverend himself was a kindly-looking gentleman who could easily have played Santa at Christmas without props. Full and fluffy sideburns, startling in their whiteness, framed a rosy face, and pale blue eyes twinkled from behind his rimless glasses. His hair, fine and thin and the color of the sideburns, grew in tiny wisps from the pinkness of his scalp.

He waved me to the chair across from him, a mate of the comfortable green leather one behind his desk.

'So, the both of them are now in custody, poor souls.' He placed the fingertips of one hand against those of the other, then laid his chin on the apex of the triangle they formed. 'You must know what you're doing, Detective, but I must admit I felt the shock. I shouldn't have, of course. This job leaves very few surprises when it comes to human nature.'

'Have you known both Branscombes for a long time?' I asked, settling into the comfortable hollows of the chair.

'I've been pastor here for nearly twenty years. They were already members when I came. I'd say two decades is a pretty long time.'

'So would I,' I agreed. 'So maybe you can help me. It's Mabel I'm most interested in. You, as a minister, often see people from a different point of view than their neighbors or their friends.'

'This will help you with your case, Detective? You aren't just asking me some questions so you can splash my answers across the evening news?'

'I'm not a reporter, Reverend Darwell. I have no reader-ship or listenership.'

'All right then.' He paused and thought a moment. 'Mabel Branscombe is a complex woman,' he began, 'and the funny thing is you wouldn't think it on first meeting her. She comes across at the beginning as this meek, mild little soul, kind and thoughtful and like a dear grandmother. And she *is* like that, too, don't misunderstand me.

'But there's another side of Mabel, one that doesn't often show. A hard, unyielding side that doesn't easily suffer fools – and by fools I mean those poor humans, like the most of us, who have weaknesses and sometimes falter and take the lower road. She is not a tolerant woman. She can be very harsh and unforgiving, very judgmental and unbending in the name of virtue.'

He rose from his chair and began to walk slowly back and forth, his hands clasped behind his back. 'I often had to counsel her on that aspect of her nature, to advise her that the true Christian accepts the foibles of others. But she could not comprehend what I was saying. To Mabel, white is white and black is black and there is nothing in between.'

I found the Reverend Darwell's words difficult to accept. It was as if he spoke of some other person, not the gentle caring woman that I knew. But I didn't fool myself, I did not deny that his appraisal of Mabel Branscombe could be correct. Too often I had found another side to a person that I thought I knew. I didn't even have to stray too far from home for an example. Look at Jonathan, for instance.

'Is she judgmental of her brother also?' I asked the minister.

'Oh, I think she can be, yes indeed. But she has a soft spot for him, there's no denying that, so their relationship is probably pretty good. Though it's my personal belief she could give him a little more leg room, a little more chance to answer to himself. Though I guess that's an invalid point now, isn't it?'

I rose and shook his hand, and left him puttering among the paper jungle on his desk.

As I walked away, down a sunny path that ran beside the sanctuary, I wondered at the dark side of Mabel Branscombe, the jarring opposites of personality within one person. But I was dramatizing, I told myself. What I'd learned about could hardly be called a dark side; we all exhibit opposing characteristics from time to time.

So that was all we were really talking about here, wasn't it? A perfectly normal human being.

'Hey, Kate!'

The deep voice bellowed at me from behind, and I spun around and found myself face-to-face with the local hardware store owner, Pete Blackwell.

In many ways he reminded me of Kenneth Branscombe – big and plain and unsophisticated. Unlike Branscombe, though, he'd not murdered any teenage girls.

'Hi, Pete, what's up?'

'Haven't seen you since you put my man in jail. Just wanted to have a word with you.'

'What do you mean, your man?'

'Just a manner of speaking, hon, that's all – Kenny and I go way back. We're both members of the Moose and the local Chamber, so I still see quite a bit of him. Or did, till you put him behind bars.'

'I suppose you're going to plead his case, tell me that he's innocent,' I said goodnaturedly.

'No, honey, I'm not gonna do that.' Blackwell scratched his head and squinted. 'I know human nature far too well to believe there's a single one of us who won't snap his cap if the situation's right. No, I was just wondering how old Mabel's doing in that jail.' He looked at me expectantly.

'She's comfortable – as comfortable as we can make her. We don't run a medieval dungeon here, you know.'

'Well, I bet it's sure a funny sight, old Mabel locked behind those bars.' The idea seemed to tickle him.

'Sounds like you have it in for her, Peter. Want to tell me anything about that?'

'Oh hell, I don't have it in for her, Kate. It's just she's always so high and mighty and leading Ken around by his big dumb nose. Now someone's finally telling *her* what to do, never mind she's probably going to have to stand trial.'

'So she gives Kenneth too much advice, is that it?' I asked.

'Advice? Hell, that's the very least of it. *Chickeee, chickeee, chickeee* – she totally dominates him, smothering him like some old mother hen sitting on her babes. She's closed him in and won't let him get away.'

'Well, whose fault is that?' I queried. 'He's a big boy now, he can get up and walk away. Or could, that is.'

'Yeah, but he's been in the rut far too long, you see. It's hard to break the pattern, even though I've seen him mighty resentful and annoyed at his predicament. Besides, I think he's a little bit afraid of her, so he doesn't like to cross her or he'll feel her wrath.

'You're right, though.' He clapped me on the shoulder and I was reminded of a large bear laying down its paw. 'He should've told her long ago to take a hike. If it'd been me, that's for sure what I'd have done.'

I turned around and saw Carl walking toward me. His hair was neat, his clothes in place, his cheeks clean-shaven. He'd heard that Lila might be bringing Betsy back to town – down south just wasn't working out – and between that good news and the company of Sandy, he'd become a happy man.

'See you later, Pete,' I said, and went to meet my partner.

'Want to compare notes, Mungers? Let's go upstairs and put our heads together.'

Kent was sitting at his desk, talking seriously into the phone. He looked worried and I strained to hear what he was saying. 'Well, maybe the formula's too hot. Did you test it the way you're supposed to? Uh huh, I can hear him crying in the background, but he sounds angry to me. Maybe he's still hungry or wants to be taken for a stroll.'

I rapped my knuckles on his desk and motioned for him to join us, and he quickly hung up. 'She can work it out,' he said guiltily.

'Figured out the diary yet, Kate?'

Carl's question made me start and suddenly Kent wasn't the only one feeling guilty. 'Nope, not yet. I thought Dan was going to have a crack at it.'

A crusty old-timer from patrol passed behind the three of us and belched. I winced, and waited till he'd taken his bag of wind elsewhere.

'I've read through it,' Dan told us, 'and I noticed those funny little entries too. But I can't help you out. I don't know why he'd write any things like that.'

'So what've you all dug up?' I asked, folding my arms across my chest and leaning far back in my chair. 'Have you done any good at all?'

'I canvassed that street in Jacinto pretty good,' Carl offered, 'but no one recalls seeing a woman fitting Mabel's description loitering across from the rooming house that Friday. Even went up and spoke to the old geezer himself, in case he'd spied her going out. Nothing.'

He clicked his tongue in disappointment. 'Of course, we're going back a few weeks now, and it's not exactly a sight that would stick in your mind even if it were yesterday – a sixty-odd woman waiting around or walking up some porch steps into a house. Perfectly ordinary occurrence.'

'How about the pawn shop? Did you go back there again?'

'Sure did, the woman couldn't give me any more than she did the first time. She'd checked the license against the person showing it, and yes, she'd swear the boy looked real close to the picture. As far as she's concerned, she did her job and she's satisfied that boy was Larry Marchand. Of course we know that can't be true, but we're no closer than before to learning the true identity of the pawner.'

I turned to Dan. 'Did you get a line on any kid named Harold from the church people?'

'Again, non-definitive. No one can tell me they know who he is, but neither can they say he was never part of the program. Apparently it's a very loosely-run affair in conjunction with the probation department and county social services. And I checked both of those too, by the way. Kids drift in and out and no one really knows who's who or where. County or probation will give them the name of the church and suggest they might look there for odd jobs, but there's never any follow-up. The church, for its part, sees no need to keep any records. Pretty sloppy, I'd say, but then the only time anyone would really need to know is when they're trying to hunt someone down like we are.'

I considered what I'd heard, which wasn't very much. 'So all we're really left with is that we know nothing new. We can find nothing to back up Mabel's story that she's an accessory to the crime. As far as taking this to trial, so far we're just blowing wind with not one substantial thing to back us up.'

'That's right,' Carl said. 'No hard evidence, and we're going to have to release her somewhere down the line.'

I told them I didn't have much to offer either, except some insights into Mabel Branscombe's nature that wouldn't travel very far in court, and we resolved to keep on digging, then went our separate ways.

CHAPTER SEVENTEEN

She sat quietly on the narrow cot, a prayerbook in her hand. Her gray hair was brushed neatly back and fashioned in a coil rather than the bun she normally wore. Her feet were set side-by-side, with the toes pointed straight ahead. As I watched, I saw her lips move silently as her eyes moved across the words.

'Miss Branscombe, may I speak with you a moment?'

I knew my approach sounded as if she were a guest in my hotel, but I couldn't bring myself to treat her otherwise.

'Katharine – Detective Harrod – of course.'

I saw a sadness in her face that I'd seldom seen before, a deep and lasting sadness that dulled her eyes as she looked at me.

'How is Kenneth?' she asked quickly. 'Tell me how he is.'

'He's doing well, Miss Branscombe. He's in good health, gets regular exercise. He's holding up just fine.'

'But you haven't let him go?'

'No, we haven't let him go, and we won't unless we're totally convinced you're telling us the truth. And, of course, we're not. I don't believe for one minute you murdered

Connie Hammond, I believe your brother did.'

She shuddered and tears welled as she turned her face away. 'Oh, Katharine, if you only knew.'

I decided to get on with what I'd come here for. 'Miss Branscombe, the day we served the warrant, we picked up a purple diary and took it with us. To whom does that diary belong?'

Silence fell within the cell, as if she hadn't heard me. But she had.

'Why?' she asked warily, searching for the trap.

'Because we need to know in order to straighten out several details about this case. Please tell me now.'

'It's mine, Detective, my personal private thoughts that you intruded on. That's why I tried to take it from you that day. Your reading it was an invasion of the worst kind.'

'And the name on the flyleaf – K. Branscombe? Surely that means it belongs to your brother.'

'No, Katharine.' Her voice softened toward me. 'I have an old nickname – Karla – and that's what the "K" stands for. I was given the diary in a Christmas gift swap of my church circle.' So this mild little woman sitting here in front of me had indeed written those dark and ominous words – those words of hatred at seeing two people together, of strong desire to wrench that togetherness apart.

'There's an entry near the back, Miss Branscombe, an entry that reads, "I can't stand the thought of the two of them together. I've got to do something about it quick, even if it's drastic action." To whom were you referring and what did you mean by that?'

She pressed her lips together, then she spoke. 'I was

referring to my foolish brother and that girl,' she explained solemnly, and then her eyes suddenly brightened and her mood perked up. 'And I meant I was going to kill her, to do just what I *did* do! There's your proof now, isn't it?' She seemed utterly delighted and gazed at me in triumph.

I ignored her mood, although inside my heart had fallen when my suspicions were confirmed. 'That line could've just been wishful thinking, Miss Branscombe. No judge would order a person to stand trial on those words alone.'

She fell back, dejected, enervated, and seemed to shrink in size upon the bed.

'I rode by the farm the other day,' I said, surprised and wondering why I was telling her, 'and the animals seem to be well cared for and doing fine.'

'Oh, thank you, Katharine, thank you for telling me that. We have good helpers – so I'm sure, then, that they'll continue to be fine till Kenneth can get home to care for them himself. It can't be too much longer now, can it?' She looked at me with pleading eyes.

'Miss Branscombe, Kenneth isn't going home, you must accept that fact. If *you* wish to make bail, you, of course, can go.'

'No, no.' She shook her head vehemently. 'I won't go and leave him here. I won't go when this is where I belong.'

I'd gained the information I'd come for, though it really wasn't welcome news, and I got up to go. I glanced around the little cell and thought how poorly its occupant suited it. And then I thought of something else, something that was puzzling me.

'Miss Branscombe, you seem to care inordinately about

all animals, to worry they might be hurt or harmed. I think it's wonderful to feel that way, but is there some special reason why you care so very much?'

Her face tightened and twisted as a myriad of emotions ran across it. She looked at me, frightened, as if I'd touched on something far too close to home. At first I thought she wasn't going to answer, but in a moment she began to speak. 'It was something from a long, long time ago,' she said. 'Something I don't really care to talk about.'

I was suddenly intrigued and knew I couldn't walk away without pursuing it. 'Perhaps it would help you to put it into words,' I said. 'If you care to, I can listen.'

'Katharine,' she began, then stopped. 'Katharine, I've never told this to anyone in my life before, but, yes, I want to tell you. You see, my father wasn't a good man at all. I lied when I said that to you. He was an awful, hard, harsh man. Nothing but a brute.'

Her voice caught and she placed a palm across her mouth. 'He used to beat my mother, beat her something awful, and I was only a little girl and I could not help her. I saw him flail her with the whip and strike her with a board and then his fists, and I – could – not – help – her because I was too small. Do you know, can you imagine, how that made me feel? So helpless, so useless. My dear kind mother suffering like that and me doing nothing.

'If I yelled to try to stop him, he only hit me too, and so I quickly learned to keep quiet. But I couldn't stand to watch, so I would run outside – to the barn, to the pens – and I would throw my arms around the animals and hug them tight and bury my ears in their hair and fur and wool so I wouldn't hear my mother's screams. They were warm and sweet and good, and they were my friends, the only friends that I could share my pain with, that I could talk to about the troubles.'

She was crying freely now and tears ran down her cheeks, but she didn't seem to notice. 'But then he hurt them too. He took them and beat them and kicked them and sometimes killed them, and I would hear their bleats and cries, but I couldn't do any more to help them than I could my mother.'

She twisted a hankie in her hands so hard I thought she'd tear it, then swung her gaze full up to meet my eyes. 'With his death he paid for what he did,' Mabel Branscombe said, 'but I can not help my mother, for she is gone. I *can* do something, though, something to atone – I can make it up to the animals. I can be kind and good to them as long as I live, and protect them from anyone who'd do them harm.' Her look bore into me. 'I do not send them off to slaughter like he did,' she said. 'We keep them just as pets or to help us work the farm. We make our living off the crops.'

I was shaken. Despite what I knew about her family background, this horrendous tale brought it home in a deeper way. I tried to imagine the agony this woman had suffered, the living hell in which she'd existed as her beloved mother was tormented at the hands of a monster while she stood helplessly by. But I knew that, no matter how hard I tried, I could only grasp a wisp of the way it must've felt – I could never know its true and total impact.

Numb and speechless, I pushed myself up from the chair. I laid a hand on Mabel Branscombe's shoulder, then walked silently toward the cell door. My throat ached, my eyes were wet. My mind saw a vivid picture of a frightened little girl burying her face deep into the wool of a tiny lamb, throwing her arms tight around the warm sweet neck of a sturdy pony. Or becoming, in her mind, the perfumed Karla, to escape the truth of who she really was. Ah, the shields of tortured children coping with their lives of pain.

It didn't matter, I decided, if Mabel Branscombe *had* written those dark words in the faded diary. I could not believe this caring, wounded woman was a killer.

'Why don't you come and talk to *me*, detective?' the voice asked tartly. 'I'll give you an earful about Mabel Branscombe.'

'Who is this?' I asked as I shifted the phone from one ear to the other.

'No mystery about that,' the woman answered. 'I'm Daisy Bender, a member of Mabel's church, and I hear you've been canvassing the other ladies asking questions about your prisoner. I hadn't heard from you yet, so I thought I'd give you a ring in case you missed me.'

I didn't particularly like the pushy manner. 'Why are you so very anxious to talk with me?' I asked. 'Do you have some information that might help me?'

'If you mean can I tell you if she murdered Connie Hammond, no. Or cover up for Kenneth? Well, not that either. But I *can* tell you she's perfectly capable of both things and I can tell you why.'

'Where do you live, Mrs Bender?' I grabbed a pencil and a piece of paper. 'Uh huh, I can probably be there in twenty minutes.'

Another side always exists. Someone always knows about

it. You just have to keep on digging till you find it or get the word out that you're looking for it, and it'll come to you.

Whether that side was true or not, relevant or not, remained to be seen, but the undeniable truth is that few people on this earth are perceived in only one way – in a uniform one-dimensional fashion.

'Okay, Daisy Bender, let's hear what you've got to say,' I muttered to myself as I drove along.

Of course, the Reverend Darwell as well as Pete Blackwell had already pointed to a few of Mabel's faults, but neither had implied those faults could lead to murder, they were simply flaws in personality that all of us possess.

Daisy Bender, though, sounded different. She apparently had nothing good to say, only bad – and bad of an extremely high degree. I began to feel slightly nervy, as if a sudden wind had blown in and signaled change. I reached for the radio and turned the volume up high, and a rocking blues-based song from the sixties filled the car. I could not be away long from my music, especially when I was feeling unsettled. It evened out the edges in my soul.

Daisy lived in a small apartment above a corner drugstore, and I parked the car in a nearby lot and climbed the steep rear stairs. The woman who answered the door looked nothing like what I'd expected – someone bold and brassy, probably with lots of rouge and bleached-blonde hair. Instead I saw a pale, homely brown-haired woman, leaning heavily on a cane. Her lips were lightly blushed with pink but her eyes were not enhanced at all. Whatever spice and color she possessed were all contained within her personality.

'Come in, Detective.' She waved me through the door into

a wide and cheery living room. 'Please sit there – I think you'll be most comfortable.'

I eased into a large plush armchair while Daisy Bender lowered herself carefully on to the end of a curving sofa.

'Polio at an early age,' she explained, waving the cane as she set it to one side, 'that's what this is all about.'

A tan toy poodle came trotting into the room, and she swept it up as it passed by and held it on her lap.

'Good Mitzy, good girl. Stay there now.'

Then she focused her attention on me. 'I have to tell you right away that I do not like Mabel Branscombe, but I also have to tell you that this fact does not invalidate anything I'm going to say. That woman, with that meek and docile act of hers, can pull the wool over eyes of people who don't know her as I do, but I've seen something else in her and I want you to know about it. Let me tell you a little story.'

She patted her hair and pursed her lips. 'A young girl lived here once, in this same town, who was a girl very much like Connie Hammond. She was naive, not too pretty, probably not too smart in love. But she was a good girl whom everyone adored. She started going with a man several years her senior – she was in her early twenties – and she became pregnant with his child. He left her in the lurch and disappeared when she was four months gone, and she was at her wits' end what to do. She couldn't tell her parents, because they were old-fashioned God-fearing folks and would've been disgraced, and she couldn't have the baby secretly then give it up for adoption.

'Somehow, as she fought with her dilemma, our brave Mabel found out about the fix this girl was in, and she made it her business to go to her and tell her she was a no-good tramp and deserved any consequences she might have to pay. She said she should be ashamed to show her face in town and that Mabel never wanted to set her eyes on her again, or her bastard baby ever. It was a real raking-over by a self-righteous, opinionated woman who harbored strong dislikes and strong beliefs of right and wrong.'

Daisy Bender sat silent for a moment, staring straight ahead while she stroked the little poodle. 'The following day the girl's body was found in the woods, hanging from the branch of a tall tree she'd played in as a child. There was no note, no explanation of why she'd chosen to take her life, but *I* knew – I always knew. Mabel Branscombe had shamed her into it, had knocked out the last small bit of hope she held and filled her with despair. She'd taken her and pushed her past the edge. There is absolutely no doubt in my mind.'

'How do you know these things?' I asked her. 'Was it common knowledge around town?'

She drew in her breath, and I could hear it stumble and falter in her throat. 'I know these things, Detective, because that girl was my sister – my little sister Sylvia. She told me what the Branscombe woman said when I heard her sobbing in her room that night. She must've gotten up and gone out when I finally fell asleep, for I never saw her again, not until the following day, when they cut her body down from that tree. Mabel Branscombe killed that girl as surely as if she'd put the rope around her neck, and I will hate her till the day I die!'

I sat silent for a moment. What I'd just heard was the story of an unfathomable act of cruelty, an act without any purpose but to mangle and destroy. 'Did you ever confront Miss Branscombe?' I asked. 'Tell her you knew what she'd said to your sister?'

'I did indeed. Just as soon as the funeral was over. I stopped her on the street and accused her of driving Sylvie to her death.'

'And what did she say? Did she deny it?'

'Deny it? Oh, quite the contrary. She started lecturing *me* – and mind you, this was one day after I buried my sister – saying Sylvie was probably best off where she was because only grief would have followed if she lived and had the child.

'I remember how she put it: "We all have choices, Daisy. She made the wrong one. At least she knew what she had to do." I wanted to punch her, to tear at her, but frankly I was too stunned to do anything but walk away.'

'I'm so sorry, Miss Bender, so very very sorry.'

'You don't have to say that, Detective, you had nothing to do with it. And besides, that was a very long time ago. The point here is that the woman is capable of anything, without remorse, if she believes she's doing it in the name of goodness.

'I know she heard the gossip about Kenneth and the Hammond girl. I know she thought his feelings were perverted. I heard her one day when she picked him up at practice, lambasting him and telling him to leave that "tramp" alone. He denied anything was going on, but that cut no ice with her – she yelled that he'd better stop disgracing them or else.

'I truly believe if she felt Connie Hammond was causing a

problem in their lives, by engaging her brother in an "immoral" situation, she wouldn't have hesitated to eradicate her – and believe that she was right to do it.'

'What is the relationship between Mabel and Kenneth?' I asked.

Daisy Bender placed the poodle on the floor, then settled back against the sofa. A marble clock in the corner chimed the hour. 'Domination, of course – and I believe he hated it. And obsession. Her thoughts are all of him and about him. It's always been that way. Also, I think she loves the attention that he gives her and was probably jealous and feeling neglected when he was absorbed with Connie.'

I thanked Daisy Bender for the insights she'd provided and walked slowly down the steep back stairs. I saw a nasty picture here, but did I see a murderer?

No, of course not, but I could not throw away what I'd been given. It was a narrow shaft of ugliness compared with the breadth of praising words, the goodness of the person I'd observed myself.

But its strength was so undeniably solid, its message so intense, that despite its narrowness, it held its own as equal among all the rest.

I had to see for myself, to witness this side of Mabel Branscombe before I went any further. Besides, I wanted to ask her something that had worked its way up from the bottom of my mind until it finally surfaced.

This time she was lying on the cot, and gentle little snores were coming from her mouth.

'Miss Branscombe?' I rattled at the bars. 'I need to see you.'

She sat up quickly and began fussing with her hair, which was no longer neat and brushed.

'When you spoke with me in the park that day, you told me you helped your brother get arrested by making sure his print got on that gun. Was there any other way you helped?'

'Yes,' she said sweetly. 'Yes, there was. There was the note. The note I placed in your mailbox. And then I called to make sure you got it.'

Just like that. So calculating. So deliberate. Just like the placing of the print. I gave a little shiver. I'd only lately begun to wonder if that letter could've come from her, and now I'd learned for sure that I was right.

'How did you know where I lived?' I asked. I naturally kept my home address a closely-guarded secret.

'You're well known in this town, Detective,' she answered simply, 'and when you're well known, other things about you become known, too.'

So much for my perceived privacy. 'But you took a risk, walking right up to the mailbox, right up on the front porch. You could've easily been seen, and then your plan to help your brother would've fallen apart.'

'I had to take that chance. I had to try to make the finger point at Kenneth right away. I took my time and I was careful. And it worked out just the way I'd planned.'

Yes, it did, I thought, but only up until a certain point.

'Miss Branscombe,' I began again, almost hating what I was about to do, 'you are obviously a very moral woman. I want your opinion on a case that's been bothering me awhile.

Oh, no case of mine – this is something that happened in New York City several years ago. Maybe you remember. A fellow and a girl were playing kinky sex games that got out of hand, and he ended up killing the girl. I don't know how I feel about the two of them, about trying him for murder. Do you?'

I watched her closely as she listened to my question. Apparently the lack of relevance to any current situation didn't register. Instead, her eyes grew hard and shining with excitement and she began to wag her finger. 'I remember that. Of course I do! I could not believe what they were up to! Well, I say she got what she deserved, and as for him, yes, he should've been put away but maybe not for murder – for acting like the animal he was before she died!'

I felt a slow revulsion fill my body and my face began to flush. 'Is no one allowed to make a mistake, Miss Branscombe? Even when they're young and foolish?'

'Not that kind, no. There is no reason to make mistakes of the flesh, no reason at all.' She tightened her mouth and sat up straight.

'And your brother Kenneth? How did you feel about him when he made the "mistake" of adoring Connie Hammond? Were you as hard on him, too?'

'Kenneth was a foolish, foolish man, Detective, and he was weak. Kenneth isn't strong like me. But he *is* my brother and so I forgave him his weakness and asked the good Lord to forgive him too.'

I didn't want to be here any longer, listening to her punishing, judgmental words.

I looked at Mabel Branscombe and saw my mother, Chrissie, sitting there – but the image wasn't strong and bright like it had been before. Chrissie had been compassionate, forgiving – she'd been tolerant of the foibles of her fellow man. Mabel, on the other hand, did not begin to understand the meaning of those words.

CHAPTER EIGHTEEN

I stumbled on to it without insight, without cunning, without using any intellect.

I'd stopped by the Reverend Darwell's to talk some more about Mabel Branscombe. To ask what? If he thought she'd murdered Connie Hammond? I didn't know, but because he'd been the first to stress Mabel's other side – and stress it so definitely – I felt I ought to speak with him again.

He was sitting in his study, reading glasses perched on his short button nose. He rose quickly, seeming glad to see me, and I sank comfortably into the leather chair across from him.

His desk was far less cluttered than before. In fact, he seemed to be engaged right now in the task of making order of the mess. His words confirmed that I'd already guessed. 'Sometimes it just gets away from me, Detective, and it all piles up till I can't find anything I want. Look.' He held up a piece of paper. 'Here's the copy of a sermon from seven months ago. Now, what's that still doing here, I ask you?'

He balled up the sermon and threw it in the trash, then

began arranging the remaining books and papers in neat stacks.

I spied some tiny brownish figures standing near the base of the Tiffany-style lamp. Intrigued, I peered closely at them and saw birds and squirrels and bears made from some speckled type of wood. They stood only a half-inch high, with a breadth no more than twice that.

I'd not noticed them before, probably because they'd been hidden in the clutter, and I picked one up and turned it all around.

'How delicate,' I murmured. 'Are these hand-made?'

The Reverend raised his eyebrows as he looked to see what I was talking about, and then his expression softened and he smiled. 'Yes, indeed they are, hand-carved from plain peach stones. Isn't it a lovely job?' He paused. 'Do you have any idea who made them?'

I shook my head. They looked like miniature carvings I'd once seen an old-timer craft in the Blue Ridge Mountains of Virginia, but as far as I knew, the Reverend Darwell had no connection with that part of the country.

'Mabel Branscombe made them,' he told me proudly. 'I'm surprised you didn't know about her hobby. Most of us have one or two of her little carvings on a desk, a key chain, or whatever.'

'Has she had this interest long?' I asked, and I heard my breathing slow and become very quiet as my concentration tunneled in on his answer.

'Just as long as I can remember, Detective. Always see her with her little knife, whittling away. I don't know how she's getting along in jail without it – I mean, you wouldn't let her have it in her cell, now would you? – because it's rarely if ever out of her hands when she's got a moment to herself.'

'Does she use a lot of different knives?' I asked. 'Or is there a special one?'

'Oh, she's got a favorite – seems almost to be part of her. A little pocketknife with a pearl inlay on the handle.'

A little knife. A little pocketknife with a pearl inlay on the handle. Just like the one found lying in the grass at the murder scene.

Talking didn't matter any more. I'd found out something much, much better than any chatter about Mabel Branscombe's nature could reveal. I'd found proof that she'd stood beside the body of the dead girl, just as she'd insisted all along.

'Thank you, Reverend Darwell,' I said hurriedly, and got up to go.

'But you've just arrived. What was it you came to see me about anyway?' He seemed perplexed.

'It doesn't really matter now,' I told him. 'I've just remembered something I've got to do. I'm sorry to have taken up your time.'

I hurried down the little path and headed for the car. I couldn't reach the station fast enough.

'I saw the little animals,' I said, 'the ones you carved for Reverend Darwell.'

'Oh, did you now?' She seemed extremely pleased. 'I'd be most happy to make you some as well, Katharine. That is, if you'd like me to.' Mabel Branscombe looked at me shyly and expectantly.

'No, not right now,' I answered, 'not right now. How do

301

you make them, Miss Branscombe? With a special whittling device?'

'Oh no, just a little penknife suits me fine. I've used the same one for a long, long time – just get the blade sharpened up occasionally.'

She reached out and touched my arm. 'It's impossible, I know, but I just thought I'd ask if maybe I could do some carving here . . . if someone watched me to make sure I did no harm. I miss it so.'

I started to say no, but then I changed my mind. 'Perhaps we could arrange that. Perhaps we could bring you that very special knife, if you could tell us where to find it.' I held my breath and waited.

'I wish I could. You see, I misplaced it somewhere several weeks before you brought me here. Another one will have to do.'

'When did you last see it, Miss Branscombe?'

'Funny thing, it was the day before the body was discovered. I couldn't find it after that.' Her eyes took on a far-away expression.

'What did the knife look like, Mabel?' I sat down beside her.

The use of her first name made her turn and look at me, and she smiled briefly. 'It was real pretty. Just a short little pocketknife, but it had a pearl inlay on the handle, shaped like this.' She formed an oval with two fingers.

'Would this be it?' I held a plastic packet toward her, close enough for her to see the object it contained inside.

'That's it! That's it exactly!' she cried in joy. 'Wherever did you find my knife?'

I didn't answer, just slipped it back inside my pocket.

'But can't I have it? For the carving?'

'Not now, Miss Branscombe. Maybe later on.'

I turned to go. Then I felt her tug at me again.

'How much longer, Katharine? How much longer must he be here? When will you believe me and let Kenny go?'

'That's impossible. I've explained it all before. *You* may leave, but he may not.' I had to wonder as I spoke if the situation was about to change – to do a turnaround, with another charged with murder and the first released. Would she get her wish after all?

'I can not go,' she said sadly. 'I can not go and leave him here, but I also can not stay myself. I can not be happy anywhere while he's in jail for a crime he didn't do. I exist in limbo.'

'The jailer tells me you've just been picking at your food for the past few days,' I said. 'You must eat to keep up your strength.'

'For what?' A deep depression seemed to settle over her. 'I can not get him out, I can not live outside without him. And I can not live here either unless you set him free. You really are not going to let my brother go, are you?' She raised her eyes and fastened them on mine, and their intensity bored into my face.

'No, we are not,' I said. 'He is standing trial.'

'And you dare ask why I do not eat? I do not eat because I no longer have a reason to endure.'

She lurched suddenly to her feet and began swaying back and forth. She wrapped her arms around herself and, as if speaking in a chant, began to murmur words strung together in a lilting monotone like a strand of beads. I bent close to her, to catch what she was saying, but her back was to me and the sounds were indistinct.

I strained to hear. One phrase reached me but it made no sense. 'Oh my song,' she murmured, just before she fell into silence, 'Oh my song.'

I moved in front of her.

'What song, Mabel? What song do you mean? A favorite from your childhood or your church?'

Her eyes pleaded with me and she reached out a hand to touch me. 'Katharine, can I tell you . . .? No, no . . .' She shook her head vehmently and her lips tightened till the blood drained from them and left them white. 'No, never, I must not . . .'

'Mabel, please, what is it?'

She only looked at me, and now a cool denial filled her eyes as she told me, 'There is nothing else to say.'

I knew it was useless to try any more to get through to her, so I left her sitting on her cot and walked away. As the cell door jangled shut and I started down the hall, the echo of the sobs rang out behind me.

'Her knife was at the scene, her words were in the diary, but it's still not enough to charge her,' I exclaimed. Dan, Carl and I had been batting this one around for nearly half an hour now. 'You've still got the witness Greenwell and you've still got the prints on the gun.'

'Damn right,' said Carl. 'She hated the girl, no doubt about it, but those words could be just words and nothing else.' He touched a snapshot of his daughter standing on a corner of his desk. 'Words, you know, to let off steam.'

'As for the knife,' Kent explained, 'that could fall right in with her story that she tried to cover up for him. She followed Kenneth to the woods, saw the killing, then once he'd gone, bent over to remove the necklace so she could pawn it. And in so doing, the knife slipped out and fell down in the grass. But it doesn't mean she murdered Connie Hammond.'

'What's next, boss?' Carl asked archly. 'We can't go around holding cellsful of suspects for the killing of that girl. If we've made a big mistake, we've got to reckon up with it.'

I knew I had to move quickly to try to sort this out. If Kenneth Branscombe were innocent after all, any time he'd spent in jail was far too much.

'I've got an idea,' I said, 'one other place I want to look. I need to know something more before I go any farther. Let's meet back here at four o'clock.'

It was just a hunch, a deep-down, nagging hunch that begged to be explored. And why not? Following hunches is a part of good police work, because often they'll be right and lead you where you want to go.

Once again I headed to the library, once again I inquired of the old librarian, once again I descended to the dusty silent vaults. Talk about a needle in a haystack. I hardly knew where to begin.

Actually, it turned out to be easier than I'd feared. I began pulling papers from the year Kenneth Branscombe would've turned eighteen and, bingo, after looking through only two months' worth of yellowed pages, there it was – the story of Jodie Simons' death.

Beneath the picture of a smiling, bold-faced girl, I read

how her body had been found lying on some jagged rocks at
the bottom of a gorge, deep within the woods behind the
Branscombe farm. She'd gone for a hike the previous afternoon, a hike that would usually have lasted several hours.
When she failed to return home that evening, her parents
reported her missing.

A search party found Jodie Simons, her neck broken and
lying crazily to one side, late the following morning. The
death was ruled accidental because it was believed she'd
simply stepped too close to the edge, perhaps to peer at the
stream below, then lost her footing and fallen over.

I skimmed along the paragraphs, running my finger
beneath each line of type. Everything certainly looked
straightforward enough. And then suddenly I saw it, near the
end. The reason the search party knew where to look for
Jodie was that Mabel Branscombe had told them she'd been
tending to the horses the previous afternoon and had seen the
girl walking on the path leading to the woods, then disappearing into them.

She'd not noticed her come out. Since no one else had
come forward with information, it seemed clear that Mabel
had been the last person on earth to see Jodie Simons alive.

I looked up and far away, my eyes narrowing in thought.
Suppose that had been true, I said to myself, but suppose
instead of seeing Jodie passing through the farm, Mabel saw
her for the last time standing on the edge of a precipice, just
before she shoved her over. Suppose Mabel Branscombe,
angered by her brother's courting of this wilful, headstrong
girl, had decided to remove this obstacle from her life. She'd
seen her chance, followed Jodie, then crept up behind her

and given her a strong hard push that made her plunge and crash on the rocks thirty feet below.

Had the unfortunate girl heard footsteps, turned at the last minute, and seen the face of her attacker, or had she not known what had happened to her as she spun and dove and twisted through the air before she snapped her neck and died?

Proof? This story in the paper was not proof of anything, but combined with everything else I knew about Mabel Branscombe, it certainly made me wonder.

And though it might not be proof, it did offer one undisputed fact – no one saw Jodie Simons alive again after the Branscombe woman saw her.

I put the papers away and asked myself this question: if my hunch was true and Mabel had removed one impediment early in her life, why would she hesitate to remove another many years later? The answer popped right up: she probably wouldn't.

'So you want me to tell you if you've got a murderer on your hands?' Martin Korman chuckled as he moved around the room. 'See all these books, Katharine?' He waved his hands at the volumes in the bookshelves that lined his office. 'They're filled with a thousand theories on human behavior, and sometimes I still wonder if they know what the hell they're talking about!

'But—' he turned to me and bowed – 'lay out your case and I'll try my best to help you.'

Korman was the department psychiatrist, and it'd occurred to me that maybe he could shed some light on the question I kept asking myself. I'd come straight here from the library. It was only two o'clock so I still had plenty of time before our meeting.

'Here's what I want to know,' I said, leaning forward in my chair and placing both hands on my knees. 'Is it possible for a woman to be a morally good person, a Christian person, truly to believe herself to be such and to be perceived as such by others, and still commit a murder?'

'That's a very broad question, Katharine,' Korman answered, adjusting his horn-rimmed glasses on his nose. He was vastly overweight and his belly flopped sloppily over his straining belt, causing him to sit slightly back from his desk. 'Can you be more specific?'

I bit my lip and searched for the words that would best get across what I wanted to say. 'I mean, if the person would ordinarily never hurt a fly, could circumstances arise where she believed she absolutely had the moral right to remove an "undesirable" human being from the world, and would see nothing wrong in doing that? And then go ahead and do it, without regret?'

'Ah, I get the drift.' Korman nodded his head. 'In the name of goodness and all that. Well, I'd say absolutely, and I think there are several classic cases to back me up. The person you describe would be criminal only in this one narrow, strictly circumscribed area, and would see nothing wrong with her actions because *she judged* the act needed to be done, and this justified its doing. In the name of virtue.'

'The name of virtue.' The same words the Reverend Darwell had used in describing Mabel Branscombe.

'But such action would be inconsistent with the rest of her

personality, her nature,' I protested.

'No, it wouldn't, not necessarily,' Dr Korman continued. 'You're talking here about a person who's very strong and very forceful of character, are you not, with very definite ideas of right and wrong?'

I nodded, fascinated by his insight.

'Well, this person doesn't long to murder, does not seek excuses to kill in order to satisfy some blood lust as others do. Rather, this person looks on killing as a distasteful but necessary surgical removal of an evil from mankind.

'And she performs the surgery, then picks up the normal average routine she followed prior to the event without missing a beat. Not because she's pretending, mind you, but because that's the way she really is, except in this one explicit area. Which, seen that way, is actually perfectly consistent with the rest of her life. Do I make myself clear?'

'Very clear, Dr Korman. Thank you.'

I had my answers, but they didn't do me any good. I still had no hard evidence Mabel had murdered Connie Hammond. What would I say to Dan and Carl at four o'clock? In the meantime, I'd pray that maybe they had come up with something better.

I drove along, musing and listening to my music as one song after another filled the car with sound. I thought of Mabel Branscombe's 'song' and wondered once again what she had meant. Perhaps it was nothing more than the babbling of a confused and saddened mind. As I realized this, I shook my head in pity.

But suddenly the echo of a voice ran through my mind, and it was as if a shade flew up and the whole scene was flooded with clear bright light, dispensing with the shadows and exposing the truth for what it really was.

I remembered Pete Blackwell that day outside the station. I remembered when he'd called Mabel 'Mother Hen'. I ran her own words back through my mind, and now I knew she'd not been saying 'Oh my song', she'd been wailing the lament of a parent just about to lose a child. 'Oh my son,' she'd agonized, 'oh my son.'

Shaken by this revelation, I pulled over to the side and stopped the car. I knew now, in the depths of my gut, that Kenneth Branscombe was Mabel Branscombe's child, not her younger brother.

Why else would she try to lay down her own life for him unless this were true? Hers was not the love of a sister, really – but rather the deep love of a mother who'd sacrifice her all to save her child. She'd tried to tell me herself back there, but at the last minute couldn't bring herself to share the dreadful secret she'd held for so very long.

And then the logical extension of that belief began to build and grow and I was consumed with the certainty that he was, in fact, both – her son and her brother, sired by the abusive, domineering half-mad man who was her father.

She'd have been only twelve years old when that child was born – a girl just about to come into maturity and newly able to get pregnant, an innocent young girl, helpless against the depraved desires of the animal who was her father.

I wanted to know. I wanted whatever sort of proof I could get. I swung the car around and raced to Sally Burnham's. She was half-way through the door when she turned at the sound of gravel crunching in her driveway.

I wasted no time on preliminaries and, probably because of the strange look upon my face, she didn't protest my abruptness.

'Mrs Burnham, did you see much of Mabel Branscombe that summer Kenneth was born?'

She pondered my question for a moment, her hand to her cheek. 'No, no we didn't. Her father said there was a heavy crop to harvest and that she had no time for play. I remember I saw her right after classes ended and then not again till school began in fall. I missed her company, but I understood. I knew what farmwork was.'

'And Mrs Branscombe? You saw her while she was pregnant?' An anxious pitch touched my voice, giving it a higher ring than usual.

'No, not her either. In fact, we didn't even know a baby was on the way. We heard toward the end of summer that a little boy had been born and we were all surprised.'

'Do you know what hospital the Branscombes used?' I asked. 'Mariposa?'

'No, no. He was born at home, as was Mabel. And as were a lot of us.'

I left her standing there and walked back to the car, my mind rocking with the ugliness, the twisted evil ugliness, of a summer hidden in the distant past by layers of years gone by.

But the ugliness had not been confined to those summer months and that unnatural birth. It'd begun long before that time and had continued for many years to follow.

Should I share my certainties with Dan and Carl or wait awhile? I wondered. Then that question paled beside the happenings of the next few seconds. I was half-way to the station when the call came out – Mabel Branscombe had escaped from custody and was on the run.

I raced up to the squad room, taking two steps at a time.

'What happened?' I demanded. 'What in God's name happened?'

Carl looked at me with disgust. 'She complained of stomach pains, played like she was going to pass out. They fell for it hook, line and sinker and took her to the infirmary, uncuffed her, and put her on the table.

'The doctor hadn't come in yet and the cow who was supposed to be watching her wandered off to get a drink of water. I guess she thought "little old lady can't do no harm" and all like that.'

He paused and stuck a toothpick in his mouth. 'Anyway, she came back and the room was empty. No sign of Mabel, no sign of her going down the hall or out of the door – just disappeared.

'So the dunce is standing there with her mouth wide open when the doc comes in, and he's the one who makes her get her act together and put out the prisoner escaped alert. There's gonna be some departmental action on this one, you betcha.' He removed the toothpick and threw it toward the wastecan.

'Why escape?' Kent wondered. 'She could've made bail any time she wanted to.'

'Because she passed the edge,' I said slowly. 'The last time I saw her she wasn't reasoning too clearly, but I failed to grasp the real truth of her condition. Something must've snapped in her when she finally realized Kenneth wasn't getting off. Have all units been notified?'

'Yep. The word's out and the sheriff's department has been alerted too. Also, there're men staking out the farm. Wanna go on out there?'

'Yes,' I said, 'but first I want to talk with the person who allowed this to happen.'

Cindy Reece was a civilian jail employee – not uncommon in California – with more than three years' experience guarding criminals. She should've known better – there was no excuse – but she'd just gotten careless. As Carl guessed, she'd thought Mabel Branscombe posed no risk. I found her sitting on a chair downstairs, flushed and shaken. She'd obviously been crying.

'Take me through it,' I told her without sympathy. 'From the beginning.'

She wiped her eyes and tried to get herself together. 'The prisoner called the guard and complained of stomach pains in the appendix area. She said she'd had a severe attack last year and knew the symptoms. I was assigned to take her to the infirmary. When I arrived at the cell, I noticed she looked poorly. Her face was twisted in pain and she kept holding her side. I practically had to support her as we went down the hall.' Reece went on to say she'd helped Mabel Branscombe up on the examining table and then had judged it safe to get a drink of water because some crumbs from her lunchtime sandwich had lodged in her throat, causing irritation. 'She was so sick and weak I didn't think she'd move, let alone flee,' the girl protested. 'I couldn't have been gone more than thirty seconds, but when I came back the lady had disappeared.'

'Did she say anything to you,' I asked, 'besides complaining about her supposed illness?'

'Only one thing,' Cindy Reece responded. 'It didn't make any sense to me. She said, "I've failed, I've failed." She kept repeating that over and over again on the way to see the doctor.'

I left the jailer sitting there, mulling over her dilemma, and started the drive to the farm. Along the way, I kept my eye out on the crowded city sidewalks and in the fields and meadows of the countryside, to see if I could spot a lone woman in prison garb making her way along.

Of course I knew I needn't really look for the county jumpsuit worn by all prisoners – jailer Reece had also told me a long tan raincoat belonging to a nurse was missing from its hanger.

I shook my head dispiritedly. It'd all tumbled out of nowhere and taken me by surprise. I didn't know if Mabel Branscombe had murdered Connie Hammond, if she was an accessory covering for her brother, or if she really had minimal involvement, if any involvement at all. I'd expected to have time to work this out – to put my mind at rest that we *were* holding the true killer – but now she'd turned it all topsy-turvy by escaping.

Where would she have gone? What was in her mind? I tried to put myself inside the skin of Mabel Branscombe and decide what she would do. I was betting on the farm, betting that she'd try to return there, at least for some money and a change of clothes.

But would she dare? She wasn't stupid, she must know we'd be watching it.

I radioed ahead to Davey Johnson, the sergeant in charge of the stake-out, and he met me at a fork in the road maybe an eighth of a mile from the farm.

'We've got men all around the property's perimeter,' he told me, 'as well as close to the outbuildings and the house itself. There's no way she can slip past us if she comes this way.'

'Okay,' I said. 'Have you checked the inside yet?'

'Yes, there's no one there. No sign anyone's been there either.'

I'd been intending to join the stake-out team, but now that I was satisfied they were well manned and organized I changed my mind. I decided to head back into town or maybe drive around the roads a little.

After an hour or so of fruitless scouring, I started back to trade notes with Dan and Carl. As I rode along, I listened to the babble of communications, which served only to verify that no one had spotted the escapee.

And then suddenly the babble changed, requesting the immediate response of any car in the area to a residence on the northeast end of town. The residence of Sally Burnham.

I gunned the motor and headed toward the little English cottage with its pastel wildflower garden. A black-and-white was already parked in the driveway, and a young officer was talking to the Burnham woman, who stood with her hand beside her head.

I cut the engine, jumped out, and ran to her. She seemed dazed.

'What's happening? What's going on?'

'She was here, Detective Harrod, she was here and she

315

took a knife, a great long kitchen knife like this.' Sally Burnham held her hands about a foot apart.

'Tell me about it,' I said.

'I was in my garden out back. I had no idea about the escape. I was bending over the flower bed when I saw Mabel out of the corner of my eye. She was wearing a big tan raincoat that reached almost to her ankles and was disappearing through my rear screen door.'

Sally Burnham paused and put her hand across her chest. 'I followed her inside and saw her standing in the kitchen, pulling out a drawer. "Mabel," I said to her, "Mabel, I didn't know you were out. What are you doing here?" Because it wasn't like her just to walk in unannounced.

'She swung around toward me, holding the butcher knife in her hand. Her eyes were wild, like I'd never seen them before, and she just yelled, "Get out of the way, Sally, I don't want to have to hurt you", and then she raced past me and out the back door.'

Mrs Burnham's breath began coming faster and I saw perspiration beading on her brow. I pulled a chair up and asked her to sit down.

'Get a glass of water for her,' I told the officer, 'or a whiskey if there is any.' Then I turned back to her.

'Did she take the knife away with her?' I asked.

'Yes, tucked inside the coat. That's apparently what she came here for and that's what she got, and she wasn't going to leave without it. Detective Harrod, what is going on?'

'I wish I could tell you,' I said slowly. 'I really wish I could tell you.'

316

What was she up to? I wondered. Why the knife? I pictured this lonely, tortured woman on the run. How had she gotten from downtown to Sally Burnham's? Swiped coins from a newsstand, then caught a bus? It was perfectly possible.

The day was lowering into night, and with night our search would become that much harder. The last long rays of the setting sun laid bands of red and gold across the western sky. A cloud rode by, dressed in pink, and then the darkness draped itself across it and the pinkness disappeared.

A silence seemed to fall around me as the night descended, and sounds that in daytime would be harsh and bright now became soft and muted. I breathed in the freshness of the evening air, then turned and walked inside the station.

The three of us unwrapped our take-out sandwiches and began to eat. We were finishing up our coffee when the phone rang.

'My wife may have given a ride to that woman that you're searching for,' a trembling voice told us. 'She knew nothing about the escape so she didn't recognize her. The person asked her for a ride, and she saw no reason to refuse her. The lady looked harmless enough.'

'Put your wife on, please,' I said, holding tightly to the phone.

A small voice told me she was Nancy Rubin. She said she'd picked up a woman fitting the description of Mabel Branscombe on the northeast side of town that afternoon, and had driven her several miles down the foothill road, then dropped her off near a dilapidated barn.

I recognized the spot where she'd discharged her cargo. It

was less than half a mile from the Branscombe farm.

'What was she wearing?' I asked.

'A long tan raincoat. I couldn't see what was under it.'

'Was there any sign of a weapon?'

'No, none,' the Rubin woman replied, 'but she kept one hand pressed to her lap while she rode along. Honestly, Detective, I feel like such a fool, but the poor thing looked so helpless and so innocent. She came up to me in the grocery store parking lot, said she'd seen me on that road many times, and asked if she could have a ride because her car had broken down. Her face looked kind of familiar to me, as if I'd seen her around too, so I said, "Sure, get in".'

'You couldn't know,' I consoled her. 'She would've fooled anyone.'

I hung up, called communications, and asked them to patch me through to Davey Johnson.

'She's on the way there, Davey, or she may be there now. I figure she'll probably lay low till dark, then try to sneak on in if she feels it's safe. Though for what reason I do not know. Watch your cover and expect us very soon. We're leaving now.'

We drove quickly down the foothill road leading to the farm, then slowed our speed as we approached. A half-moon shone from above, casting only pale and milky light on the limbs of the trees around us. I saw the vast expanse of forest in the distance – the same forest, probably, where Jodie Simons had met her fate those many years before. Was Mabel Branscombe hiding there right now? Waiting till it was all right to come home?

And then I saw the movement – the subtle, almost

imperceptible bit of motion where none should have existed.

'Stop and cut the lights,' I whispered. 'All of them.'

I peered through the thickening twilight till I felt the strain upon my eyes. Had I imagined it? Or had I merely seen an animal furtively setting out for an evening kill?

'There's something over there,' I said, pointing to a clump of trees and bushes. 'I know there is.'

'Let's check it out then,' Carl said, and turned off the engine. 'How do you want to do this?'

'I'll go straight ahead,' I told them, 'and you each take one flank to the side. Keep circling toward the rear and I'll come right up the middle.'

We separated and I began a long, low crawl through the brush. This field had not been ploughed or planted, and burrs and stickers dug into my legs and arms, despite the slacks and long sleeves I was wearing.

'Please God let it be her,' I prayed, 'and please let her come quietly.'

I saw the clump of bushes straight ahead and I slowed my crawl, waiting several seconds before each new forward motion. There was no sound, and nothing moved, but suddenly I sensed the presence of another human being, and I felt my nerves tighten.

I crept around the right side of the bush, and then I saw her – crouching low and running out the other side, away from me and far away from Dan and Carl.

'Over here!' I cried. 'Follow me!'

She straightened up when she heard me start to yell, and ran at full speed toward the woods. The stolen raincoat, though roomy, must not have been long enough to trip her up, for her progress was certainly not impeded.

Unfamiliar with the terrain, I stumbled as I went, and I could see the shadowed figure start to draw ahead of me. Behind me, but not yet close, I heard my partners cursing and struggling with the thickness of the brush.

Mabel Branscombe, on the other hand, knew this land by heart and seemed to have no trouble whatsoever navigating. Years of outdoor work had kept her in top-notch physical shape, and she showed no signs of tiring. As I plunged ahead, I saw the sturdy little woman disappear into the woods.

I couldn't afford to wait for Dan and Carl. I'd have to try to stay with the quarry and hope that they'd catch up with me.

The forest suddenly engulfed me, so thick that the pale, milky half-moon light was totally shut out. I stopped, listening, then started moving cautiously ahead.

I stepped around a tall oak tree and suddenly she came at me, a long blade gleaming silver in her hand. Her eyes, intense and mad, glowed like large round circles on her face.

I moved quickly to one side, drew my gun, and cocked it.

'Mabel, lay the knife down. Drop it!'

She turned toward me once again and ran across the little clearing in between us, the kitchen knife now shining from her upraised hand. I leveled my arm, preparing to shoot, but suddenly another face loomed up before me – the face of my mother, indistinct and undefined, but hovering like a specter there in front of me.

I hesitated just a breath, and that split second cost me. Mabel Branscombe lunged at me and swept the blade down through the air. I ducked beneath her, avoiding it, and rolled upon the ground. She slowed her momentum not one bit, and kept on running straight ahead, disappearing deep into the woods.

I heard Dan and Carl calling in the distance.

'Over here,' I yelled, 'over here. I'm all right but she got away.'

There was no use trying to follow her any farther – she was on her own territory here while we were only visitors.

'We'll have to get the dogs,' I said. 'Let's get back to base.'

The canine unit from town picked up her scent, followed it a little way, then lost it. I left them trying to sniff it up again and started to head home, where I could quietly take out my thoughts and look at them.

I poured myself a tall drink and sat down alone, my music playing softly by my side. I was sobered by what had very nearly happened tonight, and sobered by my realization that a fantasy had gotten in my way.

And as I came face to face with these realities, I also came full-up against another one – Mabel Branscombe was *not* my mother Chrissie. Was not, had not been, never would be. I'd been a fool to build upon a wish, to imagine I saw something where nothing could, in fact, exist.

Chrissie was gone and would never come back – not as herself, not as anybody else. I could count myself blessed to have known her for that brief and shining period in my life, and I'd be satisfied with that and grateful for it. I'd never try to look for her again.

Chrissie, my beloved mother, may you rest in peace.

CHAPTER NINETEEN

They found her body shortly after dawn. It lay face down upon the grass, the dew of night still wet upon it. They didn't need to touch her to know that she was dead.

She sprawled across the greenness of the little clearing by the stream, in the woods just off the Canfield road. The knife that, hours earlier, had been meant for me, had brutalized the throat of Mabel Branscombe, and she lay still in a pool of her own blood. The deadly instrument itself had fallen close beside her fingers.

'My God,' I murmured when I saw her. 'Oh, my God!'

I bent down and looked into her lifeless eyes, now dull and still and blank. I recalled how they'd appeared the last time I had seen them – wild and filled with madness running rampant.

Was it that madness, I had to wonder, or was it love, or was it hate that had driven her to plunge a knife into her own throat and let her life's blood drain away?

And then I had to wonder something else, reluctantly, unwillingly. If I'd not hesitated, had not hung back that small breath of a moment, could I have shot and wounded her and put the cuffs upon her, thereby saving her this end? I'd have to sit down and consider that a little while, and maybe live with it a long, long time.

An envelope protruded from the raincoat pocket and I carefully withdrew it. I recognized it as the same stationery I'd once seen her using in her tiny cell.

I unfolded the thin white piece of paper and began to read: 'Now maybe you will believe me when I tell you I, and not Kenneth, killed that girl. If I kill myself, maybe you will believe me. Maybe that is the *only* way to get you to believe me.

'But there is another reason, too, that I take my own life. I cannot live apart from him. We've been together far too long for that. I cannot live with either him or me in jail. We must both be free.

'And so I've failed him, just as that tramp girl would've failed him if he'd kept on with her. I've failed him because he is still in jail. And so it all gets back to this. If I kill myself, you will believe me and then you'll set him free.

'I once told you, Katharine, that the pain is sometimes greatest just before it ends. My pain is greatest now, but it will finally end. And so, thereby, will Kenneth's.'

I passed the note to Carl and then to Kent. They read it and began to shake their heads. Shake them sadly at the futility – the complete futility of it all.

'So how do you reckon it, boss?' Carl asked. 'Did she do the killing?'

'Nothing I found out yesterday afternoon indicated that she did,' I answered. 'Certain things raised questions in my mind, made me think she could have, but no, I came up with no hard evidence. I believe she may have covered for Kenneth once she found out what he did, but I don't believe she murdered Connie Hammond.'

'I'm with you,' he said. 'She knew a lot she wasn't telling, that's for sure, but I'm a long way from convinced she shot the girl.'

'So the trial still goes forward?' Kent inquired.

'Absolutely. Right on schedule.'

We sat silent for a moment, thinking back to the gruesome scene that morning.

'What a waste,' I finally said, 'what a waste. She killed herself for nothing.'

As Carl and I left the room, he laid a big warm hand along my shoulder. 'What really happened in those woods, Kate? Were you all right?'

I felt all of my defenses start to rise. 'Why?'

'Because sometimes you seemed a little funny about that woman. Oh, I don't know how to put it. Like you thought she was a friend or something . . .' His voice trailed off.

'She came at me, I thought I could subdue her without firing, I found I couldn't and she got away. I made the wrong decision, that's all there was to it. It happens to the best of us.'

He raised his eyebrows but he let it lie. He knew he wasn't going to get any more from me.

I called the coroner and told him what I wanted.

'Sure, I can determine that,' he said. 'I'll check it out and get back to you a little later on.'

'Work your fastest,' I said. 'I'll be here waiting for your call.'

My phone rang shortly after lunch, as I poured what must've been my thirteenth cup of coffee.

'I've got your answer for you, Kate. There's evidence that the deceased gave birth to at least one child in her lifetime, and the birth was a fairly difficult one, probably precluding her becoming pregnant again.'

I sat there, sipping at my coffee, while a heavy sadness settled down on me. And then, as my mind began to wander, to drift back to that twisted family of so long ago, a new nightmarish scenario began to form in my head, and build mental brick by mental brick upon itself in logical progression. What had really happened in that lonely foothill farmhouse that April night more than forty years ago? Had Jason Branscombe truly killed himself after murdering his wife, or had someone else done it for him?

I recalled Mabel's words in the jail cell. 'With his death he paid for what he did.' It had struck me at the time as odd phraseology – after all, the suicide was his own choice – but I'd thought little of it. Now the words took on a whole new meaning. Perhaps someone had made him pay by taking his life for him.

I visualized the darkness coming down as the snow fell heavy, a girl hearing her mother scream, rushing in to see her mother with her throat cut to the vertebrae, her blood pouring on the floor and splattering on the walls.

Perhaps she'd grabbed the shotgun then and forced him to the porch, or perhaps she'd hidden, biding her time, till she found her father – her tormentor – in a vulnerable position.

And the years of hate and loathing – not just for the abuse and torturing of her mother but also, for her own incestuous molestation and impregnation – had built a force behind that trigger, and she'd blasted off the head of Jason Branscombe and made it look like suicide.

I gripped the desktop as my mind continued painting pictures that I saw as vividly as I saw a crime scene of today. She'd have had time to fix things up and get her story straight – nearly all night long, in fact – and who would doubt her word? The whole county knew of Jason Branscombe's character and accepted as inevitable the turn events had taken. And two poor children left alone were only to be pitied. Never to be suspected, not ever.

I walked slowly to the county jail. I hadn't seen Kenneth Branscombe in several days and I couldn't help but look at him differently now. I found him leafing through a magazine as he lay upon his cot. If he was upset by Mabel's death, he didn't show it.

'Mr Branscombe, where were you the night your parents died, and where was Mabel?'

His eyes opened wide. I knew this line of questioning was the last thing he expected.

'I was upstairs asleep,' he said, 'until I heard the shot. I don't know where Mabel was. Not with me.'

'Did you go downstairs?' I asked.

'No, I remember I was scared. I lay there and after a while my sister came. She told me our mother was dead and our father had shot himself.'

'What did she look like, Mr Branscombe? Did you notice anything unusual about her?'

'The blood,' he answered quickly, 'all the blood all over her. I was just a little kid and it really scared me. She told me it'd gotten on her when she checked to see if they were dead.'

'What did you do then?' I asked softly. 'Did you go downstairs?'

'Mabel wouldn't let me. She said she had some things to do and she didn't want me to see our parents like they were. She locked me in the bedroom and when she came back much later, she was all clean and neat and stayed with me till it was daylight and the phones came back, so she could call for help.'

Wordlessly, I left him and started walking back. I thought I probably knew what she'd been doing while that little boy stayed locked tight in his room. She'd been tidying up the murder scene and tidying up herself, making her father's death look like suicide and Mabel Branscombe like an innocent victim. The phones may or may not have been out, but she had said they were and everyone believed her.

I had no sure proof, just as I had no proof she'd pushed Jodie Simons from that cliff or borne Kenneth Branscombe. But I thought I knew where maybe I could find some.

I found her where I'd found her so many times before, bending down beside a flower bed, clipping blooms and turning soil. She wore a wide-brimmed straw hat to protect her from the sun and a pale blue cotton cover-all to keep the dirt at bay.

I eased in beside the curb and she straightened up and looked at me. I saw the weariness behind her eyes and the pained and drawn set upon her mouth.

'Mrs Burnham,' I began, 'I'd like to speak to you again, but first I'd like to offer my condolences on the death of your dear friend.'

She nodded silently and wiped her eye with the back of a tan-gloved hand, then motioned to me to come inside. We passed through the perfect cottage and out the other side, and once again I found myself seated at the little round glass table between two L-shaped wings.

'Mabel went crazy at the end, Detective,' Sally Burnham told me, her soft voice laboring with sadness. 'She just slipped right over the edge.'

'She was obsessed with Kenneth,' I told her, 'and her obsession blinded her.'

We sat for several moments while Sally Burnham looked off into space, then I leaned forward and gently laid my hand across her lap.

'I want to ask you something; there is something I am trying to understand. I need your help and I promise your answers will be held in confidentiality.'

Her eyes swung around to meet mine and I saw a wariness move across their surface.

'Do you remember the day I came here and asked if you had seen much of Mabel the summer Kenneth was born? And you told me no?'

She nodded silently.

'Was that the truth?'

Again her head went up and down.

'I learned something, Mrs Burnham, from the coroner after he did the autopsy. I learned that Mabel Branscombe at one time gave birth to a child. I believe that child was Kenneth. Can you help me out?'

She jerked upright in her chair and her eyes shot open wide and stared at me. For a moment, I thought I'd run up against an impenetrable wall. Then Sally Burnham's body slumped and her hand went quickly to her head. 'What use is this, Detective?' she asked weakly. 'She's dead now. Let her be.'

'She was a woman I knew and grew to like,' I said simply. 'She was also part of a very sad case that was mine to solve. I would rest much easier if you would guide me through these missing pieces. It would help to bring closure to my relationship with Mabel Branscombe.'

She watched me keenly, trying to sort out the words that I was saying. Then she nodded, as if somehow something had been resolved. 'You're right,' she told me finally, in a low calm voice. 'You're right about Kenneth being her son. And you are the only one to know, aside from her parents, Mabel, and me.'

'Tell me about it,' I said, keeping my own voice low and calm as I settled back into my chair.

'I didn't learn about it till two summers later,' Sally Burnham said, her fingers playing with a thread. 'We were very close, Mabel and I. Closer than either of us was with any of the other girls. We were best friends. I'd noticed a difference in her after Kenneth was born – a strangeness, a sort of sudden growing up but with a lot of solemness about it. I feel now it was depression, but how can a young girl recognize depression? I couldn't.

'Anyway, one time we spent the night together and we

were confiding as girls do, and suddenly, as we lay there in the soft warmth sharing all our secrets, she told me Kenneth was her baby and her father was his father, too. And that Jason Branscombe had molested her even before the conception and was still doing it from time to time.'

'You must've been quite shocked,' I murmured, imagining myself at fourteen or so hearing such a thing from a friend.

'Of course I was shocked,' Sally Burnham answered, 'but I believed her. And I promised I'd never, ever tell.'

'Not even when you knew Trudy Rideout's sister was going to marry Kenneth?'

The Burnham woman choked and gave a little cry. 'No, not even then. The secret was too awful to let out. I could not do that to my friend. I'd heard that sometimes things like that worked out – marriage to a child born of a close relationship – so I took the chance the odds would be on their side and nothing bad would happen.'

'And it didn't,' I pointed out. 'They had no children and apparently lived a happy life until she died of cancer.'

Mrs Burnham nodded, as if somewhat comforted.

'Mabel told me how Jason treated her mother,' I said. 'Because of that and because of what he did to her, it's a wonder she didn't kill him.'

And the words just settled in silence, waiting to be picked up.

'She almost did, Detective,' Sally Burnham told me quietly. 'That awful night, when she saw what he'd done to her dear mother, she almost did. She told me she ran out on the porch to find him and kill him with the shotgun but he'd

331

already picked it up and put it in his mouth when she came through the door. And before she could reach him, he blew himself away and his blood flew out and covered her.'

'And you believed her?' I asked, watching an autumn sparrow wing its way across the yard. 'You had no doubt he killed himself?'

'I believed her,' Sally Burnham answered. 'I believed her because Mabel knew she didn't have to lie to me. She knew she could tell the truth to me and I would not betray her. Because, after all, I'd already kept one awful secret for nearly five long years.'

I sighed, then reached back into another past and dredged a question from it. 'What about Jodie Simons?' I mused. 'What really made her go over that cliff?'

Sally Burnham looked straight at me, but her answer wasn't quite what I'd expected. 'Go ask Trudy Rideout,' she said. 'You'd best go ask Trudy Rideout.'

She sat across from me in her tidy living room less than two blocks from the church. Her effervescent good humor had been dampened by the death of her close friend.

'Mrs Rideout,' I said, 'I'm going to ask you about something that happened a long, long time ago. You may think it strange but trust me, I need to know this. Do you remember a girl called Jodie Simons?'

Her brown eyes opened like large round buttons and her lower lip dropped slightly. 'Sure I do. The poor soul who went over the cliff.'

'Sally Burnham sent me to you,' I explained. 'She said you could help me answer some questions about her death.'

'That Sally,' the woman sputtered. 'It's not like her to go telling tales out of school. But we're grown-ups. I guess it doesn't matter now.'

'Did you see the girl die?' I asked quietly. 'Is that what it was?'

'No.' Her round body shifted comfortably on the chair. 'But we saw her pass by, on her way to that cliff. We were probably the last ones to see her alive.'

'We?' I asked. 'You and who else?'

'Oh, Detective, I told you before I was always the loud and noisy one. I was also the one who was a little more daring than the others in the group. I had a case on a fella my parents didn't like – they'd never have let me see him – so I snuck around on the sly and met him in the woods.'

Just like Connie Hammond and Larry Marchand all those years later, I thought. How little some things change.

'We'd met in there one afternoon and shortly afterwards we saw Jodie coming toward us. We didn't want to give ourselves away so we stayed real low and quiet until she passed. And then later we found out she'd pitched over that cliff.' Trudy Rideout's eyes looked far away.

'Did you see anyone follow her?' I asked.

'No, no one did, I'm sure of that. We had a clear view of the path and even though my fella and I were foolin' around—' – here Trudy giggled girlishly – 'we were always watchin' to make sure we were safe.'

'Was there any other way in or out?'

'No, only that path and no one else went down it. Poor Mabel thought she was the last to see Jodie alive and she told the authorities she'd watched her pass by the farm. My guy and I didn't let on we'd seen her too. There was no need. We didn't witness the accident and my mom would've skinned my bottom if she'd found out where I'd been.'

So now I knew the truth. Kenneth was indeed Mabel's son, but she'd killed neither her father nor Jodie Simons. And, I told myself firmly, she didn't kill Connie Hammond either. Kenneth Branscombe had done that awful deed and he was rapidly proceeding to trial.

But I was wrong. It all started to fall apart the following day. Stuart Greenwell – the sole eyewitness to place the suspect at the scene, and a man in unusual good health up till then – suffered a massive heart attack and was in intensive care. With only a thumbprint on his own weapon and a slap across the face of a back-talking girl left as evidence, my case against Kenneth Branscombe grew weaker in one bound.

The irony wasn't lost on me. One day I had too many suspects, the next I was in real danger of not even having one. Why oh why, I flailed myself in marvelous hindsight, hadn't we used him at the prelim?

'Is he expected to survive?' I asked.

'Touch and go,' the doctor said. 'The next twenty-four hours will tell the tale.'

And if he does, what shape will he be in? I wondered to myself. No need to ask the specialist. I knew he couldn't tell me.

'So what it boils down to is this,' I told Carl and Kent, 'if Greenwell doesn't make it, what's going to happen to our case?'

'Do you think any jury would go with what we've got?'

Kent answered my query with one of his own. He seemed less frazzled than before. His dad must still be getting better or the baby's eating patterns must be levelling off.

'Do you think any DA would go with it, is more to the point, I'd say,' Carl chimed in.

Their comments so discouraged me that I brought the conversation to a halt. 'There's no need tossing this around,' I said. 'We shouldn't work ourselves into a needless fit. What we should do is just sit tight and not worry about it till we see what happens in that hospital room.'

It didn't take too long to find out, only till the following morning. Stuart Greenwell died at nine forty-five a.m. without regaining consciousness, and our case died right along with him.

'There's no way I can proceed,' the DA told me, 'you know that, don't you, Katharine? There's no way I can even try to let this go to trial. I'd be laughed right out of this office if I did.'

The District Attorney, a perky bright-eyed woman, peered at me and waited for my answer. I'd seen her once at a department Christmas party, exhausting partner after partner as her dainty little feet rapped out a fast staccato beat on the wooden dance floor – and that energized picture leapt into my mind each time we came face to face.

'Are you saying you're going to move for dismissal of this case and Kenneth Branscombe will go free?' As I spoke, I wondered why I even asked. This was all just word-playing on my part. The DA had made it perfectly clear that's exactly what she was going to do.

'No choice, Katharine. This man should not stand trial unless you provide me with more evidence than you've presently got. Can you do that?'

Reluctantly I shook my head. 'You know I can't. Otherwise you'd have it on your desk right now.'

Damn, I agonized. If only we'd put Greenwell on the stand at the prelim we wouldn't be in this fix now – we could use his testimony regardless of his death. But we hadn't, and now we'd have to live with what at the time had seemed such a smart decision.

I went back to find Kent and Mungers, to prepare them for what was happening. All that work, I thought, all the zigging and the zagging of this case, only to have it end like this.

Kenneth Branscombe was released from custody at two o'clock the following afternoon. As he prepared to leave the courtroom, he began to make his way toward me, a strange expression on his face. He seemed, somehow, to stand taller, to be more self-assured, than the man I'd previously known.

As he neared me, his eyes locked on mine, and I saw a whole parade of emotions passing through them, but I couldn't even start to read them. I tried to hold his glance till I could get a fix on whatever he was feeling, but the parade passed swiftly by and, once it ended, his eyes shuttered and became unrevealing.

What was it that I'd seen? I asked myself. What elusive feelings had he been projecting? Relief, cunning, wariness? I thought I'd seen a little bit of all of those, but I could not be sure.

I turned around and watched him walk out the door and into freedom, and I noticed once again how straight he held himself, how confident he seemed as he swiftly moved ahead.

'So it was all a bunch of wheel-spinning, was it?'

Karen Windall plopped down on the sofa in my living room – the one that was just about to be replaced. 'The real killer offs herself and the one you could've hanged for it gets set free through that old devil, the twist of fate!' She was looking more like her usual upbeat self – maybe she was starting to put Steve Darrow somewhere far behind her.

'We wouldn't have hanged Kenneth Branscombe just to have someone to punish,' I pointed out. 'He'd never have been ordered to stand trial in the first place if we didn't believe he was guilty.'

'Oh, surely you buy poor Mabel's suicide note,' she protested. 'I mean, we know how obsessed she was with him. In a way, he must be glad to lose that baggage. C'mon, the way I see it is that she really *did* shoot the girl and was sacrificing herself just like she said.'

'I disagree,' I told her, as I curled my feet up under me. 'I believe she was just a devoted sister who, in the end, went mad. And what an irony if I'm right. If she'd waited just a few more days, fate would've freed her brother for her.'

'Well, you think what you like. At least *I* know who did the killing.' Karen gave this parting shot as she walked out to get more ice.

I'd been open to Karen about my beliefs, and, indeed, in my heart I did think Kenneth Branscombe had murdered Connie Hammond – out of anger, out of jealousy, probably out of knowing and reviling the thought that he could never really have her. But once in a while, after going to bed but just before the bliss of sleep, I'd remember my earlier doubts about the innocence of Mabel Branscombe.

'We know who killed her?' I asked myself, tapping my fingers on a little table. 'I wonder if we do. I wonder if we ever really will.'

But I knew three weeks later, after a late night on the wilder side of town.

I'd gone home, then gotten a phone tip that I'd find an ADW suspect mixing drinks behind the bar at Crocco's, the club where Karen had spied Darrow and his blonde. I'd waited till nearly ten o'clock, then dressed and driven to the east end of the town.

A visual check showed me my fella wasn't there – a good likeness, maybe, but not the guy I wanted. Unless, perhaps, he was on a break. I decided I'd hang around awhile, just to make absolutely certain, though I was pretty convinced I was looking at a case of mistaken identity.

As I sat at a little corner table, slowly sipping at my soda, I let my glance wander around the room, scanning all the other patrons. Suddenly I stopped, when a face seated at a table half-way to the bandstand began to look familiar.

I peered through the smoky haze till the face turned fully toward me, and I saw then I'd not been mistaken. It was Kenneth Branscombe, with a brown-haired girl sitting close beside him. She looked to be maybe thirty-one or -two – a little on the hard side but with the full and rounded figure most men found pleasing.

It'd been nearly three weeks since I'd seen him, and as I

sat there in my corner I began to size him up. He still looked like the same slicked-back country dude he'd always been, but once again I became intensely aware of a new assurance, an offhand, easy manner that'd not been there before – heightened, even, from what I'd earlier observed in court.

He was bending forward, laughing and regaling the young lady with a tale of high hilarity while reaching for his whiskey and taking hearty gulps.

The woman listened closely to every word he said and, from time to time, would touch his hand as if in deep appreciation of his humor.

After ten or fifteen minutes I saw him toss some money on the table, pull back the lady's chair, then start to work his way across the floor and toward the door.

Suddenly, for no apparent reason, Kenneth Branscombe turned his head in the direction I was sitting. Our eyes met and a startled look swept across his face, and then I saw him bend down and whisper to the girl and he started toward me, leaving her standing there alone.

'Good evening, Detective,' he said smoothly as he reached my table. 'May I sit down a moment?'

'Sure, pull up a chair,' I answered him, 'though I don't know what we have to say to one another.'

A saxophonist played softly in the background – a poignant, flowing jazz song. I glanced at the thirty-odd brunette and saw she'd turned her attention toward the music.

I looked back at Kenneth Branscombe. His face was flushed deeper than his usual ruddy norm and I could tell that he'd been drinking, though he certainly wasn't drunk. He leaned toward me – seeming eager, as if he were just about to burst with something – and began to talk in a voice loud enough for me to hear but too low to carry to the adjoining tables.

'Actually, you know, what I'd like to say would be better said outside. Would you come out to the parking lot with me for a moment?' His eyes watched my face expectantly, as if my answer meant a lot to him.

I hesitated. My instincts told me not to go; my cop's curiosity would not let me stay. I sighed. I'd gotten into this type of fix before and it hadn't always turned out well, but I knew myself and I knew what I was going to do. I'd just watch my back, that's all.

'Let's go,' I said, and we exited through a side door.

'You must've been pretty sorry to lose that witness,' he began, as he leaned back against a pickup truck and crossed his legs in front of him.

'Of course I was,' I answered. 'You know you wouldn't have walked otherwise.'

He thought a moment and I could tell there was something else he badly wanted to say. 'You know, Mabel always thought she was the clever one in the family, but I can sure be clever too.'

'Stuart Greenwell dying had nothing to do with your being clever,' I told him smartly. 'That was pure unlucky happenstance.'

'Oh, I don't mean that,' he said, rolling his eyes and looking up toward the stars. 'I mean clever to let you keep my sister, instead of rushing forward when you arrested her and shouting "I did it!" '

'And what did that accomplish, Mr Branscombe?'

'Well, Detective, it certainly made you wonder if *she* might've killed the girl – and if I'd gone to trial my lawyer would certainly have used her possible guilt, especially with her suicide, to create reasonable doubt in any jury's mind. See, I figured all that out while I sat in that crusty, filthy cell. Anyway, if nothing else, it bought me time till Greenwell died, now, didn't it?'

I knew what I was hearing but I had to make totally sure I understood. 'Are you telling me you murdered Connie Hammond, Mr Branscombe?'

He licked his lips quickly and bent toward me, the smell of whiskey riding on his breath. 'That girl made me mad, Detective. She gave me too much trouble. Sometimes women have to pay for what they do.'

'You lousy bastard!' I hissed at him. 'You lousy fuckin' bastard! And your sister! You hung her out to dry and you didn't even care!'

'My sister was a pain, Detective, always acting like she was my mother.' I shot a glance at him, wondering if he knew. I didn't think so, and nothing in his face told me otherwise. He gave a little laugh. 'Sometimes, like I say, Detective, sometimes women have to pay.'

I longed to beat the balls off him but I struggled to stay calm, to glean a true confession if I could. We'd talked all around the subject but I had to hear him say it flat-out.

'How did you get Connie to the woods that night?' I asked softly.

'Oh no, that's enough – you're not going to get to learn any details. I just wanted to let you know this much, no more.' He began moving away from the pickup's fender.

'Why? So you could lord it over me?'

'So you could see I'm not the big dumb country boy you think I am. See what I've got here now?' he spread his hands wide in front of him. 'I've got a whole new life, and *I'm* the one who says what's happening!'

He left me standing there and walked back into the club. I don't think I'd ever felt so frustrated in all my life.

I knew now who'd murdered Connie Hammond, but what good did that knowledge do me? My only witness was a dead man, and Kenneth Branscombe's skirting words would not stand up on their own.

I saw how it had all gone down. Somehow he'd lured Connie to the woods and killed her, and Mabel Branscombe had followed him and seen what he had done. She'd then scrambled to plant evidence to cover up for him – writing notes and hocking jewelry, just like she'd always told me. The only crimes that she'd been guilty of were those of being an accessory and of loving a conniving brother far too much.

But what could I do now? Absolutely nothing. Only live with the killing knowledge and let it gnaw at me every single day.

The bastard! I banged my fist down hard upon the fender, spun around, and walked away.

September passed, and then October. The days shortened and the leaves changed color and drifted slowly from the trees. The air was always cooler now, and the long and lazy days of summer were forgotten.

The girls' softball team didn't make it to the championship, not even to the playoffs in the state.

Kent's dad was back to work and feeling fine, and Dan seemed fresh-faced and relaxed – though his Spanish wasn't getting too much better.

Carl and Sandy were still a constant duo, and I was okay on my own, watching Tommy grow about an inch a month.

Sometimes I'd see Kenneth Branscombe in San Madera and I'd make sure I crossed the street to avoid him. It rankled me – it rankled me so much.

It was getting close to Thanksgiving and I was sitting at my desk, making out a shopping list for the festive dinner, when my phone began to ring. I picked it up and heard a gentle little voice on the other end asking if she could speak with Katharine Harrod.

'Yes,' I said, 'I'm here. This is she.'

'This is Sara Greenwell, Stuart Greenwell's widow. There's something that I'd like to tell you – something that I should've told you a long, long time ago.'

Every nerve in my body tightened. I straightened up and felt my fingers clench the phone. 'Go on.'

'You see, I was in the car with Stuart that night – the night he saw Kenneth Branscombe going in the woods. He'd picked me up downtown after working late, and so we *both* saw the man and the pickup truck.'

My mind reeled inside my head and I heard myself give an involuntary cry. 'Why didn't you tell me this before?'

'Because I didn't want to get involved. I'm very shy and I always relied on Stuart to do things for me. He said there was no need for me to say anything if I didn't want to because it would be enough for one of us to tell you what we saw.'

'Then what made you change your mind?' I asked.

'Because Stuart is gone and I know you had to let that murderer go free. It's been two months now since my husband's death and I've done a lot of grieving. I've also done an awful lot of realizing that I have to make my own way now, have to rely upon myself. And so I'm calling you. Would it be of any help to you, at this late date, if I testified I saw Kenneth Branscombe at those woods?'

'Oh my God,' I said, as unprofessionally as I'd ever spoken to a witness. 'Oh my God, would it ever be!'

With the print, with the crack across the face, with our little 'chat' in Crocco's parking lot . . . and with Sara Greenwell's testimony, the case that died had suddenly come to life.

I said goodbye to her, depressed the button, then released it, and dialed the old, familiar number.

'Give me the DA, please. It's urgent!'

As I spoke, I felt a weight slip off my shoulders and fall far, far away. I began to grin, and my heart beat fast in triumph. He'd live to feel the pain – the pain and misery of his actions. The bastard who had taken two good lives was going to pay in full. And do the paying with the life he called his own.

I wasn't disappointed this time. I sat in court and watched his round moon face turn pale as the jury found him guilty, I saw his shoulders slump as they led him off in cuffs.

He's on death row now, waiting to pay the price for killing Connie Hammond. I like to think that price includes a bit for taking Mabel Branscombe, too, the woman who had sacrificed so much for him.

There'll be the automatic appeal, of course, but I don't worry too much about that one. The evidence was strong and true, the presentation flawless. Not a rule was bent nor a technicality broken as the legal process flowed from start to finish.

No, I don't worry about Kenneth Branscombe's future. Kenneth Branscombe's never going to hurt another woman again.

A selection of bestsellers from Headline

BODY OF A CRIME	Michael C. Eberhardt	£5.99	☐
TESTIMONY	Craig A. Lewis	£5.99	☐
LIFE PENALTY	Joy Fielding	£5.99	☐
SLAYGROUND	Philip Caveney	£5.99	☐
BURN OUT	Alan Scholefield	£4.99	☐
SPECIAL VICTIMS	Nick Gaitano	£4.99	☐
DESPERATE MEASURES	David Morrell	£5.99	☐
JUDGMENT HOUR	Stephen Smoke	£5.99	☐
DEEP PURSUIT	Geoffrey Norman	£4.99	☐
THE CHIMNEY SWEEPER	John Peyton Cooke	£4.99	☐
TRAP DOOR	Deanie Francis Mills	£5.99	☐
VANISHING ACT	Thomas Perry	£4.99	☐

All Headline books are available at your local bookshop or newsagent, or can be ordered direct from the publisher. Just tick the titles you want and fill in the form below. Prices and availability subject to change without notice.

Headline Book Publishing, Cash Sales Department, Bookpoint, 39 Milton Park, Abingdon, OXON, OX14 4TD, UK. If you have a credit card you may order by telephone – 01235 400400.

Please enclose a cheque or postal order made payable to Bookpoint Ltd to the value of the cover price and allow the following for postage and packing:

UK & BFPO: £1.00 for the first book, 50p for the second book and 30p for each additional book ordered up to a maximum charge of £3.00.

OVERSEAS & EIRE: £2.00 for the first book, £1.00 for the second book and 50p for each additional book.

Name ....

Address ....

....

....

If you would prefer to pay by credit card, please complete:
Please debit my Visa/Access/Diner's Card/American Express (delete as applicable) card no:

Signature .... Expiry Date...............